Dragon
Slayers

Also by Lisa McMann

» » « «

THE UNWANTEDS SERIES
The Unwanteds

Island of Silence

Island of Fire

Island of Legends

Island of Shipwrecks

Island of Graves

Island of Dragons

» » « «

THE UNWANTEDS QUESTS SERIES
Dragon Captives

Dragon Bones

Dragon Ghosts

Dragon Curse

Dragon Fire

Dragon Slayers

Dragon Fury

» » « «

FOR OLDER READERS:
Don't Close Your Eyes

Visions

Cryer's Cross

Dead to You

LISA McMANN

THE UNWANTEDS QUESTS

Dragon Slayers

Aladdin

NEW YORK   LONDON   TORONTO   SYDNEY   NEW DELHI

ALADDIN

An imprint of Simon & Schuster Children's Publishing Division

1230 Avenue of the Americas, New York, New York 10020

First Aladdin paperback edition July 2021

Text copyright © 2020 by Lisa McMann

Cover illustration copyright © 2020 by Own Richardson

Also available in an Aladdin hardcover edition.

All rights reserved, including the right of reproduction in whole or in part in any form.

ALADDIN and related logo are registered trademarks of Simon & Schuster, Inc.

For information about special discounts for bulk purchases, please contact Simon & Schuster Special Sales at 1-866-506-1949 or business@simonandschuster.com.

The Simon & Schuster Speakers Bureau can bring authors to your live event. For more information or to book an event contact the Simon & Schuster Speakers Bureau at 1-866-248-3049 or visit our website at www.simonspeakers.com.

Cover designed by Karin Paprocki

Interior designed by Hilary Zarycky

The text of this book was set in Truesdell.

Manufactured in the United States of America 0521 OFF

2 4 6 8 10 9 7 5 3 1

The Library of Congress has cataloged the hardcover edition as follows:

Names: McMann, Lisa, author.

Title: Dragon slayers / by Lisa McMann.

Description: New York : Aladdin, 2020. | Series: The Unwanteds quests | Summary: Rohan leads the effort to rescue Thisbe from the Revinir, without knowing if she will prove loyal to Artimé or not.

Identifiers: LCCN 2019057354 (print) | LCCN 2019057355 (ebook) | ISBN 9781534416079 (hardcover) | ISBN 9781534416093 (ebook)

Subjects: CYAC: Adventure and adventurers—Fiction. | Magic—Fiction. | Brothers and sisters—Fiction. | Twins—Fiction. | Dragons—Fiction. | Fantasy.

Classification: LCC PZ7.M478757 Dx 2020 (print) | LCC PZ7.M478757 (ebook) | DDC [Fic]—dc23

LC record available at https://lccn.loc.gov/2019057354

ISBN 9781534416086 (pbk)

Contents

To all who started reading the Unwanteds series in its early days as fourth graders: Happy high school graduation! Thanks for sticking with me. One more book to go and then we'll all cry together.

Total Confusion

Thisbe and Fifer had been abducted by the Revinir, and Rohan was beginning to panic. Nobody in Artimé seemed to be doing anything about it. He descended the stairs of the mansion to implore the one in charge. "Florence, please help me understand what's happening," he said, stopping in front of her in the entryway. The Magical Warrior trainer and Simber, the winged-cheetah statue, exchanged a concerned glance as the young man began pacing, struggling to stay calm. Rohan finally found his words and turned to face them. "Look. It has been *days*. Why aren't we going after Thisbe and Fifer? Are we seriously planning to

LISA McMANN

sit here and wait for Fifer to contact us? What if they're dead?"

"I've told you before," Florence said firmly. "I understand your concern, and I feel it too. Perhaps even more strongly than you. But we're going to wait."

"And Fiferrr is clearrrly not dead," said Simber, indicating the mansion still standing and himself still magically enchanted. "We don't believe that the Rrrevinirrr wants to hurrrt them. Frrrom what Thisbe and Maiven Taveerrr have told me, the Rrrevinirrr wants Thisbe to be an ally. She needs at least one black-eyed rrrulerrr on herrr side to complete the rrrequirrrements of prrroperrr trrransferrral of drrragon leaderrrship."

Rohan stopped pacing. "Right." He thought hard for a moment. "So the Revinir believes she needs a black-eyed human to join forces with her, and because Thisbe is more evil than good, she thinks Thisbe is her ticket," he said, like it finally made sense to him. "And even though *we* know the truth—that the dragons have to actually choose their leader, and the Revinir can't choose herself to be the lead dragon—*she* doesn't actually know that. So . . ." He paused, putting it all together. "She thinks she can convince Thisbe to team up with her—that Thisbe will be tempted enough by the leadership position to go for it." He shook his head. "Even though *that* won't work either, because the black-eyed people need to choose their leader too. And besides, Thisbe would never, ever do something like that."

"She'd better not," Florence muttered. "I trained that girl right. If she does something—"

"She won't," Simber interrupted impatiently. "She's smarrrt and loyal. Therrre's no way she'd do that to us."

"But what about Fifer?" said Rohan. "She's way more good than evil. Won't the Revinir want to do away with her to stop her from influencing Thisbe?"

"I've thought about that, too," said Simber. "And I think she knows that if she does something to hurrrt Thisbe's twin, Thisbe will neverrr join herrr side."

Florence studied Simber. "That's actually a comforting thought."

"It's all I can think rrright now to get thrrrough this," said Simber, and finally the worry lines on his face broke through. He hated being away from his head mage, especially *days* away. He'd promised once that he'd never let this happen again, yet here they were. Shortly after Thisbe had sent a message call-ing for help, Fifer, Artimé's new leader, had sent one telling them all to retreat and wait for further instructions. And he trusted her . . . almost fully. He cringed. He had no choice but to put his support behind Fifer. She was the head mage—a good one too, unlike Frieda Stubbs—and she'd given an order. Hopefully, they'd know more soon. But if not, this might just drive them all to the brink of madness. It was hard enough to run things in Artimé these days after the civil war. But to do it without the head mage was even harder.

"The best thing we can do," said Florence, "is to be stron-ger than we've ever been, and to be in a position to help when the time comes. That means we train harder than ever. We broaden everybody's abilities. And we need to take every move, every spell, every trick up a notch. That includes broadening our minds. We need to anticipate the Revinir's moves. She is the most powerful enemy we've ever faced, and we need to be smarter than her. I'm not going to sleep until I come up with a way to beat that monster."

Simber lifted an eyebrow. "You . . . *neverrr* sleep."

"It's just an expression," Florence said with a snarl.

"Intensive training begins first thing in the morning on the lawn. We need everybody present."

"Everrrybody who?" asked Simber.

"Everybody everybody. Not just Artimé this time. I mean *everybody*."

Simber gazed at her. "Ourrr allies, you mean?"

Florence nodded seriously. "I'll go alert our friends on Karkinos and see if they can track down Spike and Talon, who are still out searching for Issie's baby. Send Scarlet and Thatcher to fetch the people of Warbler, and Lani to speak to the people in Quill. Tell Seth to get our friends from the Island of Shipwrecks." She paused for a breath, then said in her sternest voice, "We will not fail Fifer and Thisbe. We will not let Artimé down, or anyone in the world of the seven islands. Not this time. Not ever again." She turned to look into Rohan's eyes. "I'm counting on you to step up now that I've lost my two main players."

"I will, Commander Florence," said Rohan.

With that, Florence left the two standing at the entrance and turned sharply, heading out the door into the evening, marching into the water toward Karkinos.

Rohan looked at Simber, fear and awe in his eyes. They were calling in everyone the people of Artimé knew. This was a major deal.

Simber nodded sharply. "You hearrrd herrr. Let's go."

Abandoned

The Revinir and her team of mind-controlled dragons flew a lot faster than the ghost dragons had, but Fifer and Thisbe weren't sure they would survive the trip.

It hadn't been hard for the girls to figure out that the dragon-woman had been hiding in Artimé's jungle, waiting for them to take their evening walk. She'd swooped down and snatched them up when they neared the lagoon. The Revinir's six red water dragons had risen from the sea to assist, but the dragon-woman wouldn't let the twins go—she dangled them from her claws the entire journey back to the land of the dragons. By the time they crossed over the gorge, the twins were unconscious.

It worked in the Revinir's favor. She didn't want them to be aware of where she was planning to drop them off. She wanted them to be disoriented. Lost and scared. That was the only way to bring them around to her way of thinking. Make them desperate, dangle a carrot, and then they would see her side of things. Break them down and train them back up.

Once Thisbe was supportive of the Revinir as the ruling dragon of Grimere, then the true power could be transferred, and she would officially be number one in the land of the dragons. Along with Thisbe as the ruling black-eyed human, of course. Unfortunately, the Revinir needed to keep at least one of those black-eyed children around for this purpose, and maybe a backup or two. The rest, she'd come to realize, were disposable.

And there was no way she was bringing these two back to the castle or the catacombs. Neither place had been a good prison for Thisbe—she'd escaped too many times. But Ashguard's palace and the deserted wasteland surrounding it were just the decrepit mess of sheer nothingness for miles to make Thisbe and Fifer beg to be rescued. Surround them with dragons to keep them contained, and eventually they'd promise to do anything . . . even make a pact with the Revinir to rule together.

The Revinir knew Thisbe had it in her to be evil. The girl had tricked her in the past and was more stubborn than the dragon-woman had expected, but she would come around in time. It was Fifer she was more worried about. That young woman was awash in goodness. She might have to be disposed of once the plan was in place—but not before, or the Revinir might lose Thisbe's allegiance. It was a tricky affair. The dragons would keep an eye on the girl.

By the time they soared over the crater lake and the palace ruins were in sight, it was midafternoon.

"Something was stirring a moment ago," said one of the red dragons in a monotone voice. "I don't see it now. It went off toward the orchard."

"Probably those foxes, like the last time we were scoping things out," said the Revinir. "Or some other animal. Deer, perhaps."

"Probably." Drool dripped from the hungry red dragon's mouth, but he fell silent, and the moment was forgotten.

The Revinir glanced down at the twins hanging from her grip and noticed they looked half-dead. She didn't want them to die, but other than that she didn't have much pity in her, though she did feel a small pang somewhere deep under her scales. She remembered when she was about their age. Young Emma, plotting her revenge against her horrible siblings, Marcus and Justine.

Just who had the upper hand now? They were dead, their legacies no doubt soon to be forgotten with the passage of time. But the Revinir . . . Eagala . . . Emma . . . She was about to rule an entire world, and these girls were going to help her.

They circled just above the palace, and the Revinir studied the sagging, rotten roof between the four corner towers and the large center tower. "I wonder if this old roof will hold them or if it'll give way?" she mused. "What do you think?" she asked one of her companions.

The dragon eyed it. "It doesn't seem sturdy."

"Good. You four, take your positions," she called out to the dragons, and four of the six swooped down to land on the ground, one in each corner of the vast property.

"Don't kill the black-eyed ones, but don't let them get away, either," said the Revinir, circling again above the roof with the remaining two dragons. And then she let go, dropping the unconscious girls onto the rotting palace roof.

Feeling It

Thisbe and Fifer hit the roof hard and plunged through it. They struck the top floor of the castle and kept going through that one too. The next floor down was a bit stronger and stopped Fifer, while Thisbe hit a weak spot and went through one more and stopped there.

The impact woke them both, but by the time they stopped moving, they wished to be unconscious again. It took several minutes of groaning and crying out before they realized where the other one was.

"Are you okay?" Thisbe called up to Fifer. "I think my ankle is broken."

LISA McMANN

"My entire back is on fire," said Fifer, "and my left wrist is twice its normal size and turning purple. I can't move it. Is that bad?"

"I'd say so," said Thisbe. She had abrasions and cuts everywhere, and her clothes were torn. Luckily, the soft rotten wood had broken their falls, or they'd be much worse off.

"There's a stairwell," Fifer said, easing over to the hole Thisbe had broken through and looking down into it. "Do you see it? Can you make it over there?"

"Yeah," said Thisbe. "I'll meet you on the steps. Be careful so you don't break through again. Elongate your body and slide."

"Stay in the stairwell—I'll come down to help you."

Using their elbows to pull them along, they each crawled carefully across the sagging floor and made it to the center tower stairwell, which looked solid, as it was made of stone and iron. Fifer got up shakily, then sat again and slid slowly down the steps one at a time to the next level. She found Thisbe, whose ankle was puffing up. "I can't put any weight on it," Thisbe said, trying to hold back the tears of pain. "Do you have any of Henry's medicine?"

"If it didn't fall into the sea, I do." Fifer rummaged through her robe pockets with her uninjured hand, laying out all of her remaining components on the stone step in front of them. It was a pitiful amount. Two send spells. A handful of scatterclips that had snagged the inside of her pocket. And two highlighters. She reached inside her vest and pulled out a thin metal box with a hinged lid. She winced and handed it to Thisbe. "This should have something in it that'll help with the pain and swelling."

Thisbe opened it and studied its contents, then selected the proper capsule containing magical herbs from Henry's garden. She returned the medical kit to Fifer, then swallowed her pill and washed it down with a swig from her canteen. She held it out to Fifer. "I'm glad we brought water this time," Thisbe said with a pained smile. The two had fought about canteens not too long ago.

"I haven't gone anywhere without one since our first quest," said Fifer. "I think it's because I was so traumatized." She swallowed a capsule too, and then tried standing again by propping herself up against the tower wall. But her back was too sore to let it touch anything. She just wanted to lie down on her stomach and make the pain go away. "Where are we?"

Thisbe slid next to Fifer. "I have no idea. But this is definitely not any part of the castle that I've ever seen."

"I don't think it's the castle at all," said Fifer. "The construction is very different. There's no way we would have fallen through that—the floors are made of stone."

Thisbe grimaced and closed her eyes. Every movement elicited waves of pain, and at the moment she didn't really care where they were. Time would only make their injuries hurt more as their muscles stiffened up. "Being unconscious when we fell probably saved us," she remarked after a while. "We weren't tensed up for an impact. But these injuries are going to take some time to heal. I'm worried we'll starve to death before anything else takes us out. Hopefully, our rescue team will be here soon. They should have been tailing us from a safe distance. Maybe they'll be able to tell us where we are."

Fifer shifted uneasily. She hadn't had a chance to tell Thisbe that she'd ordered Florence not to come after them. She had a lot she wanted to talk to Thisbe about, but it would land better once Thisbe was feeling less pain. "Let's allow the medicine to work," she said, "and then we'll figure out what to do next."

LISA McMANN

They rested quietly for some time in the stairwell, waiting for the magical herbs to take the pain and swelling down a bit and begin the healing process. After a while Thisbe opened her eyes. She was feeling a little better, and now that the mental fuzziness was wearing off, she had a burning question for Fifer. "Did you speak to me in my mind back when we first got abducted?"

"You heard it?" said Fifer, lifting her head. "Good! You did it to me first."

"I did? How?"

"I have no idea, but something clicked between us when we were walking along the shore. I felt it. It was electric."

"I felt that too," said Thisbe. "What do you think it means?"

"Other than we have some mysterious new telepathic ability, I don't know. I'm thinking it's similar to how Alex and Aaron used to be able to feel each other's pain."

"They couldn't actually speak to each other, though, like we did. That's pretty amazing. We'll have to try again once we can concentrate." She looked at Fifer's wrist. "Your swelling is coming down."

"It feels better. How about your ankle?"

"No longer excruciating. I'm not sure I'll be walking anytime soon, though."

"I should go in search of water and food before it gets dark," said Fifer. She winced, not wanting to move, but she was desperate to know if the Revinir was lurking about. Why had she dropped them here like this? Was it a mistake? Had her limbs just grown too tired to hold on?

"We can survive on the water we have until the others get here," said Thisbe, who also didn't want to move. "Is this place totally abandoned? Did the Revinir dump us here for a reason, or did something else happen? If she did, why?"

"Yeah," said Fifer, growing consternated. "Why didn't she throw us into the castle dungeon or the catacombs?"

"Maybe because we know how to escape from those places."

"It doesn't seem too hard to escape from this abandoned dump," said Fifer. "All we have to do is make it down the stairs."

"Easier said than done."

Neither of them could see outside, but Fifer soon grew curious enough to gingerly get to her feet once more. She held her

LISA McMANN

injured wrist close to her chest to keep it from jiggling and went to a window facing east. There she took in the overgrown landscape and spied two of the dragons from their journey standing guard at the front corners of the property. "There are dragons here," said Fifer. "I can see two of them. The red ones that were with us when the Revinir abducted us."

"I'm not surprised. But I'm still not sure where 'here' is."

Fifer groaned in pain simply from walking but kept going toward another window, facing south. She could see the late-afternoon sun off to her right and determined her bearings from it. "There's a third dragon at the southwest corner of the property. I'll bet there's a fourth one on the northwest."

"Not interested in taking that bet," said Thisbe, knowing Fifer was probably right. She eased up and looked down the spiral stone steps. "How high up are we?"

"At least a few floors. I'll go find out. Hand me your canteen, in case I find water."

"Don't go too far," Thisbe said anxiously. "I'm not sure what those dragons will do." Reluctantly she held out her canteen.

Fifer took it and slipped the strap over her head and arm.

"They've had plenty of chances to kill us, so obviously that's not on their agenda. And if the Revinir is making them guard us or something, there's got to be food and water around for them. I'm guessing it can't be too far to find a source. Besides, Dev taught us that nobody builds a house where there's no water." She bit her lip, having forgotten that the Revinir had killed him. "Ugh, sorry," she whispered. Blinding sorrow gripped her. It was too much to think about, and she was mortified that she'd mentioned him and cracked open more wounds. She started down the stairs, not even able to look at Thisbe, and took one careful step after another.

Thisbe's lip quivered. She felt miserable—physically from the fall and emotionally about Dev. Just thinking of him made her not want to be alone. She felt vulnerable, unable to walk, and worried for her sister venturing out alone without being able to fight properly because of her injuries. Not to mention having so few components. "Please be careful," she called.

"I will," Fifer replied. She continued down, moving slowly as her aching body allowed.

Thisbe pressed her face between the handrail balusters, watching Fifer go until she couldn't see her anymore.

"You're on the third floor," Fifer called up through the center of the spiral. Then: "Ooh!" she said, startled.

"Are you okay?" asked Thisbe.

"Just some animals down here in the shadows under the stairs. Foxes, I think, hiding from the dragons." She was quiet for a moment, then called up in a softer voice, "Definitely four dragons, all red. They're staying still. I'll be back soon."

While Fifer was gone, Thisbe checked all of her pockets to take stock of her components. Luckily, she still had the three obliterate components, individually boxed and safe in her inside pocket, thanks to the flap and button she'd added to it. That had kept her from losing them when the Revinir had dumped her and Fifer upside down and shaken them.

They were her answer for getting rid of the Revinir. But in addition to not knowing where she and Fifer were at this moment, Thisbe also had no clue where the Revinir was. And that's what unsettled her most.

Intruders

Dev Suresh, as he now believed himself to be, sat squeezed inside a broom closet in a tiny vacant house in the deserted village bordering his broken-down palace. He'd picked a dwelling that seemed solid and was located deep inside a maze of houses that were separated by narrow paths rather than broad roads. It was one that would be harder for dragons to get to if they were looking for him on foot.

He'd stayed perfectly still inside the cramped closet, feeling every joint and muscle in his body begin to ache. But whenever he started to doubt or question his resolve, he remembered the last time he'd been forced to hide from this group. "It's better than the river" had become his mantra, and he repeated it over and over in his mind to get him through. Anything was better than that.

When hours passed and no disturbances were felt or heard, Dev began to wonder if the Revinir and her team of dragons had passed him by without stopping. Was it possible they hadn't noticed him sneaking out of the center turret and running for his life? Or perhaps they'd seen him but didn't care? He thought back to the time in the river. He'd nearly drowned and hadn't witnessed where they'd gone after that. Perhaps this palace was just a spot along their path to some other place.

Or maybe Dev was really paranoid. After all, the Revinir had thrown him out of the castle tower from a ridiculous height and called in her dragons to dispose of him. So it was very likely that she thought Dev was dead. But the dragon-woman was exceedingly tricky and evil, and Dev didn't trust anything about her. She could be toying with him right now. She could be staring in the window of this house, smelling him. Waiting for him to feel confident enough to emerge.

Dev closed his eyes as his breath grew shallow. Fear and

dread crept in like they always did. He let his head fall back against the wall, and when it made a little thud, he worried that the Revinir had heard it, and at any second, the dragons would destroy this house with him in it.

It was too many worries for anyone, especially someone who'd gone through as much trauma as Dev had.

More hours passed with no intruders or disasters. As the light from under the door became muted, Dev eased to a standing position, then quietly and carefully turned the doorknob and pushed it open an inch. He held his breath, listening, then put his eye to the crack and looked out the kitchen window.

No one was there. He pushed the door farther and eased his aching body out of the closet, peering into other areas of the house but seeing no one. He let out a sigh of relief. Of course no one was there. There was no way a dragon could be inside unless the whole ceiling or an entire wall had caved in. "Silly," Dev muttered under his breath. Everything seemed ridiculous now that he could rest assured no dragons were nearby. But the feelings and fears had been very real.

He checked the windows that overlooked the surrounding village. It was deserted, as always. Dev had sat inside a tiny closet for half the day. He was more than ready to get back to the comfort of his home.

As he slipped out onto the path, Dev looked left and right, and also above him, just in case. He wasn't about to throw caution to the wind. When he was sure the coast was clear, he proceeded toward home. The sun had set, and in the growing dusk, Dev stayed close to the houses for cover, then made a fast break for the orchard. He picked his way between trees, stepping as quietly as possible, though he was unable to avoid the crunch of leaves and the occasional stick because of the fog that began rolling in and surrounding the hill that the palace stood on.

Dev reached the edge of the orchard and paused to look again in all directions before moving across the open area to get to the palace. His eye caught a slight movement by the center tower entrance, but it disappeared inside—was it one of the foxes? It seemed larger than that. And then he swept his gaze from side to side and saw red. Two medium-size red dragons at the near corners of the property.

His heart thudding, Dev gasped and sank into the fog.

A Standoff

Dev hovered in the fog between two gnarled apple trees, his heart still pounding. Even in the dark he could see the dragons' eyes glowing and their occasional flares of fiery snorts. Surely they must smell him by now, but they didn't seem to care. They didn't move or communicate with each other that Dev could see. Why were they here? Did their presence mean he couldn't go home to his palace now? His heart yearned for the library tower. What was he supposed to do? Go back to the village and hide in the closet again?

It occurred to him that perhaps the dragons weren't concerned with him because they hadn't been ordered by the

Revinir to attack him—similar to the dragons that guarded the castle. She hadn't sent out a roaring command in many weeks. Perhaps the dragons were there for some other reason than to go after him. But why had they decided to park themselves here? Maybe they were just weirdly resting at the corners of the palace property . . . before heading somewhere . . . else. Dev blinked. He knew there was no reason for them to be out here in the middle of nowhere unless they'd been sent.

When he could tear himself away from watching the dragons for a moment, he estimated the distance to the middle tower and contemplated making a run for it. Would they chase him? Even if he made it, would he ever be able to go out for food from the river? It was sickening to think about. One false move and Dev would be a hot meal.

Yet the more he realized that he couldn't go back to the palace, the more he wanted to do just that. He finally felt like he belonged somewhere, and he'd only gotten to experience that feeling for a short time. It was heartbreaking to think he couldn't go back. This was his land now, and the dragons were invading it.

Maybe they would leave soon. Perhaps they were just resting for the night to see if anything was happening here. It was beginning to drive Dev crazy that he couldn't figure out what was the purpose of their visit, if not to go after him. But here he was, stuck halfway between them, hidden from sight by fog, and there was nothing he could do about them tracking his scent. Heck, he could smell *them* well enough, and he was only part dragon. But they weren't even looking at him or flaring their nostrils his way.

A light flashed from the onion-bulb top of the center tower, catching Dev's eye, and he gasped again. Was someone *up* there? The light had come through the south window, which was surrounded by bookshelves. Dev often looked out that window and dreamed about chopping down the overgrowth he was currently nestled in. Who was in his sacred place? It couldn't be the Revinir—there was no way she could fit without destroying the entrance and the stairwell. It couldn't be the fox he'd seen darting into the door a while ago. So was it a human? Was someone here with the dragons?

The light stayed on, and a person-shaped shadow crossed the glass. Dev strained to see, but whoever it was didn't come close enough for Dev to make out any features. Who was invading his home? He went from scared to furious in the span of a minute. An intruder! Touching his things!

And then he remembered the painting of the girl in the orchard, which he'd slipped into a book on the desk. The images from the ancestor broth flashed before his eyes as he worried about it. He didn't know why he was so worried, but he knew he didn't want anyone taking that painting. The scales on his arms and legs, which were already on alert, strained against the grain, making his skin hurt. He wanted to charge back to his home and defend it and its contents. Who was this invader? What was he doing there?

Dev's lungs froze as the image in his mind landed on the gray man. Could it possibly be . . . him? His grandfather Ashguard? Long thought dead, returning home? It could happen—Astrid the ghost dragon had thought Maiven Taveer was dead. Perhaps Ashguard had been mistaken for dead too. After all, a few of the ancient books in the library had been used and left open not long before Dev had arrived—they'd had no dust on them. Was it Ashguard who'd been up there? If so, where had he disappeared to for all this time?

Dev realized these dragons were the Revinir's mind-controlled red water dragons. So they weren't here to assist Ashguard—he'd be an enemy of the Revinir for sure. Were they here to capture him? Were they waiting for him to leave so they could attack him?

If so, Dev had to do something. The gray man could possibly be the only kin Dev had, and after spending his whole life thinking he had none, he wasn't about to let this person slip away.

He crept forward through the fog, keeping his eyes on the dragons. The one at the back corner turned his head sharply at Dev's movement and glared, two fiery orange spots set inside the outline of the dragon's spiny head. Dev froze, but the dragon didn't come at him.

Dev felt faint. What was he doing? This was the most unwise choice he'd ever made. Well . . . maybe not, but it was pretty sketchy. He knew he could get his palace back later, after whatever was happening ended. But he'd never see it again if he kept inching forward and the dragons attacked him. Ashguard or no, Dev wasn't about to risk his life again. He waited agonizing minutes for the dragon to look away, and then he pivoted on his haunches and started creeping back the way he'd come. Through the orchard. Back to the village.

He didn't see the light go out, or the girl standing at the window peering out at him.

Uncomfortable Lies

Something is moving in the fog," Fifer said, putting out her magical highlighter and squinting out of the library window. "Bigger than a fox."

"What is it?" asked Thisbe, alarmed. She sat up on the sofa in the glorious library tower, which Fifer had discovered after she'd returned with water from the pump. She'd helped Thisbe climb the stairs. And though the trip had been agonizing, it was a relief to have some comfort and warmth and books around them. But there were also some unsettling features of this room. Like the old ripped and bloodstained shirt wadded up in the corner. And the half-eaten fish that

LISA McMANN

was now beginning to stink up the room. It wasn't very rotten, though—not weeks or even several days old. More like someone had been here recently and had left in a hurry.

"I can't tell for sure," said Fifer. "But it moves like a person. He's creeping away from us."

"Must be some vagabond looking for shelter who saw the dragons and decided it wasn't worth it," said Thisbe. "Maybe he was trying to come back for his fish." She wrinkled her nose. "Do we dare eat it?"

"I'm tempted," said Fifer, who was currently, unfortunately, not carrying anything to catch fish with. "I'd use it for bait if I had a hook." She paused and glanced at the fireplace. "The fire still has embers. I'm going to light it." She stared hard out the window for another few seconds as the person disappeared into darkness and fog. Then she turned and went to the fireplace, using her uninjured hand to stoke the embers and add more wood to it. Soon the fire was crackling merrily and making shadows dance around the rotunda.

"This would almost be pleasant if my ankle didn't hurt so much," said Thisbe. "And if we weren't surrounded by dragons. Do you think we should do another send spell? I'm worried

Florence or whoever is coming after us lost track of us. They definitely should have been here by now, wouldn't you say?"

"Hmm." Fifer turned away from the fire and went over to the corner where the musical instruments were. She kept her face hidden because it was dripping with guilt. She knew she needed to come clean with Thisbe, but she was still struggling in her own mind to understand why she'd told Florence not to come. "I don't want to waste components," she said, but she knew it was a silly reason. If the others had actually followed them, as Thisbe believed and expected, of course they'd waste a send spell to make sure the twins could be located.

"But then again, if they're lost, why haven't they responded?" Thisbe sat up higher, her voice edged with worry. "Maybe they're just trying to figure out how to handle the dragons." She turned to look out the east window and could just make out the northeast corner's dragon in the darkness. "Or . . . do you think the Revinir was telling the truth about no one following us?"

"Maybe Florence is worried about revealing that they're coming," said Fifer, cringing as she lied. "They might not know that the Revinir isn't with us anymore."

"You're sure she's not here?"

"I looked all around the courtyard. In every direction. There are four red dragons, and that's it."

"Then maybe I should just send a message to Rohan again. Or Florence. What did you say to her when you sent yours?"

Fifer cringed again and picked up a roundish instrument with strings. She plucked it with one finger, making a face when she realized how out of tune it was and realizing she couldn't tune it very easily with one hand. "Ugh, this is terrible." She didn't answer Thisbe's question. She couldn't remember exactly what the Revinir had said that had triggered Fifer's rash actions. But a strange and scary idea had formed. What if they *did* join the Revinir's side?

"Fifer?" said Thisbe.

Fifer jerked around. "What?"

"Are you okay?"

"I—yes, I'm feeling a lot better. Are you?"

"Same, but I asked you what you wrote to Florence."

"Oh!" said Fifer. She explained sheepishly, "I got so annoyed by this out-of-tune lute, and I'm frustrated I can't fix it."

"It's a mandolin," said Thisbe, which wasn't a disagreement, just a classification. "Bring it here. I'll tune it."

Fifer exhaled a quiet breath, hoping she'd successfully changed the subject, and brought the mandolin to Thisbe. While Thisbe tuned it, Fifer yawned and sat down on another sofa. A cloud of dust rose up, and she waved it away, then sneezed several times. Thisbe finished with the instrument and flopped back wearily.

"We should each take another medicine capsule and get some sleep," Fifer said. "It'll help us heal. We'll feel so much better in the morning."

"But what about our people?" Thisbe asked. She felt confused by the pain, and exhaustion had taken its toll.

"They're probably just resting somewhere for the night," said Fifer. "If they're not here by morning, we'll send the spell."

Placated, Thisbe winced in pain as she adjusted, trying to get comfortable. She uncorked her canteen and swallowed a capsule, then closed her eyes. Within minutes she was sleeping.

Fifer did the same, but she couldn't sleep. Instead she stared into the firelight, thinking about the Revinir. The Artiméans had brainstormed for months and had not come up with a way to beat her. She was surrounded by dragons who would do whatever she commanded. But what if Fifer and Thisbe could

LISA McMANN

get close to the Revinir when her guard was down and sort of . . . infiltrate? Or act as double agents? What would it look like to join forces with the Revinir—or at least pretend to? If they worked closely with the dragon-woman, and if she grew to trust them, would it be easier to do away with her? Or at least figure out what her weaknesses were?

It was the most frightening proposition Fifer could imagine. But the Revinir wanted Thisbe to join her so badly that it almost appeared to be an actual weakness, which the girls could exploit if they did it right. Could they pull off the most amazing con in the history of their worlds without messing it up? Could they use their brains, wits, and creative talents to convince the Revinir that they were willing to work with her after all?

If they failed, the Revinir would exact revenge far and wide, and perhaps destroy everyone and everything in her path. But if they did it right . . . if they appealed to the angry abandoned girl named Emma who'd only wanted a partnership with her siblings . . . whose existence must still haunt the Revinir . . . it just might work. The Revinir didn't have any other clear weakness that Fifer knew about yet. But she was arrogant, and she believed she could convince Thisbe to join her even after all the times Thisbe had refused. Perhaps that was the way in. But was it worth the risk?

Fifer smoothed her robe, knowing that all of the noble head mages who'd gone before her had been so successful because of the risks they'd taken. It was a gut feeling, and Fifer wondered if she was actually using hers properly for once. She could feel it—the inner tug that told her this was right. It was what Florence had coached her to look for. What Simber had assured her was inside her.

Now Fifer had to convince Thisbe. And if Fifer knew her twin, that task would prove to be difficult. As she drifted off, she recalled the thought she'd sent to Thisbe after the Revinir had captured them: *Remember the fights we've won.* Rescuing Pan's young dragons from ten years of captivity. Escaping the burning castle. Freeing their fellow black-eyed rulers from mind control. Saving Artimé from Frieda Stubbs. Fifer was going to dwell on that mantra from now on. Based on those successes, she knew that it took more than strength. It took cunning and wits to succeed against someone who was far more powerful than the two most magical people Artimé had ever seen.

LISA McMANN

A Strange Sight

Thisbe opened her eyes to find sunlight streaming over her. At first she didn't know where she was. She moved to stretch, and the pain in her ankle brought everything back. At least she was feeling more clearheaded—yesterday had felt so foggy compared to now. She turned to find Fifer, who was standing at the east window.

"Is someone out there?" Thisbe asked. "Did they come?"

Fifer turned, but Thisbe couldn't make out her expression because of the backlight. "Thiz, there's something I've got to tell you."

Thisbe sat up, gingerly testing her ankle and finding it had improved. "What?" She looked around the library at the stacks of books, and it suddenly dawned on her where they were. "Oh! I think I know where we are—this must be Ashguard's palace!"

Fifer tilted her head and stepped out of the light. "Where?"

"This is where Maiven went to find the ancient books. The Suresh family ruler, Ashguard the curmudgeon, lived here. This must be it. I can't imagine it's anything else."

Fifer looked nonplussed. "I don't know who that is, but I'm glad you figured it out. How close is the nearest village?"

"Oh, we're out in the middle of nowhere," Thisbe said, crestfallen. "I don't exactly know, but we're surrounded by natural barriers. The crater lake is on one side, and I think there are mountains somewhere else." She was quiet, then turned back to Fifer. "What did you have to tell me?"

Fifer tapped the windowsill, then slowly went over to Thisbe and knelt next to the sofa near her feet. "Um . . . how's your ankle?"

"Not bad. A couple more doses of medicine and I should be able to hobble a bit. Did you see someone outside again?"

"No. I mean the dragons are still there, but no people. No

rescue team. And I didn't expect to see them because, well, they're . . . not coming."

"What?" demanded Thisbe. "How do you know? Did Florence send a reply?"

"No," said Fifer, looking very serious. She pressed the bridge of her nose and let out a resigned sigh. "I know because I told them not to come. That's what I said to Florence in my message."

Thisbe's lips parted, and a confused expression came over her face. "Why?" she said softly. "Why would you do that?"

Fifer faltered, then plowed onward. "I had a gut feeling, and I went with it. I— It's hard for me to explain this without sounding like I've made a mistake, and I've been trying to figure it out for myself before I tried to explain it to you. I'm sorry I let it go this long."

Thisbe could feel angry heat coming up to her face. "You lied to me?" She couldn't fathom what reasoning Fifer had for doing this. "Have you lost your mind? Fifer! We got abducted by the Revinir, and you told Florence not to help us? That's nuts!" She fumed, thinking of all the ramifications of Fifer's poor decision. "Let's call them to come now before we starve to death." She fumbled around, trying to find her component vest so she could look for a send spell. It was on the floor, just out of reach. Had Fifer moved it so Thisbe couldn't take her out when she decided to confess this atrocity?

"Wait!" said Fifer, rising to kick the vest farther away and backing up, wary of her sister's sparking eyes and fingers. "Let me explain. Please!"

Thisbe grew angrier, and she could feel her fingertips sparking. "Who do you think you are, taking my life in your hands like that without consulting me? I'm so furious right now I could spit fire. You'd better get out of my way."

Fifer hastily ran around the other side of the desk and crouched. "Thisbe, listen to me!"

"Do you think that robe gives you the right to control my life, Head Mage Fifer?" Thisbe challenged.

"What? No! Of course not! I'm—it has nothing to do with that!"

"You are on a real power trip now, Miss Stowe," Thisbe snarled. Smoke swirled up from her nostrils, and she could feel heat in her throat, begging to be released. She let out an angry dragon roar like she'd never known she could do before.

Fifer stared, and Thisbe closed her mouth abruptly. "I didn't know I could do that," she said. She got to her feet and hobbled recklessly to the desk, too angry to feel pain. She peered out the east window at the dragons.

"Don't hurt me, please," begged Fifer, crouching lower.

"Be quiet," Thisbe said, still furious, but focusing on something else outside for the moment. "The dragons heard my roar," she said softly. "They're walking this way."

Fifer muttered something unintelligible under her breath and got up. Both girls watched as the two dragons from the front corners of the property moved toward the palace. The twins turned together to look out the window that overlooked the back of the property and saw those two dragons coming too.

"What have you done?" Fifer whispered.

"What have *you* done?" Thisbe fired back. She smoothed her scales and hopped on one foot back to her sofa; then she took a drink to try to cool the fire in her throat.

"They're sniffing the air," Fifer reported. "Slowing down."

"Nothing to see here, dragons," muttered Thisbe. She dropped her head into her hands, annoyed by Fifer and wishing the dragons away. "Are they still coming?"

"They've stopped," said Fifer. "They're turning around and going back."

"Good," said Thisbe with a relieved breath.

"How did you do that?" asked Fifer.

"I got mad enough, I guess," said Thisbe, eyeing her sister through slits.

"Look, will you let me explain?" Fifer tentatively stepped closer.

Thisbe shook her head and rolled her eyes, then sank back on the sofa. "Fine. Explain your madness, please. Because it sounds pretty bonkers to me."

Fifer wasn't sure what bonkers meant but figured it was a Kaylee word. And it didn't take much sleuthing to figure it out. "Bear with me," she said. "I have a story to tell." She went to the arm of Thisbe's sofa and, when Thisbe didn't set her on fire, perched on it. "After Alex died, when we were camped out in the forest searching for you, everybody kept asking me if I could feel your presence. And I couldn't. I'd never had that feeling that I knew what you were thinking, or where you were, or if you'd been hurt—all that stuff that Alex and Aaron felt for each other. Did you ever feel a connection like that?"

"No," said Thisbe impatiently. "What does that have to do with you making a grand decision to endanger our lives without telling me?"

"I'm getting to that," Fifer explained. "Anyway, you felt it the other day like I did, right? First on the beach, then when the Revinir was carrying us away. We spoke to each other in our minds."

"True," Thisbe admitted. "I still don't get—"

"Just give me two seconds," Fifer said, getting angry now too.

Thisbe crossed her arms over her chest and shot Fifer an annoyed look.

Fifer glared back. "I think the things are connected."

"What things?"

"Will you please just—"

"Fine! Go on! Say words already!"

Fifer stood up and stomped over to the south window, staring blindly out it as she seethed. She took a moment to collect herself. "Simber told me that I had good instincts and I needed to learn to rely on them. But for a long time I didn't know what that felt like. I learned slowly over time, and my biggest

LISA McMANN

moment, where I felt like I needed to make a life-altering move, was when I killed Frieda Stubbs. I felt it deep down, and I knew it was right a split second before I acted. Part of that came from you."

Thisbe pointedly kept her mouth shut.

Fifer glanced over her shoulder to see that her sister was still paying attention, and then she continued. "The connection between you and me has grown since that moment when you first told me I needed to do away with Frieda. We hashed out our differences, and we grew closer again after being distant for a while. Only things aren't like before, when we were kids—not exactly. Our relationship grew deeper in a different way. On a different level." She paused and turned around to face Thisbe. "And as we spent more time together, talking as leaders rather than just as twins, we began to . . . connect, I guess. So much that I felt that little electric jolt when we touched hands on the shore. Is that how it felt to you?"

"I . . . yes. I just thought it was a static shock, but then later . . ." Thisbe's anger had lessened. "I heard you in my head when the Revinir had us in her clutches."

"Exactly."

"But, if I may emphasize once more," said Thisbe dryly, "I still don't understand the connection."

"This is going to sound weird," said Fifer. "But I think I've developed my gut sense that everyone kept telling me I should have." She paused to let the words sink in. Thisbe narrowed her eyes but didn't challenge it, so Fifer continued. "Simber and Florence repeatedly told me to search for it and trust it. And I think I've finally found it. It led to our tighter connection, as well as other things."

Thisbe frowned. "And the other things are . . . ?" she asked suspiciously.

"Well," Fifer said, hesitating because it was going to sound bizarre. "I got a weird feeling when the Revinir was speaking to us that we should . . . stop fighting against her. Do you remember what I said to you in your mind?"

Thisbe faltered. "I think it was something like 'remember the fights we won.'"

"Yes. And how did we win our battles? Against dragons, against soldiers, against the catacombs and the Revinir, and against invisible Frieda Stubbs?"

Thisbe grew skeptical again. "I feel like you want me to say

LISA McMANN

something profound here, and I don't know what it is, so why don't you go ahead and tell me."

Fifer stared at her sister, thinking one word over and over in her head and trying to force it into Thisbe's mind the way it had happened before. But if it was sent out telepathically, it didn't connect—perhaps because the two were at odds at the moment.

"Well?" Thisbe demanded. "Stop staring at me like a freak!"

"Didn't you hear it?"

Thisbe exploded. "No!"

Fifer lifted her arms into the air and said, exasperated, "We won with our wits. Our smarts. Sure, magic helped against the soldiers, but we are not and never will be a match against the Revinir's power and strength. We have to beat her with our minds! Don't you see?"

"And would you like to tell me *how* we're going to do that?" Thisbe shouted.

"By joining her side!" Fifer screamed.

The words rang in the rotunda. Both girls were silent for a long moment. Fuming. Incredulous. Confused.

Then Thisbe put her face in her hands and shook her head wearily. "You have become completely unglued."

Fifer let out a frustrated noise and turned her back on her sister. She was mad at Thisbe, but she was also mad at herself for completely botching everything. The gut feeling she had was clear as day, but for the life of her she couldn't explain it adequately in words. Thisbe was right. Fifer fought off tears of frustration and wiped her eyes angrily, then stared out the window, pressing her forehead against the cool glass as the fog outside was beginning to burn off.

Then her eye caught something moving through the brush at the edge of the orchard. She focused on it, then gasped. She couldn't believe it. Everything they'd just been fighting about faded. "Thisbe," Fifer said, her anger slipping away. "You're going to freak out when I tell you what I'm seeing right now."

Testing the
Dragons

Dev had spent a restless night in the village, lying on a cold floor and trying to sleep. Trying to justify the fact that he was hiding from the dragons when maybe he should be defending his palace. Or meeting his grandfather. Or sleeping on his sofa. In Grimere, he'd reasoned, people walked around without the dragons bothering them. But this seemed different. The last time the Revinir had roared, it had been a command to kill him. Did that command expire after Drock had caught him mid-fall and taken him away? Or would these dragons still have that goal in mind if they discovered it was him?

LISA McMANN

It's not like the dragons had seemed to care that he'd been standing at the edge of the property earlier. But what if he took the lengthy trek from the orchard through the brush and up the hill, and went halfway across the open courtyard to the center tower—that was the part that frightened him the most. If the dragons decided they were interested in him after all, if they came for him once he stepped onto the property, he had no place to hide. They'd catch him for sure. Whether he made a run for the tower or back to the village, he wouldn't be able to beat them.

He'd thought about food. Could he catch some fish and use it to bribe them? Or perhaps the dragons went to the river to drink and eat at some point? That was it. He'd get close enough to spy and wait for them to go to the river.

And that's exactly where he'd been sitting for hours in the early-morning fog, waiting for at least one of the dragons to go to the river so his chances of being eaten were lessened. Not long ago all four had moved toward the tower, but then they'd retreated. Dev had held his ground and continued to wait. Then he saw the movement way up in his library window. The person, whoever it was, was still up there.

He sat up as the person looked out. He couldn't make out any features. The angle was too sharp, and the sun was bouncing off the dusty glass, obscuring his view with a glare. He didn't feel afraid to be seen—humans weren't his enemies these days. Maybe Ashguard or whoever it was could help if he wasn't hiding from the dragons. Keeping his eye on the great red beasts, Dev stood up and took a few slow steps forward through the brush, trying not to make any sudden movements that might set the dragons in motion.

They looked at him but didn't move. Dev kept walking. His heart began to pound, and his scales rose on his arms and legs, snagging his new wool skirt. "Everybody just stay where you are," he muttered under his breath. "Nothing is happening here." He kept his head down, watching from the corner of his eye, first one dragon, then the other.

The front dragon made a noise and shook out its wings. It took a step toward him. Dev kept walking, picking up his pace slightly, acutely aware of where he was in relationship to safety at every moment. He reached the halfway point. If the dragon charged now, Dev was better off running for the tower than for the orchard and village.

He began the climb up the hill and two more red dragons at the far corners of the property came into view. Great. They turned toward him, and one rose up to get a better view, then rumbled and spat a spray of fire. Dev pretended he was a townsperson in Dragonsmarche going about his business and didn't slow down. He reached the edge of the courtyard and headed between two of the small towers, aiming for the larger one in the center of the property. His tower. Who would he find inside? At this point, he didn't care. If it was anyone other than the gray man, he'd make them leave.

None of the dragons took more than a few steps toward him. With his heartbeat pounding in his ears, Dev sprinted the last few steps to the middle tower doorway and darted inside. The foxes startled but then settled when they saw him. He said a few soothing words to comfort them and himself. And then he started up the stairwell as fast as he could climb.

Halfway up he heard a noise and whirled around. Had the dragons come after him? He peered anxiously out of the windows and saw they were still in their corners. With a sigh of relief he turned. And there, on the curve of the stairwell several steps above him, was a shocking sight.

LISA McMANN

"You're alive," said Fifer softly.

Dev sucked in a breath and stared at her. "Yes," he whispered. And then, overcome by the sight of an ally, he gripped the handrail and doubled over, feeling pain and hope and fear crash together inside him. "Oh gods," he whispered. "It's you." He suppressed a sob and covered his eyes, then looked again to make sure it was really Fifer. And that she was really wearing the head mage robe of Artimé. "You came."

Fifer nodded, her expression cracking with emotion at the sight of his tears. She went down one more step uncertainly, then another. "Do you . . . want . . . help?"

Dev nodded, overcome. He climbed the step to her and slipped his arms around Fifer's waist in a hug.

"Oh," said Fifer, stiffening in surprise. After a moment she reached around him, too. Then she gently pressed his head against her shoulder, feeling his sobs. His warm tears soaked into her robe. She wasn't quite sure what was happening to make him react like this. But whatever experiences he'd been through since she'd seen him last had obviously changed him.

She reckoned she'd changed a bit since then too.

Having It Out

Come on," Fifer said after a minute, and pulled away. "Thisbe is upstairs. She can't wait to see you." She took his trembling hand in her uninjured one and started up, pulling him along. "The Revinir told us she'd killed you. So seeing you in the brush was quite a shock. A pleasant surprise, I mean."

Dev swallowed hard. "Thisbe is here?"

Fifer nodded, then studied his expression, but it was unreadable. "We have a lot of catching up to do."

"We sure do," muttered Dev, as hard feelings came out of nowhere. Thisbe was way out here? Had she been looking

LISA McMANN

for him? He had a lot of questions for her. "Anyone else?"

"No, just us two."

They rounded the curve at the fourth floor, and Dev paused to look at the fresh piles of debris from Thisbe and Fifer's unfortunate fall and the new gaping holes in the floor. "What happened there?"

"That's where the Revinir dropped us," Fifer said. "We went right through the rotted roof and two or three floors before we stopped."

Dev muttered something unsavory before turning to Fifer with new respect. "How are you alive after a fall like that?"

"Luck. And soft rotten wood."

They neared the top. Dev pushed ahead, climbing swiftly to his home. To see Thisbe. He came up through the floor and spied her on his sleeping sofa. Their eyes connected, and Dev stopped abruptly, feeling a million emotions at once and not sure how to express them. Anger bubbled up first. He started toward her, balling up his fists. "Why—how?" he said, his voice cracking so much that he could hardly finish the question. "How could you!"

"Dev." Thisbe got up and hobbled over to him. She gripped

LISA McMANN

the railing for support, and tears streamed down her face. "I'm so sorry. And I'm so happy to see you alive! Please forgive me. I can explain everything."

Dev stared with doubt in his eyes for a long moment, then dropped them and noticed her limp. "Your ankle . . ."

"It's fine. But, Dev—you've been on my mind every day. I'm so sorry we had to leave you."

"I saw you go," Dev choked out. He turned away and put his hand over his face as Fifer reached the top and hung back. Then he looked at Thisbe again. "I saw all of you on the ghost dragons. I called out to you. I *screamed your name*. And you didn't turn around."

Thisbe gripped her tangled hair, distraught. "I didn't know," she wailed. "I didn't hear you. Where were you?"

"In one of the towers. Locked up. She saw right through my act." He stumbled over to the window, trying to get away from the emotion, but it followed him. "I told you she would."

Thisbe grimaced. "We couldn't risk checking for you. There were dragons everywhere. I assumed when you didn't come to our meeting place that she'd sent you to the dungeon."

"Well, she didn't." Dev sniffed hard and wiped his eyes on

his sleeve, then took a deep breath and let it out. "I warned you it wouldn't work. That I wasn't a good enough actor. She—she tried to kill me."

"She thinks you're dead," Thisbe said. "She told us so. I'm so sick about all of this. And I understand if you can never forgive me. I really thought our plan would work. But in the end . . . well, you turned out to be the sacrifice. You saved the rest of us. And we were all planning to come back, to find you and take down the Revinir just as soon as we could. But then she abducted Fifer and me from Artimé and told us you were dead. And I . . . I felt like I died inside. You're like a brother to me, Dev. You're my family now. I'm so happy you're alive. How did you escape?"

Dev narrowed his eyes and looked sharply at Thisbe, but he didn't say anything for a long moment. Some of his anger slipped away at her words. "It was Drock," he said in a quiet voice so the dragons outside wouldn't hear. "He saved my life. He's not under her mind control after all. Not yet, anyway."

"Seriously?" said Fifer, moving farther into the room. "That's great to know. Wonderful news."

Dev turned, realizing she'd been standing there. "Yes." He

looked back at Thisbe. "We have a lot of things to talk about."

Thisbe nodded. Fifer joined her sister on the sofa. The twins put their previous argument aside so they could fill Dev in on everything that had happened after the ghost dragons had brought Thisbe and her crew to Artimé, including the civil war they'd helped win. Then Dev told them what had happened with Drock catching him and bringing him to the cavelands, and his time with Astrid, and then coming here. He told them about the biggest fright of his life in the river, hiding from the Revinir and the red dragons, and the dread that came with seeing the Revinir return. So much had happened, and their stories stretched on through the afternoon. By the time they were tired of talking, some of Dev's hurt feelings were soothed. But it would take him a while to build trust with Thisbe again.

"Have you eaten anything?" Dev asked after his stomach growled loudly. "I had to leave my fish in a hurry when I saw the Revinir coming, and I haven't had any food since." He looked around. "Where is it? Did it go bad?"

"We weren't sure how long it had been sitting there," said Fifer. "So I put it in the courtyard, thinking we could use it for bait, or fashion the bones to make fishing hooks or something."

She glanced at him. "But I found the water pump. We're a little worried about what the dragons will do if we go to the river, but we don't really have a choice. So I've been trying to figure out how to catch fish without fishing line. Do you still have yours?"

"Better yet, I have a net," he said. "But do you think the dragons will come after me?"

"They've had ample chance to nab you," Fifer reasoned. "They know you're here."

Thisbe added, "We think their job is to intimidate us and keep Fifer and me from leaving. So I don't think they'll hurt you."

"Yeah," said Fifer. "The Revinir is trying to break us down so we join her side."

Dev snorted with laughter for the first time. "That's a joke," he said. "Like it would ever happen. She's delirious."

Fifer shifted uneasily, and Thisbe gave her a "See, I told you so" look. But neither started in on that heated topic again. It would have to wait.

"I'll go with you to fish," Fifer said to Dev. "The dragons didn't do anything at all when I went to get water from the pump earlier. Hey, Thiz, are you feeling strong enough to stoke the fire so we can cook?"

"I think I can manage it," said Thisbe. She handed Fifer her empty canteen, and the two exchanged a wary glance. "We'll talk later about the other thing," Thisbe added, "but Dev's right. And we're going to need to contact Florence. Soon."

Dev raised an eyebrow, not sure what that conversation was about. Fifer shrugged as if she didn't care, even though she cared deeply. She'd have to figure out a different angle to convince Thisbe. But meanwhile, she was starving. She slipped both canteen straps over her head and one arm. Dev took his along too. As they exited the courtyard, the dragons barely acknowledged them, though the dragon at the back corner by the river seemed concerned they would try to travel beyond the boundary he'd set. Still, he let them go and adjusted his position to watch closely. After a while Dev and Fifer got used to him being there.

They quickly fell into their old pattern of friendship when it had been at its best, in the forest before Dev and Arabis had fallen under the Revinir's mind control. They chatted as they fished, filling in many of the questions they had for each other and adding detail to their stories. But Fifer didn't bring up her idea about the Revinir. Instead, she had something else she wanted to express.

"Thisbe truly is sorry," she told Dev. "I want you to know that. She was sick about leaving you behind. She cares about you . . . and so do I. I think she felt like it was all her fault when we heard you were dead. She would have never forgiven herself if it had been true."

Dev was taken aback by Fifer's kind words and couldn't look at her. The Revinir had told him that no one cared about him. That sentiment had echoed a lifetime of abuse as a slave for a selfish princess who only liked him when he was assisting her in making mischief and taking the blame for her misdeeds. Could the Revinir be wrong? Or was Fifer lying just to appease him?

After a minute Dev grunted, then checked the position of the nearest dragon, wanting to be careful what he said in its presence. That the dragons had seen him alive was already a risk, because if the Revinir thought to ask them if they had, they'd answer truthfully. But it was too late to change that, so he wanted them to have as little information about him as

LISA McMANN

59 « Dragon Slayers

possible. He scooped the net swiftly and pulled out a flopping fish, then slid it on the grass for Fifer to handle. He leaned toward her, then whispered, "I'm just not sure where we go from here. We can't let the Revinir know I'm alive. And I'm sure she'll be coming back for you eventually."

By sunset the three were full and feeling more comfortable physically. Thisbe's ankle and Fifer's wrist and their other injuries and aches from the fall were healing nicely, thanks to the magical medication Henry had made sure the head mage carried. They were settling in with one another too, but kept the conversation light—they were all still dealing with the emotional reunion and new situation of living in this onion bulb together, and figuring out what life looked like from here.

And Fifer's mind was distracted by something else entirely: how to convince Thisbe of what they needed to do . . . and somehow include Dev without revealing to the Revinir that he was very much alive.

Resolved

In Artimé, Rohan did his best to step into a sort of leadership role, though it was weird because this wasn't his island or his people. He observed as more and more people and creatures from other islands began to arrive in Artimé, and he knew without a doubt that the good mages of this land had more than a surface knowledge of their neighbors and a relationship with them. They had strong bonds that could only have been built over time. The people from Warbler, Karkinos, and the Island of Shipwrecks were clearly dedicated to the Artiméans. And so were a surprising number of the people in Quill. When they heard that Florence was

LISA McMANN

calling for their help, they flocked to the shore in such great numbers that Aaron had to take a moment to magically extend the lawn so everyone could fit. Even some of the former dissenters begrudgingly joined in, for their lives had been saved multiple times by the fighting teams of Artimé. And perhaps seeing what a civil war could do to their precious land had changed a few of them along the way.

As Florence trained everyone, Rohan watched the seasoned generation of leaders, like Lani and Samheed and Aaron, and the elder scientists like Ishibashi, as well as Queen Maiven, with reverence and respect. He absorbed their moves and decisions and tried to figure out the mental steps they took that led them to make the choices they made. He was a sponge in the middle of the lawn, soaking up the expertise of the ones who'd built such a great example of leadership. And he took Florence's request seriously. He didn't want to let her down.

But he missed Thisbe. Desperately. Achingly. She'd brought out the boldness in him, and now that she was gone, some of his courage had left him. He knew he had to flesh it out again on his own, but it wasn't easy. He was in a foreign land. Anxious about his *pria*. His love.

Rohan was a young man. Fourteen, on the verge of fifteen at his best guess—he wasn't sure of his age. But his connection with Thisbe was electric. It was life changing. And he knew she felt something for him, too, though it might not be on the same level. She was driven by duty, as was he, and that in itself seemed enough to make them compatible. When separated, they were strong. But together they were stronger. Fluid. Dare he say it? Unstoppable. Whether they worked together as friends or something more was to be decided by fate. But working with Thisbe for life was no longer an if. They had formed something, an unbreakable bond, that couldn't be removed no matter how much distance was between them. Thisbe had changed Rohan's life. And even if he could only admire her from afar, so be it. But he knew that their connection had solidified something incredibly powerful between them that no human nor beast nor dragon-woman could sever.

Love was a strong word. He knew that, too, and anyone who hadn't experienced this feeling couldn't possibly relate to it. If what Rohan felt for Thisbe wasn't love, it was a step above it. Something transcendent that hadn't yet been named.

Luckily, he could concentrate on other things, though it

was difficult at times. But when it came to assisting Thisbe's people and statues that she counted on most, he was all in. Whatever it took, he would do it. His passion and drive had the wondrous ability to shove aside his weariness and fatigue. And his desire to be as powerful as possible against the Revinir was so strong that he would do anything . . . to learn everything.

That's why staying in Artimé wasn't quite as painful as it could have been, though he knew Thisbe had been captured again. He agreed with Florence and Thisbe that there was only one chance to beat the Revinir. And at first it seemed like their chance had been fumbled or lost because of Thisbe and Fifer's capture. But Florence and Maiven didn't waver, so neither did Rohan. The two of them knew that they all had to be at their strongest in order to continue on. And Rohan wouldn't stand by and let anyone eclipse him. This was his duty to the land of the dragons, and his duty to Queen Maiven Taveer and the crown. He wouldn't let the Revinir or anyone supporting her stand in his way. He was ready to be a great warrior like Florence. To assist Thisbe and Maiven. And to eliminate anyone who sided with the evil dragon-woman, for no doubt she was recruiting people left and right while holding all the dragons hostage. There was no question about putting an end to her. And he would convince his fellow black-eyed slaves of this too. They had one chance to knock out this monster, and they had to succeed. There was no alternative except to lose everything, including wiping the black-eyed rulers out of existence. And with so much life left to live, Rohan wouldn't take that as an answer. The upcoming weeks would be the greatest education Rohan had ever received. And he was ready for it.

There was nothing that could possibly make his faith in Thisbe and her people waver. They were going to win. He could feel it—things were going to go their way eventually. But in the meantime, without Thisbe there, the chasm of loneliness in Rohan's heart was growing deeper by the day.

He only wished he could talk to her. Just once. Just for a moment. He had a slew of send components now, but he knew what Florence had said. Under no circumstances should anyone contact Fifer or Thisbe. It could endanger their lives. So with great reluctance, Rohan kept his components safely tucked away next to his heart.

Meeting of the Minds

A week passed in the palace surrounded by red dragons, and every day Fifer had to fight Thisbe to not call on Florence to come for them. To convince her to hold off from communicating at all for now. "We only have a few send components," Fifer argued. "We have to save them for when we really need them. But right now, Florence is probably training everybody and making our army stronger, and you and I are living a pretty good life here with Dev while the Revinir thinks we're suffering. Do you see what I'm saying?"

"I get that," said Thisbe impatiently, "but if we call Florence now, she can send someone for us and we'll all be in Artimé training together."

"Ah, but then the Revinir will find out, and she'll be even angrier. And you're assuming our people can fight off four dragons. I feel confident they will attack if we attempt to leave, and even if we succeed in escaping, they'll follow us if we don't slay them! We can't have our people fighting those dragons when they're not the ones who matter. There's only one dragon who matters, and we need to save our fighters for her. I really wish you'd listen to my idea."

By now, Dev had heard bits and pieces of Fifer's backward-sounding plan to join the Revinir's side, and he'd agreed strongly with Thisbe. But he hadn't heard Fifer explain it directly. "All right," he said from across the room. "I'll take the bait. What *is* your plan exactly, Fifer?"

Thisbe rolled her eyes and turned away, but didn't try to stop Fifer from answering.

Fifer fidgeted with her robe, not expecting the abrupt question and not wanting to mess up the answer again. But she'd been mulling things over for a long time, and she was ready.

"Okay," she said. "Here is where we stand. From our best

deductions, based on what all three of us know, the Revinir came here some time ago to scout out the area and discovered that it was remote and deserted—that was when Dev hid in the river."

Dev nodded. "Agreed."

Thisbe didn't indicate she was listening.

Fifer continued. "She probably scouted out other areas too, and decided that since Thisbe was so good at escaping the castle, she needed a new place to keep her from which she couldn't escape. So she chose this palace—she could easily station dragons around here to keep her locked in the area, but she wouldn't starve to death, and she could find shelter from the weather. She doesn't want Thisbe dead, but she wants to break her. She believes that because Thisbe's level of evilness is greater than her level of goodness, she's the easiest nut to crack of all the black-eyed rulers. And rightly or wrongly, she concludes that because of this, Thisbe will be the one most likely to join her. In her mind, they will successfully create the bond between dragon and black-eyed ruler that is necessary to take over authentic leadership of Grimere and the land of the dragons."

Dev frowned. "What is necessary to do that? I've never known the rules."

"Maiven Taveer said that the dragons must be of sound mind, which they are not, and they must vote for a leader, which they have not done. And the black-eyed people appoint a ruler, which they *have* done—it's Queen Maiven Taveer, not Thisbe. We don't think the Revinir knows these rules, because she believes she can just assume the position of head dragon. And she doesn't know that Maiven is alive, much less that she's the reigning queen of Grimere."

"Okay," said Dev, trying to keep up.

Fifer continued. "But she does seem to know that the ruling dragon and the black-eyed ruler must also officially choose each other to be partners in order to restore the leadership of the land. Without that agreement, the rightful rulership cannot be restored, and the ghost dragons won't be able to pass on to their next life."

"And you think the answer to this is for Thisbe to pretend she's ready to make that commitment to the Revinir?" asked Dev. "So it gives Thisbe the power and the title of ruler alongside a tyrant—which would make Thisbe look like a terrible person."

"Exactly!" said Thisbe, turning sharply. "And even if I wanted to do that, which I don't, the bigger problem is that the black-eyed people choose their ruler, and so do the dragons. We've already got our ruler in Maiven—"

"Whom the Revinir doesn't know exists," Fifer reminded her.

"—and," Thisbe went on, "the dragons, in their right minds, would never choose the Revinir to lead them!"

"That's exactly my point," said Fifer. "They're not in their right minds. So the rulership won't actually transfer, and all will be fine. But the Revinir knows nothing of this! Think of it from her perspective. She believes she has everything she needs except the black-eyed ruler to give her the blessing of the partnership. She's so close to it that she's practically drooling."

"So . . . ," said Dev, thinking hard. "But wait. If Thisbe *isn't* the proper leader, because Maiven is, then the partnership won't go through."

"That is what I've been trying to say," said Fifer, and she began ticking things off on her fingers: "The dragons aren't in their right minds to choose a leader. Even if they were, they wouldn't choose her. The Revinir doesn't know about Maiven being the chosen pick for the black-eyed rulers. So she won't know that this plan will fail in a variety of ways."

Thisbe looked highly skeptical. "Then what good is it to do it?"

Fifer pressed her lips together, trying to stay calm and choose her words properly. "Look at where we are. We're stuck, far away from her. The Revinir has one hundred percent control of us from afar, and we have no way of stopping her—and let's be honest. We know that killing her is the only way to break the spell. But if she comes to check on us, or if you tell one of the dragons to take you to her, you can say you're feeling desperate and starting to change your mind. You tell her you want to consider entering into that agreement with her . . . with a few conditions, just so it's not suspicious. Then you take up residence in the castle alongside her, and she puts trust in you, and you have chances to be alone with her." Fifer gave her a hard look.

Thisbe stared at the fireplace for a long time. "And if I'm alone with her," she said slowly, "I can use the obliterate spell to destroy her without hurting anyone else."

Fifer held her breath. After a moment, she let it out. "Yes," she said softly.

"That's a lot of ifs. And it's a huge risk, when she could

freak out and kill me at any time. What happens when we get to the point of agreement and the partnership doesn't take effect because Maiven is still alive? She'll know something's up."

"You can say you didn't know the rules either."

"She'll never believe me," Thisbe muttered.

"You've lied to her successfully before," Dev said quietly. "I think you're the only one who can do it. For some reason she can't read you like she can read the others. She told me that when I was in the tower. It seemed like she begrudgingly admired that in you."

Fifer nodded. "She said as much when she abducted us."

Thisbe closed her eyes and sighed. "It's dangerous."

"Well," said Fifer, "we'll have a backup plan then. Yes—so maybe we *will* alert Florence and ask everybody to come, or at least a few of them at first. But," said Fifer, growing serious, "we can't tell any of them that you are faking this partnership. The Revinir could use dragon-bone broth and get the truth out of any of them. And she'll need to see that our people are truly upset about this venture between you two—that's exactly the kind of proof we'll want to convince her that you've really changed your mind. She's going to want to crow about this, not keep it secret. She'll *want* all of the seven islands to know that one of their beloved mages has joined her in ruling the land of the dragons."

Thisbe shook her head. "I don't know about this."

Fifer leaned in. "Remember what she said when she abducted us? She wants all of our people to come to her so she can fight them at home. I'm saying we give her exactly that and beat her at her own game. She'll never know what hit her."

The three were silent as their thoughts whirred crazily.

"It's not a bad plan," Dev admitted.

Fifer shot him a grateful look. Then she turned back to Thisbe and reiterated, "We have to convince everyone that you've entered this agreement willingly because you are more evil than good. So that if they ever get captured, they won't give it away."

"Even Rohan?" Thisbe whispered. Something wretched pounded behind her eyes.

The fire crackled sharply, and sparks shimmered and settled.

"All of the humans, for sure," said Fifer. "Since they are all vulnerable to the broth. It'll take some work to convince them. But I have ideas for how to do that, too."

LISA McMANN

Dev glanced at Fifer with renewed respect, but he could see why Thisbe would be so against this plan. It seemed difficult, yet what a gloriously smart way to beat the Revinir.

Agitated, Thisbe got up and limped over to the fireplace. "How do you get Florence and everybody here?"

"Sometime after you're gone," said Fifer, "I'll call them in with a send component. I can feed them the lies."

"So now you're not going with me?" asked Thisbe. "I have to do this alone?" New fears struck her—fears she'd been able to tamp down until now. One in particular left her incredibly unsettled. She didn't want to entertain it and tried to smother it.

Fifer frowned, thinking hard. "I want to go," she admit-ted. "But it'll be more realistic without me—she's not going to believe that I've changed my mind. In fact . . ." She squeezed her eyes shut and imagined how things would play out. "In fact," she said again. "Yes. It's better this way. We'll have you sneak off. I'll send for Florence, and I'll be devastated and furi-ous that you are doing this. I'll say that I tried to talk you out of it, but you were embracing your evil side. Everyone will believe it if I'm the one to say you betrayed us. Because they think I never lie."

"I know that's not true," Thisbe retorted.

"Yes, but they don't." Fifer smiled sweetly, then got up and went to Thisbe and placed her hand on her sister's arm. "Just think about it," Fifer said. "I know it's a lot to process."

Thisbe shook her head slowly. "I don't know," she muttered. She looked at Fifer, and something electric passed between them again, restoring their connection that had been lost during their massive argument. It gave Thisbe a moment of relief from her fears.

Fifer felt it and sucked in a breath—it seemed like a good sign that this was the right thing to do. Thisbe might not be sure yet. But Fifer was. And they had a lot of work to do before they could put this plan in motion.

Coming to Terms

Thisbe rolled the thoughts over in her mind for a few days, trying to convince herself that Fifer's idea wasn't strong enough. That it would never work.

Because for Thisbe, the whole "measuring one's good and evil levels" had been a bit of a sensitive issue ever since she'd learned of this dragon concept. She knew that Dev was exactly half-good and half-evil. And his personality had imitated that, coincidence or not.

She also knew that Fifer was way more good than evil, and it had shown throughout her entire life. Though there were exceptions. Killing Frieda Stubbs, for example. And this recent infiltration idea Fifer had come up with was pretty much something straight out of an evil person's playbook. So maybe someone's level wasn't totally indicative of what their actions would be like.

When the Revinir had told Thisbe she was more evil than good, it had felt really strange and unsettling. Rohan had heard this pronouncement. He hadn't seemed bothered by it, but it had bothered Thisbe quite a lot. She didn't feel evil . . . or particularly good, either. But the Revinir's assumption that Thisbe, because she was more evil than good, would automatically want to be like the dragon-woman, or even work with her? It was insulting and borderline horrifying.

There was a lot to consider regarding Fifer's proposal. But there was one thing that bothered Thisbe the most. Something she hadn't voiced. Something she'd barely allowed herself to worry about over the past year or two. It was a preposterous fear, yet Thisbe couldn't shake it. And now the question pounded her: If she joined forces with the Revinir, would that somehow trigger this purported evilness inside her? Would Thisbe try being evil . . . and like it? And worse, did Thisbe secretly *want* to be in partnership with the Revinir because she was more evil than good, but she just hadn't realized it yet? Maybe she was on the brink of falling into an abyss of evil. Was that what had happened to Emma, the girl who had turned into the Revinir?

She thought about the journals she'd read in Artimé. She hadn't gotten as far as she'd wanted to before the dragon-woman appeared out of nowhere in the jungle. But what she'd learned was that Emma was a pretty normal girl who'd felt distanced from her siblings. And when they'd left her behind to do bigger things, she became angry and turned a corner that led her down a really horrifying path of revenge.

What if that happened to Thisbe? What if she turned into someone as horrible as the Revinir? Was that the kind of person the Revinir had seen in her from the first day in the catacombs? Someone just like her?

Thisbe tried to push these thoughts aside. She hated that the Revinir had gotten inside her head. She could recall her voice too easily from the awful catacombs, and it swam through her ears. Cajoling her. Telling her she was her secret weapon. Now she finally understood what the dragon-woman meant. And that made it even worse. How could Thisbe do this—pretend to join the Revinir, to be the one to carry out her plan? And what would that do to her mentally and emotionally?

And besides all of that, what would others think of her? Rohan and Simber and Florence and Aaron and Maiven and the rest? Those thoughts were the worst. Sure, they'd find out the truth eventually. But they would be so disappointed in her. If there was anything Thisbe couldn't stand, it was someone being disappointed in her. Like Alex had been the last time she'd seen him. A pain speared through her.

"I'm going for a walk," she announced abruptly. Fifer and Dev were across the room, examining sticks from a pile Dev had gathered. She didn't want them to come with her, and she made that clear in her tone, for they didn't offer. Thisbe needed to get out of there, no matter how her ankle felt. She'd been cooped up since they'd been dropped here. Maybe some fresh air would do her good.

It took her a long time to get down all the flights of stairs, but she finally made it and began a slow walk across the courtyard. The fresh breeze and sunshine lifted her spirits immediately, but now Alex was on her mind. Maybe that was why she'd had such a hard time with his death—his disappointment in her.

And yet he had come after her when she'd needed help. Had he died still feeling that same way? Had her mistakes, which had brought him to Grimere, caused his death? And did he realize that at the end? Was his final thought before he died about his continuing disappointment in her?

And now all the rest of Artimé and Grimere would be disappointed too. They'd hardly had a chance to see that she'd grown and accomplished things. Alex had never seen it. Fifer had barely witnessed it. Thisbe pictured what it would be like when Fifer told everyone that she had left to join forces with their worst enemy. She imagined Aaron's face at hearing that news. The thought made her sick.

And then she pictured Rohan, and her heart tore. He would feel personally betrayed. It could hurt him so badly that he might never forgive Thisbe when this was all over. When she could tell him the truth. Would anyone believe her? What if they didn't? Could Rohan ever trust her again after this? The decision was potentially life altering, and Thisbe didn't think she could do it. It would be the hardest thing she'd ever done. And she could lose the one who filled her soul . . . forever.

Thisbe blinked hard in the sunshine and checked the

location of the dragons. They had their eyes on her, but they didn't come for her. The fog that she'd seen every morning and evening from the windows had burned off for now. She continued over the grass and headed toward the back of the property to the river until her ankle ached, and then she stopped and watched the water flow. Watched it wash away everything in its path.

She thought about the story Dev had told about hiding from the Revinir, and about how one of the images he'd seen had come to happen in his life, just like what had happened with her. Dev had been so brave, so desperate, so totally unwilling to be caught by the Revinir, that he'd been ready to die rather than be captured again.

Thisbe didn't really know how the people of Grimere and the surrounding villages were feeling about the dragon-woman, but they certainly had to be scared too—the ones the Revinir hadn't fed the dragon-bone broth to, anyway. Then there were Thisbe's fellow black-eyed friends, whose lives were in danger. Would they be willing to do anything to avoid capture like Dev had done?

Thisbe thought about Fifer's plan. If Thisbe didn't go along with the Revinir, would the Revinir go after one of the others instead and try to force them into the partnership? Thisbe didn't like that idea either. That could turn out frighteningly bad for everyone involved.

She closed her eyes, tipped her head back, spread her arms wide, and let the breeze flow over her. The land of the dragons was hers—the land of her people. Her grandmother should be ruling it. And maybe Thisbe or one of her friends could be the ruler someday if they ever got it back. But if they couldn't stop the Revinir, the black-eyed rulership would end forever. All of them were in danger—not just her and Fifer and Dev. Not just the rest of the black-eyed humans and the dragons. Everyone in the land of the dragons, plus everyone in the seven islands, was threatened. And no one could come up with any other viable way to overthrow the Revinir.

Fifer's plan had a few holes in it. But together, maybe they could fill them. And it seemed possible they could succeed. Thisbe was an excellent actor—she felt pretty good about being able to convince the Revinir she was joining her side. But could Thisbe come to terms with how hard this would be mentally when everyone she loved would think she had betrayed them? Rohan's face kept coming to mind. How could she even look at him again, knowing how wrecked he'd feel? He'd be devastated. That was by far the worst part of all of this.

Yet after months of brainstorming with the best warriors they knew, this was the first idea about how to defeat the Revinir that actually sounded like it could work. And Thisbe was the only one in the right spot and with the right creative skills to do it.

She let her hands drop to her sides and opened her eyes. It seemed like everyone in two worlds was depending on her. It was a heavy load to bear. And that tiny but awful worry about actually liking the evil side continued to sow doubts in Thisbe's mind. Is this how it had begun for Emma? Or for Aaron? Was there any way to control that, or was it her destiny?

Thisbe turned back to the palace and started walking. Her ankle didn't hurt quite so much going back—perhaps she'd loosened it up a little. And maybe the sunshine had helped her spirits overall, despite the gravity of the fears Thisbe wrestled with. Going up those stairs would be a challenge. But she was pretty good at facing challenges head on.

Once Thisbe neared the top, she called out. "Fifer?"

"What is it?" said Fifer, coming to the landing. "Do you need help?"

Thisbe shook her head. She'd done so many hard things alone. And this was just one more. "I'm going to do it. Your plan, I mean. I . . . I'll do it."

Filling in Some Pieces

While ships continued to arrive in Artimé filled with Warblerans determined to support Florence and the rest of her team, Fifer, Thisbe, and Dev strategized in Ashguard's library without telling anyone what they were doing. They lived fairly peacefully with the four red dragons, whom the humans had decided by now must have been instructed not to harm anyone on the property, but to keep them from leaving. And as long as they didn't step outside of the dragons' boundaries or cross the river, the three black-eyed schemers were safe and free to roam.

LISA McMANN

"How does it begin?" Thisbe asked. She lay sprawled on her stomach on the library floor with papers surrounding her. She and Fifer and Dev had sketched plans, discarded them for other plans, then returned to the original ideas.

"First, we wait awhile," said Fifer. "Not just so we can be strong and fully healthy again, but also to get the Revinir chomping at the bit."

"She's going to expect me to be suffering and ready to give up," Thisbe said. "So I can't look too healthy."

"True," said Fifer. "But I want your ankle fully healed."

"Fair. And I agree, we want her to be getting anxious and wondering if I'll ever come around. The more time that goes by, the better the chances she'll believe I've come to work with her." Thisbe hesitated. "She'll ask about you, Fifer. What's our plan there?"

Dev chimed in. "Play up the good-evil thing. You're evil; Fifer's good; you left her behind. She loves talking about that stuff. It's like how some people talk about astrology and the stars—she's a true believer that it means something."

Thisbe glanced at him. "Don't you believe in the good-evil levels?"

"Pfft. It's bollocks."

"Really?" said Fifer, sitting up. "But what about you? You're fifty percent good and fifty percent evil, and your actions totally fit that."

Thisbe flashed Fifer a warning look, and Dev's jaw dropped. "I'm . . . what now?" he asked. "I don't think I knew that." He frowned, thinking it over.

"Hux said not to tell him," Thisbe muttered. "The knowledge can really mess with your mind. Believe me."

Dev tapped his lips. "Exactly half? That's unusual, isn't it?"

"It's probably not even accurate anymore," Thisbe said. "That's just what Hux told us when we first met you. These levels must change all the time."

"I didn't think it was still a secret," said Fifer sheepishly. "Sorry, Dev. And Thisbe's right. You've changed a lot since we first met you. You seem to be more good than evil now."

"See?" Thisbe exploded. "Now you're making assumptions! You're saying that just because Dev is nicer to you than he used to be, it means he's somehow gotten more goodness in him. And that is not at all an indicator! *I'm* nice to you. Does that mean I'm mostly good? Obviously not."

LISA McMANN

87 « Dragon Slayers

"You're being kind of a snot right now," Fifer remarked.

Thisbe fumed. "You just feel like it's no big deal because you see yourself in the clear, based on the assumption that having more good inside you is better. You're someone who's been told they're more good than evil. So you don't see the impact this has on people like me, who have a bias automatically applied to them. I'm more evil than good, so therefore you expect me to do bad things. You probably even pity me, you annoyingly righteous do-gooder. That's not fair. What if you ignored your inner goodness and only focused on the sliver of evil inside you? I firmly believe people do this all the time."

"I would never do that," said Fifer primly.

"You totally used your evil side on me when we arrived here, you big liar."

"That was to protect you, so I see that as using my good side, actually," Fifer retorted.

"This whole plan of yours is pure evil!" Thisbe said.

Fifer gasped. "It is not. It's—"

Thisbe turned away in disgust. "Can we not talk about this?"

Dev's head ping-ponged between the twins. "Um, okay, so if anyone cares, we have some work to do." He tapped the plans.

"I want to get through this. I've got to work on my weapons."

"Right," said Fifer, settling down.

Thisbe wrinkled her nose at Fifer, and Fifer sneered back. Then they both chuckled softly.

Dev did a double take. "Okay, laughing now. Is that . . . good? Or is that the sound you make before you rip each other's heads off?"

Thisbe growled, and both girls pounced on Dev. The three wrestled on the floor playfully for a moment before straightening up again. Fifer held her sore wrist but didn't seem to regret how she'd reinjured it.

Dev scooted back and blew out a breath. "Whew. I'm not sure I have it in me to handle both of you together. Sparring one at a time was a little more manageable."

"You'll have your wish soon," Thisbe said. The words dropped with a thud.

"On that note," said Fifer, fixing her hair, "let's get serious about this. Where were we?"

"I was asking how this plan begins," said Thisbe. "More specifically, what is my motivation? And why do I go alone? I need to build my character."

"I'll say," Fifer said snidely.

Dev snorted.

"I didn't mean it like that," Thisbe said, then started laughing hopelessly again. "You're awful. I was talking as an actor. I'm playing a role here." A shadow crossed her face as she found herself questioning, *Am I, though?* She frowned and shoved the thought aside. Of course she was. But once again the niggling doubt was there on the edge of her mind. If she was more evil than good, would joining the Revinir and diving headfirst into this role, body and soul, unleash something inside Thisbe that she couldn't control?

"You'll sneak away at night," Fifer suggested. "Say you knew I wouldn't come and you didn't want me there anyway, being all judgmental about things."

Thisbe glanced sidelong at Fifer. "Tell the truth, you mean?" The snickers started up again, but this time they reined them in. "Yeah," Thisbe continued, "I think that's the best angle. And I can't come across too strong or she'll be suspicious. But I'll want to surprise her with some sort of changed demeanor, because that will throw her off. Maybe I go there not quite having made the decision to join her, but revealing how obvious it is that she needs me, which would make me quite confident. And so I'd ask for something first before I say I'm willing to join her."

"Yes," said Dev, looking up. "Ask for something big and be willing to settle for something less. Negotiate a bit."

"Like maybe tell her that if you join her as she wishes, she must agree to leave the seven islands alone. Well, I mean, she can have the Island of Graves."

"Heh," said Thisbe, scribbling things down. "I like it, I like it." Then she wrote, *Too confident to negotiate? Play it out.*

"At the very least, perhaps the Revinir will agree not to bother Artimé," Fifer said, with hope in her voice. "I'd really like to not have to worry about our island for a bit."

"I won't give too much away," Thisbe murmured, feeling the beginnings of her character forming. "She wants this partnership badly. And we have a lot of friends on other islands to protect."

"True," said Fifer. "Use your instincts."

"And then once we strike a deal, you call in Florence."

"How will we know when it's time?" asked Fifer. "I feel like sooner rather than too late is best."

"I'll do a send spell to you with all the details."

Fifer's stomach twisted as she imagined Thisbe in the castle with the Revinir, trying to activate a send spell without seeming suspicious. "That seems awfully risky. What if she sees it? Or if someone else does?"

"Hmm . . ." Thisbe thought about that. "I don't know. I mean, I won't send one if it's not perfectly safe."

Dev raised an eyebrow. "But then how will we know what's going on? Do we sit here waiting and wondering? I don't know if that's a good idea."

"You could look for Drock and try to have him deliver a message to us," said Fifer.

"That's something," said Dev, looking up. He wouldn't mind seeing Drock again. He felt a special bond with him now that he'd had the dragon's teeth implanted in his flesh . . . and they'd had a moment or two back in the cavelands when Drock had made him feel like he was really someone special.

"I promise I'll let you know what's up somehow. Maybe if you don't hear from me in a certain amount of time . . . you can just send for Florence anyway. And then . . . someone can drop Kitten into the castle to look for me?"

Fifer frowned. It was way too convoluted. "This part of the plan needs work. Let's figure it out later and move on for now." She took a moment to reset her mind. "So, let's recap. You get one of the dragons to take you to the Revinir in the night. You tell her that you decided to sneak away and do this thing because you didn't trust me to go along with it. You ask for her to leave the seven islands alone in exchange for you joining up with her. After some amount of time we send for Florence. It'll take them a few days to get here. . . ." Fifer trailed off.

"Then what?" said Dev. "I think Thisbe is just going to have to play things by ear. We won't be able to respond to her without the Revinir getting suspicious. She could easily inter-cept a magical message."

"That's scary, but I think Dev's right," said Thisbe. "I'm just going to have to move at whatever pace the Revinir wants to set. Meanwhile, you assemble the troops . . . where, exactly? Here? What about the red dragons?"

"Hmm," said Fifer. "They let Dev in."

"But they won't let us out again, I'll bet," said Thisbe. "Unless we say we want to be taken to the Revinir. That's the only way I can see them letting anyone go."

LISA McMANN

"Florence and the rest could assemble in the cavelands," Dev suggested. "There's lots of room out there."

"Okay, but if they're not here in person, how do I tell them that Thisbe betrayed us?" asked Fifer. "I can't possibly do that all by send components. It's going to be a tricky conversation to have."

"But if they come here, the red dragons will attack and inform the Revinir that everyone arrived," said Thisbe. She was starting to feel anxious again about the plan to lie to everyone about her loyalties. She got up and started limping around, then went to the fire to get it going for the evening.

"That's another thing we need to figure out," said Fifer. She thought for a long moment. "Maybe it actually would be a good idea to use send components to tell Florence about Thisbe's betrayal. That way we can be sketchy about the details, and when they bombard us with questions, we can take a minute to come up with answers." She tapped her chin thoughtfully.

"If you think that'll work," said Dev, sounding skeptical. "Won't they just come barging over here if that happens? It's kind of a big deal to tell them something like that."

"Not if I tell them not to," said Fifer. "I'm the boss now."

Thisbe brought fire to her throat and slowly blew, lighting the kindling. The more she listened to Fifer and Dev talking about how they'd explain Thisbe's betrayal, the more Rohan's face popped into her head. It made her stomach hurt to think about it. She could hardly stand to make these plans. It was the most horrible thing she'd ever had to do . . . and after all she'd been through, that was saying something. Yet there was a tiny part of her that was thrilled to be playing this trick. Was that her evil side nudging her into this?

"Let's adjourn this meeting," Thisbe said suddenly. "I think we've had enough for today. I . . ." She was about to say she changed her mind and wasn't going to do this. That she couldn't. That it was just too much—too hard. But the tiny thrill remained, and she swallowed the words. "I'm hungry," she said weakly. "Let's get out of here for a few minutes. Get some fresh air."

Fifer looked over at her, about to protest—they were just figuring out the important stuff. But then she saw the look on Thisbe's face and sat up. "Yeah, okay," she said kindly. "Let's go fishing before it gets dark. We could all use a break."

Putting Things Together

A rtimé was full to the brim with people, but in a good way. Somehow bringing together willing fighters from Warbler, Karkinos, and the Island of Shipwrecks was working to unify the magical land in a way that might not have happened had they been left alone to heal and grow after the rift. Everyone gathered there had one purpose in mind: protecting the seven islands and helping the neighboring world. The grumblings from any remaining dissenters were drowned out by the camaraderie and enthusiasm that spread through the mansion and across the lawn.

Florence began training the newcomers alongside the veterans, teaching magic to those who possessed abilities and combat to those who didn't. Samheed, Lani, Seth, and Carina all assisted Florence in demonstrations and teaching beginning magic. Kaylee, Sky, Maiven, and Ishibashi taught nonmagical combat and, in their spare time, created more throwing stars and other small weapons. Rohan and his friends from Grimere assisted with the weapon making and grew stronger and more adept magically, too. And, after so many years of oppression in the catacombs, the black-eyed children were finally learning how to socialize.

The mansion had been repaired after the civil war destruction, and now that everyone had arrived from the other islands, things began to settle down in Artimé. In the evenings after training there was time for everyone to relax and learn about each other. To keep their minds off of Thisbe and Fifer's troubling absence, Rohan and Maiven and the other black-eyed people often sat and talked with new friends like Seth and his family, or Henry and Thatcher and their children.

One evening Rohan, Maiven, and Asha met up with Seth, Henry, Ibrahim, and Clementi in the dining room for a late snack. Clementi, an Unwanted, and Asha, one of the black-eyed children, sat together, for the two were like long-lost friends from the instant they'd met during the civil war. Aaron wandered past, and Maiven urged him to join them, so he did.

"I've been meaning to see you anyway," said Aaron to his grandmother. "I was wondering if you would tell us more about . . . my mother. And how everything happened with her." He glanced around, realizing a little too late that she might not want to talk about it in front of so many people. "Or would you prefer not to?"

Maiven Taveer reached out and gave Aaron's hand a squeeze. She smiled sadly. "I've come to terms with her death," she said. "I'm willing to share what I know in case it brings peace to anyone who needs it. And perhaps you'd be willing to share what you know as well."

"Of course."

"Well," said Maiven, shifting in her chair and dabbing the corners of her mouth with her napkin, "as most of you know, I was the queen of Grimere when the usurpers began their rise to power. A fine dragon named Suki was the ruler of the dragons, and she and I got along very well until her unfortunate death at the hands of the rebels." She went on to give a short history lesson about that rogue group who took advantage of a strange natural disaster, the meteors, to seize control of Grimere. "I hid my daughter, Nadia, in the castle while I commanded the army to fight against this group, but the usurpers were clever. They kidnapped black-eyed children and used them to get to her. Then they forced the other children to deliver Nadia to the pirates, threatening to harm their parents if they didn't comply. Before I could get to her, she was gone."

"Wait a minute," said Rohan tersely. "And please excuse me for interrupting, but did you say that the other black-eyed children were *forced* to kidnap your daughter? They didn't do it willingly?" His expression betrayed how important this detail was to him.

Maiven studied him. "Yes, I'm sure of it. They were her friends. I knew most of them by sight if not by name, and I knew they wouldn't do anything like that unless they were coerced or threatened, which all of those children were. Why do you ask?"

Rohan seemed beside himself for a moment and couldn't speak. Then he said quietly, "As you know, those of us who have taken the ancestor broth have experienced images pulsing through our minds. One of mine that I've been ashamed to tell you about is of my mother . . ." He paused to steady his voice. "My mother," he continued, "as a young girl, helping to push Nadia onto the ship."

"I have an image like that too," said Asha. "And so does Reza. We didn't know what it meant. Are those our parents by the sea? And is the captured girl Maiven's daughter?" She turned to Aaron. "She's your mother?"

Maiven reached out to Asha and Rohan. "Listen to me," she said. "Your parents are not to blame for Nadia's capture. That rests solely on the usurpers, especially the one who called himself king. Whatever the images show you . . . please believe that your ancestors are not at fault."

Rohan rested his face in his hands as he absorbed this new information. He'd been feeling bad about that scene in his mind ever since he'd first taken the ancestor broth. He knew the girl was Thisbe's mother, and he felt terrible that his mother had done something so horrible to a fellow black-eyed person. He couldn't fathom anyone betraying their people in such a terrible way, and he'd all but written his mother off as a traitor. But now . . . maybe she wasn't as horrible as he'd thought. Perhaps he'd been too quick to judge based on that image and the foggy, conflicting memories of his childhood. He winced and looked up. "Thank you, Maiven," he whispered, and sat back. "Please continue the story."

"There isn't much to tell after that," she said. "The pirates chained my daughter to their ship. My assistant tried to stop them. She screamed for me to come—I can still hear the awful echo of her voice in my head. My army ran with me, but we were too late. The ship sailed. I saw Nadia . . ." Maiven stopped and cleared her throat, then pressed a crooked forefinger to her lips for a moment before speaking again. "I saw her strain against the chains to look back at me. And then they were gone." Everyone was quiet for a long moment as the queen collected herself.

"We weren't prepared for such a thing," Maiven continued after a while. "I commanded my ships to organize. Within hours they were going after her, and I was preparing my own ship as well when the earthquake came and split the worlds. Our ships were lost in the gorge. But Nadia's ship made it to this world."

"I wonder how she got to this island," said Aaron. "The pirates wouldn't have sold her to Quill—there's no money system, and the High Priest Justine would've been too paranoid to intentionally bring strangers in. Frieda Stubbs told me once that my mother snuck in through a break in the wall while it was being repaired. Frieda's neighbor in the Wanted quadrant must have felt some pity for her and taken her in."

"Maybe she escaped the ship," said the queen. "We may never know the truth if she didn't confide in anyone."

"Confiding in anyone would have been frowned upon in Quill," Aaron said. "And punishable. I wonder if my father had a clue that he'd married a princess."

"What else can you tell me about her?" asked Maiven.

"She was mostly quiet and reserved. But she seemed proud of me when I was declared Wanted," Aaron said, "though she didn't say anything about it. I could tell it in the way she helped me pack for university. The pride was in her touch. Her . . . step, I guess. Perhaps she lifted her head a bit higher after that. Glad that I'd be treated properly after what had happened to Alex, being Unwanted. I wonder . . ." He shook his head. "I wonder what went through her mind all that time.

Stuck in Quill with no way to escape. Staying silent and living that oppressed life. Then having the girls and finding out they had her black eyes . . . That must have been so meaningful to her. We never knew any of it." He looked at the black-eyed people gathered there. "No wonder she gave up her life to save them when the wall fell. She must have known they had an important future. And perhaps a way out that she couldn't fathom for herself."

"She must have known we'd need them," said Rohan reverently.

"I wish I had more answers," said Aaron. He thought about the wall coming down and the leadership changing, and how that must have given his mother hope all those years later. A new will to keep the girls alive so they could go back to her land. She'd never had the chance to tell them about it.

Henry looked up, wearing a sanguine expression. "So many stories were lost in Quill forever. What a soul-sucking place it was."

Maiven's eyes were glossed with unshed tears. "Thank you for telling me about her."

On that melancholy note, the party broke up, and most

slipped away to their rooms. But Aaron headed upstairs to the kitchenette tube to go home to the Island of Shipwrecks for the night, which he could easily do. He was feeling an urgent longing to hold his wife and son, and to thank Ishibashi for believing in him.

No One to Tell

Rohan lay down, but he couldn't sleep. The newly revealed truth about his mother swirled around him. She'd been forced by the usurpers to help the pirates abduct Princess Nadia Taveer. She hadn't been working for them by choice. It changed everything about that image, and Rohan was shaking with eagerness to explain it to Thisbe after feeling so bad about what his mother had done to hers. Beyond that, he'd kept the story of his parents close to his heart and hadn't shared much about them with anyone before, because his memories were few and unsettling. For the first time, Rohan wanted to tell Thisbe everything but couldn't.

After tossing and turning for an hour, he got up and found some linen blotting paper in the living area of his magical apartment. He sat in a chair and began to write Thisbe a letter.

My dear pria,

I have two memories of my childhood before I ended up in the catacombs. They are fuzzy, and they don't make sense together. I've never felt comfortable telling anyone about them—you are well aware of this, I know. And I'm grateful you gave me the space I needed. But I want to talk about them now. If only you were here with me! I will write them to you instead, with the hope that someday I'll be able to hand you this letter and watch you read it. That's an image I'm going to affix in my mind to help me through these uncertain days.

The first memory is of my parents and me. I was about four years old. We were together in a house with several other people, but my father only had eyes for my mother. He looked at her like her eyes were a portal to a heavenly place. He stroked her cheek and whispered, "I love you, pria."

That is where the word originates in my mind. The love between my parents. When I saw the way Sky spoke about

Alex, it reminded me of that kind of love. The kind that lasts a lifetime and beyond. I guess you know it means so much to me to use that word for you.

The second memory is jarringly different and has caused me much consternation ever since. It happens not much later than the first. The memory is of my mother. She's angry. Screaming. At me, I thought, and I was devastated. She kept yelling "Go! Go!" and pointing to some strangers in blue uniforms. "Get out!" She was hysterical, and I kept running back to her, apologizing for whatever it was I'd done. Begging her to stop screaming and let me stay. But she shoved me at the soldiers. They scooped me up and took me away. That was the last time I saw her.

Rohan paused to press his fingers into the inner corners of his eyelids. A wave of emotion washed over him. Then he continued writing.

Why would she do that? Why would she change like that? Had she turned into a different person so suddenly? I couldn't make sense of anything. When I took the ancestor broth, which made the image appear of her helping the pirates capture your mother, something cold entered my heart. I'd held on to the thought that my mother was good once and had turned bad. But this image shattered that. Perhaps she'd been evil all along and had only had that one tender moment with my father before revealing her true self. It made me sick.

I tell you these memories because I found out more information today about that image. Maiven said that my mother didn't willingly help the pirates capture your mother and chain her to the ship's deck. Maiven knew her! My mother was friends with your mother. Reza and Asha have similar images of their parents doing the same thing, but they didn't know what the images meant. Maiven told us that nearly all of the black-eyed children had been taken away by then—they were our parents, obviously—and were forced by the king and the other usurpers to kidnap their friend Nadia, your mother, and deliver her to the pirates. The usurpers threatened the lives of their parents if they didn't obey.

I'm not sure why it's so important for me to tell you this right now. I know you never blamed me or held ill feelings for me because of what we thought had happened. But I still felt strange *about it. And I miss you. Writing this makes me feel nearer to you.*

It makes me want to share more with you—everything with you.

He stopped writing, his pen poised over the last phrase. Was it too much? Should he be telling her just how strongly he felt about her? He wasn't sure he liked how vulnerable that made him feel. He also wasn't sure she felt the same. He knew they had a special connection. He knew she liked him. But they were both very young, though based on their experiences, they'd been through more than most adults. Somehow that aged them in his mind. And the torture and death-defying feats they'd performed together were enough to cement them for life. Rohan felt like he could tell Thisbe anything.

Now that she was gone and he didn't know where she was or if she was safe, he threw his fear of vulnerability out the window and decided to be reckless. He wasn't going to hold back. What if he never saw her again? He continued writing, pouring his feelings into it.

I'm scared, Thisbe. I don't know where you are or what

you're doing. Florence and Simber are convincing me to

trust what Fifer wrote, but I'm so conflicted about it. I'm tempted to write you a send spell every day. I don't want to put you in danger, but why aren't you letting us know what's happening? Are you trapped? Did the Revinir take your components away? Are you even . . . alive? I can't dwell on that thought. I wish I had some answers. I wish you could reassure me that you're okay—I think that would help me cope with this. Everyone here is being wonderful—that's not the problem. But right now I feel stuck in a strange land, waiting in limbo for something terrible to happen. Not having a home to go to. And hoping my whole life isn't about to get upended because something terrible has happened to you.

I can't imagine my life without you in it. You're gone . . . and I'm hollow.

Ever yours,

Rohan

Rohan put the pen down. He'd look at the letter again later; tweak a few things, maybe. Or rip it up and throw it away. He knew he'd needed to write it, but now that he'd gotten it all out, he wasn't sure if he wanted Thisbe to read it. What kind of pressure would baring his soul put on her, especially if she didn't feel the same way about him as he felt about her? Maybe he'd hold on to it. Read some of it to her later—the part about their mothers. And let the love part come naturally if it was meant to be. When he saw her again. That felt better.

He yawned and went back to bed. This time sleep came.

Another Story

While Thisbe, Fifer, and Dev bided their time in Ashguard's palace, the Grimere group gathered again in the dining room in Artimé's mansion, joined by Henry and Thatcher and their family. Rohan had been thinking about Asha's revelation about how she and Reza both had an image similar to Rohan's flashing through their minds. He'd meant to call everyone together so they could describe their images and talk through them, but he hadn't had a chance before now. With all of them together tonight, he brought up the idea.

They'd all been thinking similarly and were eager to discuss it. Asha began, briefly describing the image that a number of them had seen of Nadia being forced onto the ship. She went on to describe an image of an old gray-haired man with a beard, whom she declared to be Ashguard the curmudgeon. She was one of the few who knew for a fact that Ashguard was her grandfather.

"How do you know so certainly?" Rohan asked her.

"Because my mother told me so. She was Ashguard's daughter."

"And . . . you remember your mother well?" asked Prindi, leaning forward. Like many of the others, she had no memory of her parents, so it was fascinating to hear from someone who did.

"I was seven when the Revinir bought me at auction," said Asha. "I remember my mother well. She was in the crowd, at the back. My father had already been killed. She was in danger."

"Was it your mother who sold you?" asked Reza, incredulous.

"No, of course not," said Asha. "I was free for my early years—no one knew about me. We lived in hiding near the foothills that separate Ashguard's village and property from the cavelands, though we visited him sometimes at the palace when it was safe. One day, dragon hunters strayed off their path when I was collecting sticks for the fire. They startled me and noticed my eyes. They came at me, and I barely had a chance to scream. My father came running and attacked them. And then . . . they killed him."

"Oh, Asha," Clementi murmured. "That must have been horrible."

Asha didn't answer at first and kept her head down. "We have all seen a lot of things we wish we hadn't." Then she lifted her chin, glanced at her new friend, and tried to smile. "It has been years. I don't dwell on it. It's too hard." She reached out her hand and took Clementi's. "It's better to think on what can be done, rather than what can't."

Clementi nodded. "And your mother?"

"I assume she's dead too."

Maiven Taveer looked up. "In the image you see of Nadia's capture—was it your mother at the scene?" The memory of that scene was burned into her mind. Watching her daughter's friends being forced to do something horrible hurt Maiven, too—she knew they would never get over it.

"Yes. My father didn't have black eyes." She paused. "They

killed him anyway to keep him from coming after me."

"Asha," said Maiven, leaning forward, "I believe I know who your mother was. We called her Adhi—was that her name? Adhira? Ashguard's second daughter?"

Asha stared at Maiven. "Yes," she whispered. "You knew her?"

Maiven smiled warmly. "What a charming girl. She spent nights at the castle. She and Nadia were very good friends from the time they were barely able to walk." She hesitated, seeing Asha's face. "That image in your mind—that was the last time I saw Adhi. The usurpers captured me soon after and threw me into the dungeon. I am glad to hear she survived long enough to find love and have you. Though I am so sorry for the life you were forced to live."

Asha smiled. "It makes me so happy that you knew her, Queen Maiven," she said. "And that you thought she was a good person."

"Did you . . . ," Maiven began, then seemed to think the better of it. She shook her head. "Never mind."

Asha gazed at the queen. "You may ask me anything. I don't mind. What were you about to say?"

"I wondered if you had any . . . siblings?"

Asha sat back. Her face turned gray. "I . . ."

"Oh dear," Maiven fretted. "I shouldn't have asked! My humblest apologies. Please forgive me."

"No," said Asha. "It's all right. If you had asked me before I took the ancestor broth, I would have said no."

Clementi narrowed her eyes. "So you've seen another image? One you haven't mentioned?"

Asha shifted. "I . . . Yes. There is one more image. It's . . . confusing." She brought her hand to her mouth, fingers trembling, and went silent.

Rohan's face filled with concern. "You don't have to talk anymore if you don't want to," he said. "No one among us from this point forward will be forced to do anything against their will ever again." He said it almost angrily, defying everything he and the others had experienced for most of their lives.

Clementi, who still held Asha's hand, gave it a gentle squeeze. "Shall we take a walk? Get an orange cream or a cup of tea? Or some fresh air?"

Asha nodded. "I'm sorry, everyone," she whispered. "I thought I was fine until I started talking. And then I realized

LISA McMANN

just how ill we all must be after what we've been through." She looked at Henry. "If only there were a doctor who could fix this kind of pain."

Henry, who'd witnessed his own mother's death when he was ten, agreed. "If only," he said, his eyes misting over. "Perhaps we could all use a break."

Just a Little Bit

Asha and Clementi slipped past Simber—he noticed, of course, but didn't let on—and went outside. The stars were out, and light from the mansion reflected on the sea. The two new friends started walking along the shore together. After a minute, Simber went outside to keep an eye on them. He wasn't about to have another black-eyed person abducted by the Revinir and her dragons.

The girls didn't go far and soon found a spot on the lawn to sit. They talked quietly about everything except the image Asha had seen—they steered clear of that topic for now. But

LISA McMANN

they had plenty of other questions to ask. Asha, who'd had little exposure to the arts in her lifetime, wanted to know everything about Clementi's talents and what it was like to live in a place like this when war *wasn't* on everybody's mind.

In turn, Clementi wanted to know more about what Grimere and Dragonsmarche looked like. She'd heard so much about those places but hadn't actually seen them because Drock had urged Aaron and her and the others to turn around and go back.

Asha had little to tell her. She'd only been free for a couple of days in Grimere before they'd boarded a ghost dragon and left to come here. And she didn't have any memory of the other times she was outside of the catacombs, because she'd been under the Revinir's mind control. But she filled in what she could, using a mixture of both languages. Friends in Artimé were learning the common language at the same time as the black-eyed people were learning theirs. Between Asha and Clementi, they could communicate fairly well by now.

After a while they grew tired but didn't want to go inside. "I love being outside," Asha said. She lay back in the grass and spread her hair out. "I missed it so much in the catacombs."

"I can't imagine," said Clementi. She lay back too, next to Asha, and their elbows touched. "You lived outside for seven years and inside for seven years."

"Outside is better," Asha said. She turned to look at Clementi's profile. Her dark brown skin was splashed with starlight. "I like being here with you."

Clementi's face grew warm. She liked being there with Asha, too. A lot. She turned her head and saw Asha looking at her with her long eyelashes half lowered and a lazy smile on her lips. It gave Clementi butterflies. "Me too," she said. "I've never had a friend like you before."

Asha held Clementi's gaze for a long moment, then squelched a playful grin and turned back to study the stars. "Being in this magical world with you makes me not want to leave."

On the lawn near the front door, Simber rested his head on his paws, feeling a distinct melancholy longing inside him. He was a sucker for a sentimental moment, and moments like this had been too scarce lately. Simber would never tire of seeing people find a little bit of comfort in others.

Now all he wished was that he could experience the comfort of having his head mage safe and sound at home. But he feared that moment would be a long way off, and there would be many troubles along the way before that time came . . . if it ever did.

Moments of
Normalcy

A few weeks passed and Thisbe's ankle was healed, but her dread was building. She felt a little nervous to take on the Revinir, but worse was thinking about the other part of the plan—the part that would make her look like a terrible person to everyone she cared about, especially Rohan. And Maiven. And Aaron . . . ugh. Aaron. He'd be more disappointed than Alex would be if he were alive. And Sky . . . Thisbe closed her eyes wearily. "Stop," she said under her breath. She couldn't stand it.

As she and Fifer and Dev talked about options, went through various scenarios, and imagined questions the Revinir might have, they continued to make improvements to the enormous palace. Cleaning up debris, patching holes with whatever they could find to make the place a bit safer and easier to navigate. They talked about what might happen to Fifer—would the Revinir want to leave her in the palace with the dragons? Or do something else? That was something Fifer would have to play along with, whatever happened. And Dev would be forced to deal with it too. If the Revinir came after Fifer, Dev would need a foolproof place to hide. They assumed he could go to the village, but they weren't sure what the dragons would do. So they explored other options too, just in case.

The twins divvied up their remaining components: four send spells, seventeen scatterclips, twelve heart attack components, three blinding highlighters, and a backward bobbly-head. And Thisbe had her obliterate spells—all three had stayed safely inside her inner pocket. They had no invisibility paintbrushes. No clay shackles. No magic carpets.

Fifer could call her birds once they needed them. And she could use her voice to shatter glass if that became necessary. Thisbe had her eyes and fingertips to send bolts of fire and sparks, and her fiery dragon breath. They both could cast

LISA McMANN

unlimited freeze spells and could throw glass barriers and invisible hooks.

There was one more thing the twins had. Their new mental ability to send thoughts to one another. It wasn't consistent, at least not yet. They confirmed that if they weren't fully in sync—if they were cross or frustrated with each other—they wouldn't be able to connect. They spent hours each day working on it, sending messages and figuring out the range and length of the phrases that worked best.

Whenever they ran out of things to say to each other in their mind messages, Thisbe would relay stories she'd read in the Revinir's journal. In one session she told Fifer all about young Emma standing on rocks watching her siblings and their friends practice elemental magic in a stream on Warbler Island. Emma had written about not being invited to join them that time . . . and not really wanting to anyway. Thisbe told Fifer that this story stuck out to her because it seemed inconsistent with the rest of her journal, in which she was always wanting to be with her siblings. The twins speculated about why she'd felt that way on this particular day, but neither had answers.

When they weren't sending mind messages, Thisbe and

Fifer taught Dev a few basic spells. He spent the rest of his time by the fire, carving wooden weapons from thick branches. He meticulously shaved the end of a sword into a sharp point, then twisted and knotted some of his old clothing into a belt that would hold the sword at his side. On the handle he carved the symbol of the Suresh family, which he'd found on the steins in the alcove. Then he started making daggers. Thisbe and Fifer hadn't been carrying weapons when they'd been abducted, so Dev wanted to make sure they each had one as well.

Sometimes Thisbe got frustrated when all of the worries became too large in her head. She began to pull back from Fifer and Dev emotionally to protect herself. And she began acting in character as she prepared for the role of a lifetime. Some days she stayed in character all of the time, wanting to experience life as the one who betrayed her people. Wanting to know how it would feel to be the person who joined ranks with the evil Revinir. She needed to become that person in advance, so that she would know what to do and how to act when faced with unexpected circumstances. Because the Revinir was anything but predictable. She was bound to make Thisbe's life difficult no matter what, even if she was delighted that Thisbe had decided to join her. Thisbe had to be ready for anything unexpected . . . and that was the hardest kind of character to play. That was why she needed to be the one to do unexpected things too—to keep the Revinir guessing.

As Thisbe receded into her mission, spending more and more time alone in her thoughts and planning, Dev and Fifer grew closer together, taking care of the palace, providing food and water, and planning the best way to keep Dev hidden if the Revinir showed up. He told Fifer about the village and the little house with the closet he'd hidden in. And he told her about the alcove where he'd found the drawings but described how hard it was to access it.

Together the two of them went to a lower floor and pried up some sturdy floorboards. They brought them up to the level where the alcove was and lined the perimeter of the floor to make it easier to access the space, for it could make a good emergency hiding place in case they ever got discovered and couldn't escape the palace. They began to stockpile dried fish and extra water in the alcove, treating it as a storage room as well. They even stored the ropes there in case they needed to escape out the window—fire was always on Dev's mind when it came to being surrounded by dragons. He never wanted to be trapped. It reminded him of all of the people in the dungeon, like Maiven had been for so many years.

"Do you think any of the people in the dungeon escaped during the fire?" Dev asked randomly one day as he and Fifer were fishing.

"We wanted to release them," said Fifer, "but the smoke was too thick. We barely got out of there alive with Thisbe and Maiven and Rohan. I don't know if any of the guards were generous enough to unchain them . . . or if they survived the smoke and are still down there."

Dev nodded and repositioned his chain-mail net, then scooped up a flopping fish and deposited it on the grass for Fifer to process. "I hope some of them got out," said Dev. "There were some nice people down there. Some who were very old, who'd been there for decades. And people that shouldn't have been there. Like Maiven. I'm really glad you went back for her."

"Did you know she was the queen?"

"I suspected it. The guards rumored about it. I didn't know her last name for sure, though, until Thisbe said it after the mind control was broken."

"She hardly looks the same as when we rescued her," said Fifer. "She's a powerful woman. Very strong and commanding. You should see her collection of weapons."

"I hope to someday. I want to . . . thank her."

Fifer looked up from the fish. "For what?"

"For being kind to me. If I were her, stuck in a dungeon for all of those years, I wouldn't be feeling very kind toward anyone. Especially not the guy with the disgusting slop."

"Aw, Dev," said Fifer, feeling cheeky. "Who were you with? And you shouldn't call yourself disgusting."

Dev's mouth opened. "You are a horrible person." He slapped the river, sending an arc of water at Fifer and dousing her.

She ran off, laughing and wiping the water from her eyes. "I deserved that." She came back to gut the fish as Dev turned back to the river, looking for one more fish so they could eat well that night. As she watched him work, she smiled to herself. He was such a lovely friend. She was really starting to enjoy spending time with him.

Then she thought about kissing him. The idea made her gag. Nope. Not a chance.

Waiting in the Castle

The Revinir had been impatiently waiting inside the castle for the twins to break and either come to her or send one of the dragons to fetch her. And while the dragon-woman was confident in her plan, she questioned herself a few times. She'd even chided herself for taking Fifer along. This might have been easier if she'd only snatched up Thisbe and left her alone at Ashguard's old palace. Then she could have used Fifer's future safety as a bargaining chip. But having the twins right there in front of her had been too tempting. What a feat, getting them both. She hadn't expected it, so when the opportunity presented itself, well . . . how could she pass it up? At the very least they were valuable. But she had no plans to put them on the auction block. At least not unless they failed her.

But what were they doing all this time? Having a twin holiday at that rotten falling-apart monstrosity? The Revinir hadn't made many mistakes along the way. But maybe she shouldn't have let Thisbe have a companion while she was trying to break the girl down. It could potentially be much longer before Thisbe was ready to say good-bye to isolation and compromise with her.

She felt confident in Thisbe's ability to convince her sister of what needed to happen here, though. Fifer might be less evil than her sister, but she still had a wedge of it in her. And the Revinir could wager that Fifer was getting antsy to go back to her little magical world, since she was the head mage and all, which might provoke a concession just to make things happen.

One unanswered question was whether Fifer's people had come after them. When the Revinir had dropped the girls through the roof of the palace and returned to Grimere, she still hadn't seen anyone. If the people of Grimere had come after the twins, they hadn't gotten close enough to them yet to trigger the dragons to act or to send a message back to her.

Perhaps the hints the Revinir had seen in Artimé of something bigger happening there pointed toward some severe trauma, enough to keep the key players at home even though their head mage had been abducted. She'd been waiting in Artimé for a full day, hiding behind the jungle, far enough away so the ghost dragons and Simber couldn't detect her. Did they really not care enough to go after the twins? Maybe they were just tired of having to rescue the incompetent teenagers after being forced to do it so many times.

Whatever was happening, the Revinir had received no word from her team of four reds about anything suspicious or dangerous going on . . . and they knew what kind of threats their boss wanted them to put an end to.

If something didn't happen soon, perhaps it would be time for the Revinir to pay a little visit.

Time to Go

Finally the day came when Thisbe felt like she couldn't take it anymore. She either had to set this plan in motion or abandon it forever. She and Fifer and Dev had prepared all they could. And they were increasingly worried about someone else making a move and wrecking everything. They needed to control the situation as much as possible, and that meant they didn't want the people of Artimé coming or the Revinir returning.

Fifer and Thisbe had figured out most of the parameters of their new telepathic ability. They couldn't be at odds with each other. And they could only send short thoughts or else the words would get jumbled. They'd tested out how physically close they had to be and discovered that for perfect accuracy they had to be in the same room or within speaking distance. And being across the property from one another, each of them at the boundaries set by the dragons, was a little more difficult, and sometimes not all the words transmitted from one mind to the other, but it worked for the most part. They hoped there was some way to communicate between Ashguard's palace and the Revinir's castle. That would keep them from having to use any sort of magic with a visible component . . . which could also save their lives. Unfortunately, they wouldn't be able to test it until it was too late for Thisbe to turn back.

The three of them spent their last evening together going over the details of their plan and talking through all of the what-if scenarios they could come up with. When Dev and Fifer went to the river to catch dinner, Thisbe sat down at the desk. She laid out all of her components in front of her alongside her wooden dagger and looked at them, then slowly repacked her pockets so that she'd know exactly where everything was in case she needed them.

She left the three obliterate components for last and stared at them for a long time as she remembered Florence's instructions. She tried to picture a scenario in which she'd actually use one. Perhaps she and the Revinir would stroll down the road together and Thisbe could get far enough away to attack her with one. She slipped the first one inside her interior pocket and picked up the second, then turned the little box over in her fingers. She hesitated, then put it inside the pocket as well. The third one she studied for a longer moment. There was no way she could imagine needing three. If she messed up with the first one, she was probably never going to have a chance to use the second, much less the third.

Thisbe glanced out the east window, seeing the dragons in their corners. She knew Fifer and Dev had no defense against them. Thisbe heard Florence's voice in her head, telling her that the obliterate components were for her use, and her use only. And that she trusted Thisbe. Thisbe had promised to keep them safe and use them strictly when appropriate.

But things had changed, and the threats around them were growing. So, despite that promise to Florence, Thisbe pulled a sheet of paper and a pen from the desk. In great detail she wrote out the instructions, range, and effects of the spell, making sure to emphasize just how deadly and dangerous it could be. Then she wrapped the instructions around the component box and slipped it inside one of the pockets of Fifer's robe, which the head mage had left draped over the railing while going out to fish. Hopefully, Fifer would find the component sometime after Thisbe left so they wouldn't have to have an argument about it and risk messing with their current state of oneness.

Fifer and Dev returned. Dev cooked dinner, and the three ate in strained silence. Reality was hitting them in the face, and they wondered if they could really pull this off. As night fell, they gathered by the stairs to say good-bye.

"Remember," said Fifer, who felt responsibility for things going wrong because it was her plan, "the Revinir wants this to happen. And her ego is big enough that she'll buy into it more easily than we expect—she'll give herself the credit for succeeding at another one of her ventures."

"The only way she'll hurt you is if she thinks you aren't useful anymore," said Dev. "Or if she thinks no one cares about you." He frowned. "That's why she threw me out the window. If you can prove that others will listen to you, she'll keep you around."

"I hope that's the case," said Thisbe. "But I want to say once more that I'm doing this willingly, Fifer. If something happens to me, it's not your fault. I am in control of this. Okay?"

Fifer wanted to shout, "Nothing's going to happen to you!" But she knew that wasn't the kind of comfort Thisbe needed to hear right now. "Okay," Fifer said. Deep down the understanding remained that if anything happened to Thisbe, she would feel responsible for it. This had been her plan, and she'd talked the other two into it. She bore the weight of it.

But Fifer still felt like it was right. They hugged all together, then two and two. They turned out the lights so the dragons would think they were sleeping. In the darkness, Dev slipped away to give the girls a moment.

"What if I fail?" Thisbe whispered.

"You won't," said Fifer. "I believe in you."

"But what if I actually do fail?" Thisbe said. Her voice was worried.

"Then we're no worse off. We'll figure it out. We always do. Have confidence."

That was the answer Thisbe needed. They whispered their last good-byes.

Thisbe descended the stairs with her rucksack, canteen,

hidden dagger carved from wood, and her two obliterate components tucked away in her pocket, plus a few other components. As she walked out into the fog toward one of the front-corner dragons, her heart began to pound. *Confidence*, she repeated to herself over and over. She had to show the dragon that she was in charge. She was black-eyed ruler Thisbe Stowe, co-equal to the Revinir. And she wasn't going to be disrespected by anybody. Not even an enormous red dragon.

As she drew close, she let out a dragon roar like she'd done early on in her stay here. Showing her dominance . . . or something. She kept walking as the dragon stood up and faced her, making the ground shiver. The dragon approached.

Thisbe roared again, and the dragon dipped his head.

Fifer and Dev watched breathlessly from the window. "He's bowing to her," Dev whispered. "She roared, and he's trying to decide if she's in charge of him." His mind began to whir, but he kept quiet.

Thisbe stopped walking a few feet from the dragon's enormous face. She stared into his eyes, finding them dead-looking even in the cover of darkness. "Take me to the Revinir," she ordered in her most commanding voice.

Everyone held their breath. Fifer gripped the windowpane. Dev could barely stand to watch. And Thisbe stood there, ready to ride or be attacked. The dragon's hot breath made her skin hurt. He narrowed his eyes and sniffed her.

Thisbe's eyes flared and sparked. She let out another roar, with fire this time. The dragon reared back as the flames touched his tender nostrils. He swung his neck around, then turned his massive body and let down a wing for Thisbe to climb up.

She boarded the dragon. As they lifted off the ground, Thisbe heard a whisper in her ears. *I am with you.*

Thisbe turned to look back at the palace. She couldn't see Fifer and Dev, but she tapped her chest twice and sent the same words back to Fifer, hoping she wasn't out of range. Then she faced forward, scrutinizing the path before her and wondering where this most risky choice would lead.

The Summons

As Thisbe disappeared into the darkness on the dragon's back, Fifer kept sending short mind messages to her, and Thisbe sent some in return. They came through fairly well at first. But the farther away Thisbe got, the more words were missing. When Thisbe sent "I can see the castle," Fifer only heard "I . . . see . . . castle." Usually Fifer could figure out the missing words and guess what Thisbe was saying. In this instance, she assumed Thisbe was saying "I *can* see *the* castle," instead of "I *cannot* see the castle" because of all the other clues that went with it: Thisbe had left on a dragon after commanding him to take her

LISA McMANN

to the castle. Dev and Fifer had watched as the dragon flew off in its direction. And they both knew that was where Thisbe intended to go. But what would happen when they no longer knew what Thisbe was doing?

It made Fifer uneasy. She stayed by the window as time ticked by, questioning the plan. Were they doing the right thing?

Long after the dragon was out of sight, Dev came up beside Fifer. "We should get some rest," he said.

Fifer nodded. She sent another telepathic message to Thisbe, but this time she didn't get a response. "I think she's out of range." Fifer sighed and turned away from the window. After finally having been so close with Thisbe again, Fifer was emptied out. She looked at Dev and felt a sudden surge of warmth and appreciation for him. "I'm really glad you're here. I'd be very lonely without you."

Dev's mouth twitched and he almost smiled, but he was feeling something strange inside of him too. He was worried about Thisbe, but it was more than that. Like the three of them had become a family in the time they'd spent here in this dilapidated palace. It was something Dev had never had before. And now that Thisbe was gone, he experienced a loneliness that was unlike what he'd felt in the past. Worse than when Shanti had died. This was much sharper. Deeper. More personal. He was as glad to have Fifer by his side as she was to have him. He was aware of a new level of emotion that he'd never encountered before, and he wasn't quite sure what to do with it. It threatened to bubble out and spill all over the library if he wasn't careful to rein it in.

Back at the castle, if he'd ever let his emotions out, he'd have been punished or ridiculed. But Thisbe and Fifer carried no judgment about such things. They cried freely when they felt like crying. And when Dev had lost it in the catacombs, Thisbe had accepted it as if it were normal. It felt liberating and somehow stifling all at once. Like, now that it was okay to cry or shout or be angry, he had some burden to do it. Yet he still felt the urge to batten it down.

He turned away without saying anything and went over to his sofa, leaving Fifer puzzled as she watched him go. She knew Dev had been raised differently than she had been. But she'd expected some sort of a response. After all, she'd just said something quite kind to him. It made her wonder if maybe he didn't want to be here with her . . . or maybe, after all he'd been through, he was just afraid of getting close to anyone ever again.

In the morning Fifer went to the desk according to the plan they'd finally decided on. She removed one of the send spell components from her vest, took out the pencil that accompanied it, and wrote:

Dear Florence,

I only have two send components and didn't want to use one until it was absolutely necessary. Unfortunately, that time has come. I am sickened to have to tell you that Thisbe has joined the Revinir's side—she stole away during the night. Please come if you can. I'm trapped at Ashguard's palace surrounded by dragons. Maiven will know how to find it. Just . . . please. Come.

Your friend,

Fifer

Fifer showed the note to Dev. "Does that look right? It's time to send it."

Dev read it. "Just like we talked about." He scrutinized it

again. "Yes, it's good. She's going to ask why Thisbe would join the Revinir when she knows the two of them can't take control of things due to the rules."

"Exactly," said Fifer, looking up at Dev. She took a deep breath and let it out. "Ready?"

"Whenever you are," said Dev.

Fifer replaced the pencil and rolled up the note, then concentrated on Florence. A moment later the component flew from Fifer's hand, down the staircase, and out across the yard. It went due east, leaving a tiny trail of smoke behind it that soon disappeared. The risky plan was in motion. Time would tell whether they were ready for the consequences.

"Well," said Dev after a moment. "That's done. Ready to call in the birds?"

Fifer nodded. "Since we're not sure how long it'll take them to get here, I think we should do it now." She let out a shrill whistle that nearly pierced Dev's ears. "Let's go outside near the orchard. That'll be a good place for them to roost."

The two friends went down to the yard. It was strange to have one of the dragons missing, leaving a long gap almost big enough to make a run for it. They both noticed it and looked at each other, but neither said it. It wasn't needed. There was nowhere to escape to. Every civilized place available would be too difficult to navigate. And it would take only a few steps or wing flaps for a dragon to catch up to them.

They sat on the grass and waited. The last time Fifer had seen the birds was right after the Revinir had abducted her and Thisbe. The dragon-woman had tragically killed several of them, and Fifer had ordered the rest to retreat. They were magical, so there was a chance they could travel much faster than normal birds. And sometimes they followed her, but she hadn't seen so much as a single red-and-purple feather since they'd retreated, so she assumed they were still in Artimé, waiting for their next command. Fifer hoped they were able to hear her whistle from this far away. They hadn't failed her yet.

After a while a glowing ball of light came zooming past the dragons and stopped in front of Fifer. She reached for it, and it melted into a note in her hand.

Dear Fifer,

What? How? Doesn't Thisbe understand that without support from the dragons and the black-eyed people, they can't rule anything? This is madness! Something sounds fishy. I'm coming with a small contingent. Stay safe.

Florence

Fifer grimaced. "Yikes. She doesn't believe it."

"We expected that," Dev pointed out. "Now you respond."

Fifer took the pencil and added on to the conversation.

Florence,

Thank goodness you're coming. Yes, Thisbe knows that. But she took a hard fall early on and has been a bit out of sorts ever since, talking about being more evil than good. Then she mumbled something yesterday about there being another way. . . . I didn't know what she meant by that until she disappeared with one of the Revinir's dragons. I'm afraid she has something sinister in mind. I'm sick about it—this isn't the Thisbe everyone knows.

Fifer

She sent it. Then she sighed deeply and looked at Dev. "Tell me this is going to work."

Dev held her gaze. And though his face remained troubled, he answered, "It will."

While they waited for the birds, both of them a little on edge, Fifer studied Dev. He'd seemed especially moody since Thisbe had left. Dev didn't notice her—he was staring at the nearest dragon, the one at the back corner where the orchard met the river. He could feel his scales rise as he brought heat and fire to his throat and let it simmer there. After a minute he made a low growling sound.

Fifer grew alarmed. "Was that you?"

Dev nodded, not wanting to speak as he tried to make the roar come out louder and more forcefully. All the while he watched the dragon. It was hard to roar like a dragon without feeling ridiculous. He wasn't sure how to get the grisly roll of sounds to build and expand in his chest rather than in his throat.

He tried again, and it came out a little louder. The dragon didn't seem to notice. Then Dev got to his feet. He jogged in place for a minute, then swung his arms wide to open his chest. Fifer watched him, half-intrigued and half-amused. What was he trying to do?

Dev took in a deep breath and held it while he brought the

LISA McMANN

fire back up to boil in his throat. Then he flung his arms back and opened his mouth, letting out a mighty roar that surprised both of them.

It surprised the dragons, too. The nearest one started toward them.

"What are you doing?" Fifer whispered harshly. When the dragon kept coming, Fifer got up and started dragging Dev to the palace.

Dev pulled his arm away. "Watch," he whispered. "Let's see what happens."

"What did you say to it?"

"I have no idea."

Fifer watched as the dragon continued toward them. "This is a bad idea, Dev," Fifer said. "It's not part of our plan."

"I know, but it could make the plan better."

The dragon let out a roar of her own. Dev's eyes widened. He roared back, and the dragon stopped and stared at the two of them. Then she opened her mouth and sprayed a line of fire at the grass in front of them, scorching it.

"Dev!" said Fifer, abandoning him and making a run for the palace. "Please don't mess up everything!"

Dev glanced after her, then looked back at the dragon. He couldn't tell if the creature was angry or if it was ready to obey, like the one at the front corner had done when Thisbe had roared. But he didn't want to mess up everything, like Fifer had said—especially not if it would put Thisbe in danger. So he went after Fifer, waving off the dragon in case that would help end whatever it was that was happening. He could try again another time. But it was good to know he could roar like Thisbe.

Back in the library, Fifer was mad. Between huffs from the speedy climb up the stairs, she said, "You could have gotten us killed."

"They're not going to kill us," said Dev, breathing hard too. "You, especially. And they don't seem bothered by me, either. They haven't been ordered to kill. That's obvious by now. At least not while we stay on the property."

"But there's no reason for you to call them to us," said Fifer. "We don't want to go to the castle like Thisbe did, and you definitely don't want these dragons to tell the Revinir that you're alive." She lowered her voice. "That was really reckless. Just because they haven't hurt us yet doesn't mean they aren't dangerous. They're dragons."

Dev frowned, then conceded the point. "I'm sorry. I just wondered if they'd listen to me if I roared like Thisbe did. I was thinking maybe we can command them to do other things."

Fifer tipped her head thoughtfully. "I doubt that. They're under the Revinir's control. Not ours."

"But Thisbe did it, so why can't I? I have scales and black eyes, and I managed to roar. What other dragon qualities does Thisbe possess that I don't? I was just trying it out."

Fifer considered it. "That's a good point," she admitted. "Maybe we can use them somehow. What if . . . what if all the black-eyed people who have taken in the dragon-bone broth can affect the mind-controlled dragons in some way? That would be phenomenal! What a breakthrough—and the Revinir probably doesn't know."

"I wish I knew if Thisbe had just roared at that dragon randomly, or if she felt like she was saying something to it." Dev turned to ponder it and spotted movement out the front window. He rushed over to get a better look. "Something's coming," he said, his voice strained. He could see several dots heading their way.

"Are they dragons?" asked Fifer. She moved to stand next

to Dev and peered out. "Is it Thisbe? Or the Revinir?"

After a strained moment, Dev shook his head. He turned and looked at Fifer, who was as close to him as she'd ever been, barring their hug on the stairs when Dev had found them in his library. Something in his stomach flipped, and he caught his breath. "It's your birds," he said. "They're on the way. I nearly forgot."

"Oh, of course," Fifer said. "That's a relief."

They watched them coming in and realized they were carrying the hammock, like usual. As they approached, the front dragon turned his head sharply. He stood up and faced them, as if he found their approach threatening in some way. And then, as Shimmer and the rest of the birds came swooping down over the dragon toward the palace, the fire-breathing creature let out a mighty roar, throwing flames from his mouth a hundred feet into the air.

"What? No!" Fifer screamed. She gripped Dev's forearm. "Stop! Oh no!"

But the billowing flame caught the flock and the canvas hammock as if they were made of tinder. Everything went up in a cloud of smoke.

When the smoke cleared, there was nothing left of them.

Things Get Real

F ifer stared in horror. Then she turned and ran across the library to the stairs and started down. "No!" she yelled again. "My birds!"

Dev started after her. "Where are you going? Wait!"

Fifer kept moving.

"Fifer!" Dev shouted. He tried to catch her, but she was too fast. "Fifer, stop! There's nothing you can do! The dragons—"

Fifer couldn't think straight. How could this have happened? The property was filled with birds, and the dragons had never done anything to them. She'd never seen the dragons even pay attention to them. And now all of her precious birds were dead. Shimmer . . . She stopped at the bottom of the spiral staircase, sending the foxes running. Shimmer was dead too.

The dragons had done nothing to the foxes. They'd never gone after a bird. Was it the hammock that had spooked the dragon? Did they suspect these birds were more than just casual neighbors on this property?

Dev caught up and stopped behind Fifer, breathing hard from the chase. "I'm so sorry," he said. "Are you okay?"

Fifer was so angry she couldn't begin to cry. She wanted to murder the dragon for what he'd done. She covered her face, shocked by her own violent reaction. But it was true that Fifer was a killer now, after taking down Frieda Stubbs. She looked up. "I'm so furious!" she screamed, more at the dragons than in response to Dev's question. "Augh!"

Dev stayed back. His face wrinkled up in angst. What could he do besides being angry too? Dev loved animals. He'd spent much of his time in the forest. He cared for the foxes as if they were his charges. He could only imagine the pain Fifer must be going through. He knew the birds were more than just a means of transportation for her.

Fifer moved to the doorway, scowling at the dragon who'd killed her flock. She was glad that Dev had come after her, because she might have kept going straight to the dragon to attack him. But that wasn't safe, especially now that the dragon was riled up. And while she'd known never to trust one of the Revinir's dragons, she and Dev and Thisbe had grown lax about them being here since they could roam freely within the perimeter of the property.

"You killed my birds!" she screamed at the dragon.

The red creature was not impressed by her shouts and didn't seem to notice how upset Fifer was. Fifer gripped her hair and tugged at it in frustration. She whirled around to look at Dev on the bottom step. "I can't believe I've lost them all," she said, softer now. "They died because of me." Her face fell. She wasn't able to unsee the fiery disaster, and it went through her mind over and over. Her shoulders slumped. She pushed her hair back, and a tear slipped down.

Dev had noticed that Fifer wasn't a touchy-feely kind of person. She didn't seem to like giving hugs unless she really knew and liked a person. But he was at a loss for what else to do. And now her bottom lip was quivering. "I'm sorry, Fifer," he said. "Do you . . . do you want a hug? Or . . . anything?"

Fifer's lip kept quivering. She nodded and dropped her hand from her face.

Dev stepped down off the stair, went to her, and wrapped his arms around her. She pressed her face into his shoulder and sobbed.

They stood there for a long moment, intertwined, until Fifer's sobs stopped. She pulled away, and Dev hastily let go and shoved his hands into his skirt pockets. "You okay?" he asked.

"Thanks," said Fifer, sniffing and looking up at him. "Yes. Thank you."

He pulled a wadded-up handkerchief out of his pocket and handed it to her. She took it and wiped her eyes and blew her nose. Then she held on to it and stared at it, not sure what to do. "I'll . . . go wash this now."

"It's okay," said Dev weakly, even though he really didn't want it back in its present condition. "You can keep it. There are more upstairs."

"I—thank you." Fifer shoved the handkerchief into her pocket and wiped her hands on her pants. She closed her eyes and shook her head. She couldn't believe what the dragon had done. "I'll meet you upstairs," she told Dev.

Dev narrowed his eyes. "Um . . ."

"I won't do anything crazy," she said. "I just need a minute. I'm going to the water pump. That's it."

Dev smiled grimly, and as Fifer slipped out the doorway, he turned and started back up the stairs. As he went, his mind began to whirl with questions. What did it mean that the dragon had attacked Fifer's birds? Had he seen them as threatening? Or had the Revinir given them very specific instructions on who or what to attack?

When Fifer came back to the library, she hung out the freshly washed handkerchief over the railing to dry. Then she turned to Dev and said clinically, "This new development throws a wrench into things."

"Right," said Dev. "We just lost a means of transportation."

"More than that," said Fifer. "We assumed since you managed to walk onto the property without the dragons harming you, anyone could come in without a problem—that the dragons are only here to prevent Thisbe and me from leaving. But now . . . I'm not exactly sure what to think. Did the Revinir program the dragons to attack anything from the air?"

"That doesn't make sense. There are birds all around that fly in and out as they please."

"So was it the hammock?"

"Maybe," said Dev.

"Or maybe the Revinir gave specific instructions and descriptions of all of our friends and allies," said Fifer. "In which case we are totally—"

"Oh no," said Dev, turning sharply. "What about Florence? Your team! They're coming here. You have to warn them."

"I hope Florence writes me back soon," said Fifer gravely. "Because I only have one send spell left."

They Meet Again

The red dragon Thisbe was riding reached the castle and landed near the moat. Thisbe's scales rose and stayed up, and she could feel the Revinir's presence in the air. Familiar guards stood at attention on either side of the drawbridge. When they saw who had arrived, one of them hurried inside. Thisbe remained on the dragon's back for a moment, steeling herself for what was to come. She was in character. Playing a role. She was about to fake joining forces with the most evil thing their worlds had ever known. And part of her . . .

She tamped down the thought.

LISA McMANN

But seriously, part of her . . .

She wrestled with her feelings.

Because part of her . . . was excited about it.

She liked the risk. She liked the power. She liked that there was no one else the Revinir wanted to work with. It was Thisbe or nobody. That gave her a rush. It was scary to think that way, but Thisbe liked that aspect of it too. A thrill. Who didn't like a thrill?

But she was scared, too. More scared than she'd ever been before, outside of the first time she'd met the Revinir. Back then she'd been taken from the auction block, dragged into the catacombs, and locked inside a cell full of dragon bones. Later she'd been branded—a signature move by the Revinir, who'd done a few similar things when she'd been Queen Eagala in Warbler. At least now Thisbe thought the Revinir might treat her properly, especially since she wanted something from her. She could always walk away, she told herself. Though . . . she grimaced to imagine it. What would the Revinir do? Just let her go? Hardly.

Last night she'd surprised herself by communicating with the red dragon through roaring, and she wanted to try that again. She let a soft rumble percolate in her throat, trying to project to the dragon to put his wing out so she could disembark. She let the growl grow and made it more urgent sounding. Eventually the dragon paid attention and let his wing unfurl. She slid down over the webbing to the ground, landing with a hop. Then she straightened her component vest and walked across the drawbridge toward the huge castle entrance.

The giant entry room had been cleaned up and repaired after the fire. There was still a mild smoky smell, enough to make Thisbe's sinuses sting. She moved inside, remembering all the times she'd come through here before. She was at her most confident this time, which was saying something. But she had to be, for that was the kind of character she needed to play in order to beat the Revinir at her own game. She walked with an air of ownership, letting her boots click loudly on the green malachite floor and coming to a stop in the center of the grand vestibule. She crossed her arms over her chest and waited.

It didn't take long for a servant to come toward her. "Come with me," the man said. His eyes were glazed over. Remembering that the Revinir had probably drugged hundreds of people of Grimere with the dragon-bone broth was depressing. It made everything just that much harder. Would the antidote of ancestor broth work on them? Or did that only work on the black-eyed people? They'd have to figure out what to do with them, too. Would the mind control break automatically once Thisbe took the Revinir out?

She was getting ahead of herself. One thing at a time. Thisbe followed the man, enjoying the echo of her footsteps. Imagining the Revinir hearing her coming. What was in store for Thisbe? She had no idea. She'd imagined several scenarios but didn't want to spend too much time on them. She wanted to experience this without rehearsing any specific reactions—she'd be more authentic that way. More believable.

They went up several flights of stairs—the same ones they'd climbed before when trying to escape the drawbridge fire. Finally they entered the grand ballroom, where many of the king's old servants had escaped to when the smoke became too thick elsewhere.

The large doors to the balcony were open wide, and the Revinir was standing with her wings and tail toward Thisbe. A few attendants surrounded her. "Here you are, Revinir," said the man dully. He left the room, leaving Thisbe standing there.

Slowly the Revinir backed into the room and turned around. She wore a smug smile, revealing her rows of teeth. Thisbe stood firm.

"So," drawled the Revinir, "what brings you here? Have you had enough of the palace already? I was just thinking of paying you a visit."

"I've come to work with you," said Thisbe. "On one condition."

The Revinir snorted in surprise. Fire flew from her lips. Thisbe let out a warning growl and shot fire back. The attendants ducked.

"Well!" said the dragon-woman, clearly delighted by the exchange.

Thisbe glared. "I can leave."

The dragon-woman tried to hide her smile, but she wasn't very good at it. "No, you can't," she said matter-of-factly. "You're here now, and here you shall stay. But let's talk about your 'one condition.' What's that all about? I'm not sure I like that idea."

"If you want me to help you fulfill the deal to make us true rulers of Grimere, you'll have to do what I ask."

The Revinir looked condescendingly down her snout at Thisbe. "You have become so bossy," she said. "It's not a pretty look on you."

"I'm not here to be pretty. I'm here to rule this world."

"Well!" the Revinir said again. She was continuously surprised by Thisbe. Suspicion crept in. "Why? What changed your mind?"

Thisbe, who was still gauging just how confident and straightforward to be, took a moment to meander to the sideboard where a teapot sat on a silver tray. "The last straw was being stuck at that place, whatever it was. I had plenty of time to think."

The Revinir eyed her carefully. "And what has become of your sister?"

"I left her there. She's . . . not exactly on board with my plan." Thisbe shifted, then turned and folded her arms defiantly. "But then again, you never expected her to go along with this, did you?"

The dragon-woman turned away and moved through the ballroom, thinking hard. She'd been studying Thisbe. Trying to detect if she was lying to her. She knew the girl had lied to her once before—she'd pretended that the ancestor broth had no effect on her. But since the time in the tower when Dev had revealed the truth, the Revinir had been ruminating over it. And she'd concluded that the reason she'd believed Thisbe so easily, so errantly, was because the girl gave the answer she'd been hoping for. She hadn't wanted the ancestor broth to affect Thisbe, because it hadn't affected *her*. And that was why she'd been so easily swayed that time. But was the girl at it again? She oozed confidence. Is that how someone would act after being stuck in a dilapidated palace for a month, guarded by dragons?

The Revinir narrowed her eyes at Thisbe. The girl looked healthy enough, though a bit ragged. But she didn't seem to have a clue where she'd been staying all this time. Or . . . was she lying about that? Questions pounded her. What had made her come here? "Why haven't your people come after you?"

"I told them not to come," said Thisbe. "In the note I sent after you snatched us up."

"Why would you do that? Weren't you afraid of me?" The dragon-woman seemed offended.

Thisbe lifted her chin. "Maybe I'd already been thinking

about joining you. You've asked me enough times, you know. You think it hasn't been on my mind?"

"You said the opposite back then," the Revinir accused.

"Because Fifer was there. What else could I say?"

They both fell silent as the Revinir contemplated Thisbe's story. It was plausible. But was it true? She still wasn't sure. Finally the Revinir went back to the balcony. "What's your one condition?" she asked.

"That you leave the seven islands alone."

The Revinir snorted out over the railing. Fire rained down on yard crews below, but she didn't care. "Of course," she said, her voice dripping with sarcasm. "Why wouldn't you want that?" She chuckled long and low. "Oh, my dear girl. There's no way I'm interested in granting that."

"Then I'll be leaving." Thisbe turned abruptly and started toward the doors.

"Stop!" shouted the Revinir.

"You need this more than I do," said Thisbe over her shoulder. She didn't stop.

"Halt!" the dragon-woman shouted. "I'm not finished with you."

Thisbe kept going. "Don't call your guards, or I'll never join you in this endeavor. It's time you treat me like a partner instead of a slave. Where's my room?"

"What?"

"My room. I'm going to let you think about this for the rest of the day. I'm tired from traveling all night on your stinky dragon."

The Revinir growled. She hadn't been pushed around like this since . . . well, since Marcus and Justine had forced her to stay home when they left for Quill, back when she was a child. And she didn't like it very much. But she sort of admired it too. She knew she'd seen strength in Thisbe from the very beginning, when she detected that the girl was much more evil than good. She'd chosen her future partner well. And now here the girl was, finally willing to help make the Revinir's dreams come true, and she was letting her walk away? What was happening?

"I'll . . . find a room for you," the Revinir said. "Wait here."

Thisbe stopped and folded her arms as a smug smile played at her lips. "The best one you have," she called out. She eyed a guard who stood at a hallway intersection. When the Revinir was out of sight, Thisbe let out a breath of relief. Everything was going smoothly. Her instincts on how to play this seemed to be pretty good—or close enough. She was keeping the Revinir on her toes. That was working. She straightened again and put on an impatient expression.

A moment later Thisbe could hear the Revinir barking directions to someone. Then the dragon-woman reappeared. "Right this way to your suite," she said coolly. She turned around, her haunches and tail slamming into the sides of the wide hallway as she navigated the tight space. Little bits of the wall were left crumbling.

Thisbe followed her to a wing of the castle she hadn't been in before. Finely appointed, completely empty suites sprouted off from both sides. The Revinir stopped at one. "Here you are. I've borrowed a servant from the kitchen who will attend to your needs. She'll be coming shortly with water and food for you. And she'll be watching your every move, so don't be sneaky with your spells." The dragon-woman couldn't help but smirk. "You'll notice I didn't try to disarm you."

"You'll notice I didn't try to kill you," Thisbe retorted.

"Indeed." The dragon-woman gave Thisbe a scornful look. "Anything else?"

LISA McMANN

"What's my servant's name?"

The Revinir scowled. "How should I know?"

"That's going to change." Thisbe pushed past the dragon-woman into her little apartment. It was well appointed with a sitting room, small kitchen, and bedroom. Doors led from the far wall to a balcony. "That'll be all for now," Thisbe called out over her shoulder, and dropped her rucksack on her bed. Then, when the Revinir didn't leave, Thisbe closed the door in her face. Gently. Because she wasn't a monster. Yet.

Stressing Out

M aybe Florence will respond to your last send message," said Dev. "Then you can reply to that one, right? That way you won't have to use your last component."

"That's what I'm hoping for," said Fifer. "Either way, they won't be here for a couple of days, so we have time to decide whether to use this last send spell. I really want to save it in case I need to reach Thisbe, though."

"Florence will be bringing more with her," said Dev. "Won't she? She's the head of your army, after all." Dev hadn't ever met Florence, but he'd heard plenty about her over time.

"I'm sure whoever comes will have extra. But I don't feel good at all about using the last one until I'm one hundred percent certain more are in my possession. As we both know, plans can change. And I'm not at all positive we'll be able to have Florence come directly to us." She balled her fists and pounded her forehead. "I can't believe my precious birds are gone forever. I feel terrible. Shimmer was my friend."

Dev didn't know how to comfort her. She was distraught over it. So was he, but Fifer's loss was much more personal. Plus, they'd been counting on the birds for later. Not having them would mess up their plans. And now, with Florence and whoever else was on the way, they had to figure out where to send them so that the dragons wouldn't attack as they'd done with the birds.

And there was also the question of what to do with Dev. Because he was supposed to be dead, they didn't want anyone from Artimé to know quite yet that he was alive. This was for the same reason that they needed their friends to truly believe Thisbe had joined the other side—because in case anyone was captured and forced to take in the dragon-bone broth, they couldn't tell the Revinir the truth. Dev was safer dead than alive at this point, at least in the minds of every-one potentially vulnerable to the Revinir's schemes. But now Dev was second-guessing his intentions to attempt to cross the property line shortly for his hideout in the village. He'd figured he'd be able to leave just as he'd been able to come, but now he wasn't so sure. Besides, he wanted to be here for Fifer if she needed him, especially now that she didn't have Shimmer. He also wanted to be in on the action. It was a risk, though, because he knew the truth about what Thisbe was doing. And if the Revinir captured him, that had the poten-tial to mess up everything.

They went out to fish. Neither spoke for a long time, both lost in their thoughts as they crouched side by side along the bank, patiently holding the chain-mail net. Fifer was trying to figure out what to do with Florence and her team. And Dev was weighing the risks of staying at the palace. There was always one thing at the back of his mind . . . the fact that he felt like this palace belonged to him. And now that he actually had a place that was his, he was reluctant to leave it. And a little bit selfish, too. Because Fifer was forced to stay here, she got to remain in the comforts of the library. *His* library.

"Maybe I could hide out in the alcove," Dev said suddenly, breaking the silence.

Fifer looked up, feeling an unexpected surge of hope at the idea. She didn't want Dev to leave. It was too hard to communicate. Then she frowned. "Actually, if Florence and her team don't come here, you might as well stay."

"But where are you going to send them?"

"I don't know. I was thinking maybe the foothills on this side of the mountains. But I don't know where the river flows."

Dev plucked a stiff blade of grass and started chewing on it. "Why not reroute them to the cavelands? The land there is flat, the river flows through it, and there's room for them to find shelter in the caves. Plus, they can talk to Astrid and the other ghost dragons."

"I've never been there. How far away is it?"

"Half a day's journey via ghost dragon."

"That's a bit far."

"But it'll be totally safe for them there. They can't stay in Grimere. And the forest might be too dangerous with such a large party—the Revinir would learn of them soon enough, and the dragons use the dragon path. Besides,

LISA McMANN

that's probably just as far from here as the cavelands."

Fifer spied a small fish coming their way and pointed at it. Dev nodded and slowly repositioned his end of the net. The fish got close, and the two scooped it up in one smooth motion. They pulled it onshore, and Fifer went for the fish knife to kill it and clean it while Dev returned to try for a second one. They made a good team. Everything would be harder if they were separated—like fishing, since there was only one net. And since neither of them knew when anybody else would be able to reach them because of the red dragons, it would be silly for Dev to leave now. It was a relief.

"I'm staying," Dev whispered over his shoulder, barely catching Fifer's eye before turning back to the river.

Fifer shoved a stick through the fish's mouth. "Good." She felt a weight lift off her shoulders. "Besides, have you even tried to leave since you got here? The dragons might not let you."

Dev was quiet as he spied their second course. He scooped up the fish and brought it over. "No. That's been on my mind too. But I do want to try talking to the dragons a bit more."

"Talking?" Fifer scoffed. She handed the knife to Dev, then

LISA McMANN

went to the water to rinse her hands. "They just ignore me when I talk to them."

"Roaring, then," said Dev. He glanced at the dragon nearest them. The creature was alert but not looking at them. They'd made this trip to the river so many times that the dragons no longer seemed to get worried about them being so near this particular boundary. Perhaps they even thought that the two of them couldn't or wouldn't cross it. "At least they react to my roars. Don't you think that indicates something?"

"Like what?"

"That I'm actually getting through the mind control."

Fifer, who didn't have much experience with the mind-control part of the Revinir's powers, could only shrug. "All I know is that these are not nice dragons. And if they can scorch a flock of magical ravens into ash, they can do the same to you." She stood up and turned to him. "And I wouldn't be able to handle it if something happened to you."

Dev felt something thick rise to his throat. It wasn't fire. It was something emotional. He remembered what the Revinir had told him. And he was angry that he kept thinking about it. That she had retained that amount of control over him.

"When the Revinir . . ." His voice came out gravelly, and he cleared his throat. "Before she threw me out of the window, she said not one person in the world cared about me."

Fifer looked up. Her eyes grew shiny. "And did you believe that monster?"

Dev's bottom lip twitched, and he fought to still it. "Yes."

Fifer held Dev's gaze. "Well," she said, "she was wrong."

Sound the Alarms

Receiving Fifer's first send spell after so many weeks without a word had been a relief until Florence opened it. Florence and Simber had read it together in utter confusion, then called in Aaron and Maiven and Rohan. And then Ishibashi and Sky. And Carina and Seth. And Lani and Samheed. Nobody could make sense of the shocking turn of events, especially Rohan.

"Could this be some sort of a trick?" Rohan asked. He couldn't fathom it.

"I think we have to treat it as real," Lani said. She glanced at Aaron, who'd sunk to a chair and covered his face.

Florence had immediately responded, and then she'd prepared a small rescue contingent to head out on the ghost dragons. Leaving Lani in charge of Artimé and Samheed and Kaylee to take over magical and combat training, Florence, Simber, Aaron, Maiven, Rohan, Ishibashi, Sky, Carina, and Seth departed Artimé in various stages of disbelief, having had little time to absorb and comprehend Fifer's words.

Fifer's response came in while they were flying on Gorgrun's back to the Island of Fire. Florence called an emergency meeting with Maiven and Rohan and the rest of them. Simber flew next to them, and Quince beyond, carrying luggage and supplies. Florence opened the send spell and read it silently while the others waited.

Rohan's face looked as gray as it had been when he'd lived in the catacombs for years. "I just . . . I can't believe this is happening," he whispered as he prepared himself for more atrocities.

Florence looked up, then read the message aloud:

Florence,

Thank goodness you're coming. Yes, Thisbe knows that. But she took a hard fall early on and has been a bit out of sorts ever since, talking about being more evil than good. Then she mumbled something yesterday about there being another way. . . . I didn't know what she meant by that until she disappeared with one of the Revinir's dragons. I'm afraid she has something sinister in mind. I'm sick about it—this isn't the Thisbe everyone knows.

Fifer

"Sinister?" Rohan said, his eyes widening. "Not the Thisbe everyone knows? What is going on here? She was injured . . . ?" He shook his head angrily. "More evil than good? That's *not* an indicator of anything! I kept telling her that!"

Maiven touched Rohan's arm. "We'll get this straightened out."

"Clearrrly the Rrrevinirrr has put the twins thrrrough something horrrible," Simber said. "We should have gone afterrr them earrrlierrr."

"We had an order from the head mage," Florence reminded him.

"But why didn't Fiferrr contact us beforrre this happened?" Simber lamented. "Maybe we could have done something!"

"I still think something odd is happening here," Rohan said. "Thisbe would never do this!"

"It's not impossible for me to imagine Thisbe going this route," Aaron muttered. His expression was distraught. He didn't know what else to say. A pang of guilt went through him. Was his sister taking after him?

Maiven looked from Florence to Simber and back again. It was heartbreaking to see their reactions. "Florence," she said, "how do these notes strike you?"

"I didn't track with any of this at first," said Florence. She glanced at Rohan. "I understand your disbelief, Rohan. Maybe Fifer is somehow compromised. There's no telling what people will do when injured and threatened or bullied." She thought for a moment. "But Fifer knew she didn't have to make up a shocking story to get us to come—she could have just asked, and we'd be on the way immediately. So why would she need to lie?"

Rohan closed his eyes in defeat.

"A lot of time has passed, and we don't know any details," Florence said gently. "I'm withholding judgment for now. But . . . I have little reason to doubt what Fifer is saying."

"I agree," said Sky quietly.

Seth nodded. "Fifer doesn't lie." A shadow crossed over his face. *Unless it was for Thisbe.* He shook the thought away—it didn't make any sense. How would Fifer lying to all of them about this help Thisbe in any way?

Ishibashi spoke up. "'Another way' . . . what does that mean?"

"I assume it means another way to take over leadership."

"Impossible," Maiven said. But her eyes narrowed, and she didn't seem 100 percent sure.

Rohan remained quiet and withdrawn. Everything about this strange development seemed completely off. And he was furious that Florence and the others hadn't gone after the twins when he'd suggested it, right after they'd been abducted. Back when he'd tried to convince them that it was the right thing to do. Nobody knew the Revinir like he and the other black-eyed children did. Why hadn't they listened to him? Why hadn't he pushed harder? He sank down into the dragon's soft back, feeling stunned. How could Thisbe possibly do something like this? Not just to him, but to their people? It made Rohan sick enough to want to throw up. He thought he knew her.

179 « Dragon Slayers

Maybe this was Fifer's way of saying something else. Was she being forced to send it? Was Florence sure that it sounded like Fifer? What if the note was really from the Revinir? "Are you sure Fifer wrote these?" he asked, desperate to make sense of this.

"She would have had to be the one to write it and send it magically," said Florence. "No one else could do it and imper- sonate her."

"But if a dragon were hovering over her, she might write whatever the Revinir told her to write," Rohan argued. "I just can't believe this is true. Thisbe would never, ever do this." He felt like he was repeating himself, but he couldn't let it go.

"I can't fathom it either," Maiven said. "Florence, could Fifer be compromised?"

"Absolutely," said Florence. "And if she is, the Revinir will be anxiously waiting for our response."

Seth glanced up. "So it would torture the Revinir if we don't answer right away?"

Florence raised an eyebrow. "Could be a good technique. Maybe not quite yet, though. We want to reassure Fifer in case she's really in a dire situation."

"We have to at least act like we believe what Fiferrr is telling us," Simber said. "In case Rrrohan's position is corrrect."

Simber's comments made Rohan feel a little better. But what Fifer had said about Thisbe being more evil than good stuck in his craw. He'd waved off that argument since the beginning. But he remembered when the Revinir had announced it—he'd been with Thisbe in the catacombs, near the river. And Thisbe had clearly been bothered by it then. But he thought she'd gotten past it. Maybe she hadn't after all. Had the dragon-woman worn her down so much that she'd started to believe her?

"What other way could there possibly be?" Rohan asked suddenly. "Surely Maiven or the ghost dragons would know if there's another way to take over the rulership of the land of the dragons."

"Without support from either body of residents," Maiven explained, "there isn't another way. I've been racking my memory trying to think of what she could possibly mean."

Florence tapped her chin, making a clacking sound. "Perhaps she thinks the rest of you can be coerced to vote for her."

LISA McMANN

Rohan and Maiven looked at each other with doubt in their eyes. There was no way any of the black-eyed children would turn their backs on Maiven Taveer. It was impossible. And Thisbe knew it.

Rohan began to despair again. "Nothing makes sense." he said.

"Any thoughts on how I should respond?" Florence asked.

"We rrrespond as if we believe Fiferrr," said Simber. "Whetherrr she's telling the trrruth or trrrying to send us a hidden message, we must go along with it to keep herrr safety intact. She's intelligent. I don't believe this is a game in any way. Something's verrry wrrrong, eitherrr with Thisbe orrr with Fiferrr."

"Or both of them," said Sky.

Florence glanced at Maiven and Rohan. "Agreed?"

"Yes," said Maiven.

Rohan hesitated, then added, "Is there a way to give her a clue that we are skeptical about all of this? So she knows we're not swallowing it whole?"

"I think so. Let me work on this." Florence wrote her response and showed it to the others:

LISA McMANN

Fifer,

We're shocked beyond belief. We are on our way to Ashguard's
palace, hoping to arrive tomorrow morning. Don't despair—
we're coming to help.

Florence

The group agreed that the "beyond belief" part conveyed
what they wanted to say while still being clear that they sensed
the danger she was in and were taking it seriously. Florence
sent it, and they dispersed to brood individually.

Aaron had no words. Only the questions pounding him.
Was this somehow his fault? Could he have detected this kind
of behavior, having turned on everyone himself at one point?

Rohan took to a quiet spot near the back of the dragon to
be alone. He still couldn't get over what Fifer was saying. If it
were true . . . Ugh—he could hardly even imagine. His heart
would be broken forever. There was no worse betrayal in his
mind. Thisbe knew how dedicated he was to getting the land
back to the rightful owners. She had to know how much this
would hurt him. Didn't she care? If only he could talk to her.
Find out what was happening.

He could hardly get through the suspense one minute at a time. He didn't know if he could last until they found Fifer the next day. Where was Thisbe? The castle? Would she be alone? He glanced at Quince. Perhaps Rohan could go to the castle to check things out while the others went to find Fifer. That would be risky, though. He'd have to clear it with Maiven and Florence, and he could already predict the answer to be a hearty "no." But he just wanted to talk to Thisbe so badly his head ached.

A few weeks before, Florence had awarded Rohan his very own loaded component vest. He slipped his fingers into one of the pockets and drew out a send spell component, then turned it around in his hands.

He knew it was a bad idea to send anything to Thisbe, knowing that she was probably with the Revinir. Yet . . . he couldn't stop agonizing about everything. How could she do this to him? He clutched the buttons of his shirt, near his heart, as if that would stop the pain from oozing through his chest.

But it only intensified. He'd never felt more abandoned in his life. Not even when his mother had forced him to go away.

Thisbe's betrayal was worse than that. It felt cold-blooded. Calculated. Almost impossible to believe. But what if . . . what if it was true? What if her evil side had taken point for the first time? What if all this time her evil levels were increasing and Rohan just hadn't known? What if her turning to work with the Revinir was just an inevitable thing that Rohan had convinced himself wouldn't ever happen? How naive of him.

He pictured Thisbe, the way she looked at him. There was never any evil in her eyes. Only kindness. Gentleness. Even . . . love. He let out a low moan as tears sprang to his eyes. His heart was breaking right here, on a ghost dragon's back, and he couldn't stop it. He would do anything to end the pain. He had to know if Thisbe had really betrayed them. He couldn't stand it. Taking the component, he removed the pencil and hunched over so the others wouldn't see. Through tears he held it poised, then wrote:

Thisbe . . .

A sob escaped him just from writing her name. How could she hurt him like this? He remembered the letter he'd written to her. It was folded up inside his pants pocket. He'd poured his heart out to her in that letter, and now he wanted to rip

LISA McMANN

it up. Burn it. Throw it into the ocean. She didn't deserve to read it.

Rohan hated himself for feeling this way when they still weren't sure what was happening. But along with that feeling came an instance of clarity and acknowledgment. A reluctant moment of awareness of the danger he could cause by sending a spell to Thisbe. He stared at Thisbe's name on the paper and let out a breath. Then he replaced the pencil and slipped the send component back inside his pocket. He curled up on his side with his back to everyone, his eyes on the sea, his tears lost in the silvery ethereal skin of the dragon.

A Perilous Step

Thank goodness," said Dev when he saw the send spell zipping up the stairs toward Fifer.

Fifer hastily reached for it and opened it. The latest letter from Florence melted into a note in her hand, and Fifer read it aloud:

> Fifer,
>
> We're shocked beyond belief. We are on our way to Ashguard's palace, hoping to arrive tomorrow morning. Don't despair—we're coming to help.
>
> Florence

LISA McMANN

She read it again, pausing on the first line. "We're shocked beyond belief." She looked up at Dev. "Is that supposed to mean something? Is she saying they don't believe me?"

"I don't think we can parse each word right now, do you? You have to tell her to steer clear of this place."

"Right, right," said Fifer, who was already preparing a response.

Florence,

Do not come to Ashguard's palace. Go to the cavelands instead and remain there until I can figure out what to do. It's too dangerous for you to come here. There are dragons waiting to attack anyone who approaches. They've just killed Shimmer and the rest of my birds.

Fifer

Fifer read it to Dev. "Sound okay? I don't have much more room to explain further."

"It's a bit shocking," Dev said. "But it conveys the urgency of the situation. Get it out there."

Fifer sent it, and they were left to wait agonizingly again.

Dev excused himself. "I'm going to try to communicate with the dragons again," he said.

"It's so dangerous, Dev," said Fifer. "Can't you do it from inside? When Thisbe roared by accident the first time, she was up here."

Dev shrugged. "All right. I hope it's not too annoying."

Fifer was more relieved than she cared to admit and totally willing to tolerate Dev's roars if it meant he was safe inside. She wasn't sure why she was feeling so clingy toward Dev lately. Probably because Thisbe was gone and in danger. Fifer didn't normally need to rely on anybody—she was somewhat of a loner anyway, especially lately. But maybe it was the severity of the situation that made Fifer really appreciate having a friend around.

Dev began making grunting and growling noises by the back window, trying to get the dragons to notice him without setting the curtains on fire. Fifer went to the bookshelves. Maybe something here could give her an idea about what else they could do to put them in the best position to escape these dragons in case Thisbe called on them to fight. She looked up at the shelves that were far above her head and wondered if there had ever been a ladder here. If so, it was long gone.

Spying a potential foothold at eye level, Fifer went to get the desk chair to help her get to that height so she could look at the books up there. She climbed up, hanging on to the shelves and anchoring a few invisible hooks as well, and started reading the titles. "*Caring for Dragons*," she said. "*The Keeping of Dragons. Dragon Rulers.*" All of the books on one shelf were about dragons. She continued. "*Living in Harmony: A History of Dragon and Human Interaction in Grimere.*" She pulled it off the shelf and dropped it to the floor with a loud bang. Dev gasped, startled by the noise.

"Sorry," said Fifer with a smirk. The next book didn't have any words on the spine, so she pulled it out and blew the dust off. The title on the cover was in strange old-fashioned curly letters, and the words were that of the ancient language. But the illustration showed an army of humans fighting a single dragon and apparently slaying it. Her eyes widened. She dropped that book on top of the other and climbed back down to the chair and the floor.

Dev let out a gravelly howl that did absolutely nothing. Fifer laughed, and Dev muttered something under his breath, clearly annoyed. "I can't remember how to do it," he said, this time loud enough for Fifer to hear.

"It's got to come from deep inside you," said Fifer, trying to remember how he and Thisbe had sounded before. "Let it roll around a little in your chest at the beginning."

Dev raised an eyebrow but said nothing, even though it was somewhat annoying to have Fifer, who had no clue about how to roar, give him directions. Still, he tried doing what she said, and, surprisingly, the growl seemed deeper and more intense. He let it roll in his chest and then build and shoot from his throat. It sounded like a real dragon—a small one, but a real one.

Fifer clamped her hands over her ears, her eyes going wide. "That's it!" She went to the window and looked out. "They heard you. They're coming!"

Dev looked out. He watched for a second and then roared again, shooting fire toward the ceiling. The dragons kept coming. "I'm going down there," Dev said. "I think there's something to this. I don't know what yet. But maybe we can use them to help us leave the property and then somehow escape from them."

Fifer sighed. It had to be almost impossible to escape a dragon. But maybe Dev was onto something. "I'm coming with you," she said, and she took off after him down the stairs. Round and round they went until they neared the second floor. One of the dragons was poking his face into the second-story window. Dev and Fifer slid to a stop and stared at the creature. He was about twice the size of the Revinir, but not nearly as big as the ghost dragons. He eyed the two teenagers, his giant nostrils dripping and flaring, his lip curling defiantly.

"He doesn't look happy," Fifer said.

"No, not really," said Dev. He inched toward it, then roared again.

Fifer cringed and ducked her head. The red dragon seemed agitated by the sound, and he reared back, then roared in response, sending a wave of fire at them.

Dev swore and dove on top of Fifer as he tried to shield her and get away. His shirt caught and lit up the staircase. He screamed in pain and tried scrambling even more, stepping over Fifer in a blind attempt to escape the dragon. Fifer slid out from under him and threw herself on Dev's back to suffocate the flames; then she grabbed him around the chest and pulled him up the stairs. He got his footing, and before the dragon could shower them with more fire, they rounded the curve and kept going, moving on sheer adrenaline all the way to the top.

Dev collapsed in the library, out of breath and his back beginning to throb. He swore in the common language and started shaking, curling up on his side and writhing. Fifer whipped open her smoldering robe and fished out the healer's kit. "Lie on your stomach," she said, glad that she'd spent at least a little time in the hospital ward learning from Henry and Carina. "I'm going to remove what's left of your shirt, okay? I've got some medicine. It'll make you feel better pretty quickly, but I've got to clean you up first."

Dev's teeth started chattering. Fifer ran for a blanket and covered his lower body, then pulled out the wooden dagger Dev had carved for her and started ripping through his shirt to get it off. Some of the fabric had melted onto his skin, and when Fifer tried to remove it, Dev squealed in pain. She cringed and removed it anyway, trying to hold him still. Then she found a clean shirt and wet it down with water from Dev's canteen. She dabbed Dev's back to clean it. He screamed.

It was the most horrible thing Fifer had ever had to do, and the way Dev was screaming rattled her, but she continued diligently. Finally she applied the salve from the kit and silently thanked Henry for making her carry it with her. It had come in handy multiple times already.

Dev's moans quieted as the salve numbed the pain and began to heal him. Fifer fetched her canteen for Dev to drink from and gave him a capsule of herbs to swallow, then she brought him a pillow from the sofa to rest his head on. When she had done all she could, Fifer sat back and wiped the sweat off her brow. "That could have been disastrous," she murmured. She shook her head slightly, looking at Dev lying on the floor facing away from her. She pleaded silently for the medicine to work fast, because she was going to need him. They'd already lost the birds. Now this. Was everything going to fall apart? She hoped things were going better for Thisbe than they were for her.

A Moment of Weakness

The team from Artimé was approaching the Island of Fire when Fifer's latest message arrived. Before she read it, Florence directed everybody to land on the volcanic island so they could wait for it to submerge and take them to the crater lake in Grimere. Sky and Seth planned to lead the way for those who hadn't traveled in this fashion before. It would shave a day off their travels, and the mouth of the volcano was big enough for the ghost dragons to travel through as well. While Sky gave instructions to aim for the first portal, Florence opened Fifer's message and had a look.

LISA McMANN

"Simber!" Florence called. Rohan and Maiven came quickly as well.

"What is it this time?" asked Rohan nervously. His world had turned upside down in an instant. Was this just one more thing?

"Now Fifer says we *shouldn't* go to Ashguard's palace, which is where she supposedly is. She says it's too dangerous, and . . ." Florence looked up with grave concern. "She says the dragons have just killed Shimmer and the rest of Fifer's birds."

"What?" whispered Rohan. The birds? He caught Seth's troubled gaze. Neither boy knew what to think.

"Nonsense," said Simber. "Now I'm cerrrtain the Rrrevinirrr is dictating these messages. She doesn't want us to come."

Florence studied the note. "It sounds like Fifer's way of speaking, and it's her handwriting. But you're right, Simber. This is too suspicious. Maiven?"

"If she's telling the truth, the dragons could harm us if we approach. Is she suggesting an alternative location?"

"The cavelands."

"That seems like a reasonably safe place," Maiven pointed out. "But I agree the sudden change seems suspect."

Rohan looked at the note. "So, wait. I'm confused on where we think everyone is. If we believe Fifer to be at Ashguard's palace, and we believe the Revinir is holding her hostage there and forcing her to write these notes . . . where is Thisbe? Also at Ashguard's palace, despite Fifer telling us she went to the castle?"

"Potentially," said Simber. "If so, the Rrrevinirrr has set up a strrrange and unnecessarrrily complex rrruse to keep us frr- rom finding them."

"Why would the Revinir tell Fifer to make us come, and then try to keep us from finding them?" Florence shook her head wearily. "This is getting complicated."

"I'm starting to think we're the ones making it compli- cated," said Ishibashi in a quiet voice.

Aaron looked at the man. He knew the old scientist didn't speak often in situations where someone else was leading. But when he did, it was usually something impactful. So Aaron took Ishibashi seriously. "The simplest answer is often the right one? Is that what you're saying?"

Ishibashi's lips tightened into a line. "I don't want it to be true, but perhaps it is."

Rohan was growing more distraught over it all. And the

LISA McMANN

evolving discussion now seemed to swing in the direction of all of this really being true. He had to get some answers. Find out the truth about all of this. His broken heart longed to know, one way or another. Was Thisbe really betraying all of them? Or was something else going on?

He slid down Gorgrun's wing onto the island, too caught up in the Thisbe and Fifer saga to spend much time worrying about traveling via volcano. He pulled the component out of his pocket again and looked at the note he'd barely started. His heart was heavy. Could he risk this? What would happen if he did? But also . . . what would happen if he *didn't* reach out? Maybe, if Thisbe had really followed her dark side to the Revinir, he could be the one to stop the worst from happening.

He sat down in a quiet spot and pulled out the pencil, then continued where he'd left off.

Thisbe,

How could you do this? To me, and to all of us? Please reconsider. I'm devastated. I await your explanation while clinging to hope and love.

Roban

The ground shivered. Sky shouted a warning and a reminder to everyone: "Be ready! Just a minute or two and we'll all go down. Stick together if you can and aim for the first portal!"

Rohan quickly reread the note. His hands were sweating. Should he send it? Or not? Did he sound desperate? Afraid? Angry? He shouldn't have said "love."

The pencil had no eraser. As Rohan's heart pounded faster and faster, the ground began to shake more and more. "Rohan!" Maiven called out. "Come join me, please."

Rohan gripped the component and rushed toward Maiven just as the volcano shook again. He grabbed the queen by the hand and tried to take a few deep breaths. When the volcano began to descend, Rohan squeezed his eyes shut. He concentrated. And as water came up around his ankles, he whispered, "Send."

A Major Wrinkle

Thisbe opened her room door and ran into her servant, who'd been newly assigned to her apartment to watch Thisbe's every move. "Oh," said Thisbe. "Hello. I'm ready to speak with the Revinir again." She hesitated. "What is your name?"

The woman, whose eyes were glazed with mind control, didn't answer. She went down the hallway and stopped, then turned and looked at Thisbe as if she expected her to follow. Thisbe hastily grabbed her wooden dagger, shoved it into her belt, and closed her door. Then she went after the servant, straightening her vest and double-checking her

LISA McMANN

inner pocket. Everything was where it should be.

They returned to the ballroom, where several servants awaited instructions that might never come. Thisbe's servant went out to the balcony to let the Revinir know that the girl had returned. The two came back inside.

"Have a seat," the Revinir said, pointing to a table set for dinner. She sat on her haunches and worked her curly front talons together like a chef sharpening knives. Thisbe didn't doubt they were just as sharp. Was the dragon-woman trying to intimidate her? If so, it wasn't a smart tactic. They would have to be on equal ground in order to enter into a partnership, and Thisbe wouldn't hesitate to remind the Revinir of this every time she tried to take the upper hand.

Thisbe remained standing and put her hands on her hips. She studied the Revinir. "Are you planning to murder me with those glorified fingernails? I'm not sure that's how a good partnership works."

The Revinir stopped sharpening her claws. "No. They just . . . hurt sometimes. When they grow quickly." She frowned, as if unsure how to handle Thisbe's bolder personality.

"Great," said Thisbe. "Then I expect you won't do that

again in my presence. How do we proceed? What has to happen before we can go forward with this plan of yours?"

"I— Just wait a minute," said the Revinir, sounding frustrated. Smoke drifted from her nostrils. "I'm not sure about this."

Thisbe stared at the dragon. "You're . . . what? I'm sorry. Did I hear you correctly? You've asked me more times than I can count to join you. You've kidnapped me on multiple occasions with the intent of convincing me to help your selfish cause. Most recently you dropped me onto some falling-apart monstrosity of a palace and left me to fend for myself with the hopes that I would come crawling to you, broken, and finally see the wisdom of your plan. Am I exaggerating?"

"No, but—"

"And now that I have done exactly what you wanted me to do, *you* are the one having doubts? Is that what's happening here?"

"I have questions!" the Revinir said sharply. A shower of sparks flew from her mouth and made tiny burn marks on the carpet. The dragon-woman rose to her tallest height.

Thisbe dodged the sparks but didn't back down. "You have

wasted and ruined enough of my life. I don't care if you have questions." She held out her arms, covered in scales, and then blew an arc of fire into the room. "You did this to me, and I'll never be the same again. And now you can't decide if you want to be my partner? It's a little late for that, *Emma*."

The Revinir recoiled at the use of her given name. She hadn't heard it in a very long while. "What? H-how?" she sputtered. A roar rose up in her throat, but she held it back, not wanting any extra dragons and servants to come running in right now. She was confused and furious and insecure all at once. And she needed to take back control of this conversation.

The Revinir wrinkled up her snout scornfully. Just as smoke started pouring from her jowls, a ball of light zipped in through the balcony doors and stopped in front of Thisbe.

Thisbe froze and stared at it. And then both of them lunged for it. Thisbe's touch opened it, and as it melted into her hand, the Revinir grabbed it before the girl had a chance to read it.

"Give me that!" Thisbe screamed. Fire shot from her eyes and fingertips.

"'Thisbe,'" the Revinir read in a mocking voice. She stood tall and kept the letter out of Thisbe's reach. "'How could you do

203 « Dragon Slayers

LISA McMANN

this? To me, and to all of us? Please reconsider. I'm devastated. I await your explanation while clinging to hope and love. Rohan.'"

Thisbe's face burned.

The dragon-woman began to chuckle. "Wow," she said. "Hope and *love*? So dramatic." She eyed Thisbe, who had stopped clawing at the dragon and had given up once she realized who the note was from. But she couldn't let on how devastating this was. She couldn't show that she cared the Revinir was reading anything anyone sent her, because that could give away her secret. Thisbe had to act like she'd abandoned everyone in her past life and that this was easy to explain away. The young mage stood tall and narrowed her eyes. Sure, the words from Rohan had hit her hard, and she could almost hear the disappointment and shock in Rohan's voice. She could fall apart later. But now she had a job to do.

The Revinir moved around Thisbe, studying her closely and trying to get some sense on how the girl was handling this note. Was she moved by it at all? Or had she been playing Rohan all along like she'd played her sister? It was impossible to tell with Thisbe, which frustrated her, but at the same time, it was the thing she most admired.

The dragon-woman read the note again. "Poor Rohan," she said bitingly. "You've devastated your dearest friend. How does that make you feel, Thisbe?"

Thisbe stared straight ahead, fixing her gaze on a large plant that rested on a bejeweled table in the corner. How did it make her feel? Horrible. Awful. Terrible. Like giving up. It made her feel like running away. Like abandoning the plan. Like going in search of Rohan and telling him everything. It made her feel like her chest had been ripped open and her heart sliced by those awful curling claws. It made her want to crumple up in a ball on the floor and die.

She didn't look at the Revinir. Her eyes didn't weep, and her voice didn't waver. She just stared at the plant on the table. "How does it make me feel?" she said, hearing the pride swell up, though she felt none of it. "Of course I'm sad my friend doesn't understand. But his *love* guarantees he'll be on my side eventually." She turned to look at the Revinir with a gleam in her eye. "Our side, that is. So everything is falling into place."

Regret

Florence, Simber, the two ghost dragons, and all of the humans exploded out of the first portal and landed in the crater lake in Grimere. Simber and the dragons plucked the humans out of the water and brought them to the narrow path on the shore to collect themselves. It was a bittersweet moment for Rohan and Sky—they'd spent a lot of time here with Thisbe. But they were glad they weren't staying.

The team was much closer to their destination now, but the skies overhead were filled with dragons in flight. Some of the dragons were watching them. "This isn't good," Maiven said, wringing the water out of her braid. "The dragons are everywhere. I'm sure they've already gone to tell the Revinir about our arrival."

Rohan's expression was slack, and his eyes were half-dead. He didn't care about the dragons. He could hardly muster up a sense of guilt for employing the send spell to Thisbe. He hoped it didn't cause a problem, but really . . . Thisbe was the one causing all of the problems right now. So he didn't feel too bad about it. "We're doomed anyway," he said to Maiven. "It doesn't matter."

"Stop that," said Maiven, harsher than she'd intended.

But her tone seemed to penetrate Rohan's funk, for his eyes focused on her. "If the simplest explanation is usually the correct one, and if what Fifer is saying is true, then Thisbe really has joined the Revinir and we've lost her forever . . . and possibly our future, too. And if Fifer is being manipulated by the Revinir, we're all heading for a huge amount of trouble. There's no good side to any of this."

Carina spoke up. "You've left out the possibility that Fifer is lying of her own accord."

Seth looked up.

Simber growled. "She wouldn't do that."

Carina lifted her chin. "I know it's hard to hear, and I know she's not known for lying. But I'm just laying out all of the possibilities," she said. "We would be foolish not to consider everything."

Simber nodded. "That's fairrr. I apologize." He turned away. "I still think she wouldn't do it," he mumbled. Carina let it go.

"She would lie for Thisbe," Seth said quietly.

Carina glanced sharply at her son. "Do you think that's what she's doing now?" she asked. "If so, why? She's not making Thisbe look very good."

"I don't know. Maybe they're plotting . . . something. Together. It wouldn't be the first time."

Carina frowned, thinking about the notes Fifer had sent. "If they are, I can't imagine what it could be."

Rohan glanced over. "Do you mean plotting together against the Revinir? Without telling us?"

Seth nodded. "Yeah," he said, though nothing made sense.

"I . . . still don't see it," said Carina.

"No," said Rohan sadly after a minute. "Carina's right.

They wouldn't do that without telling us. Why would they lie about it when we could help them carry it out? It doesn't make sense. Nothing does."

Seth sighed. "I know. I've just—I've known Thisbe and Fifer almost my whole life. They're my best friends. I guess I'm looking for any reason to believe that something other than what Fifer wrote is happening. I was . . . grasping." He shook his head. Ishibashi was right. The simplest explanation was probably the correct one—that Fifer was telling the truth. And Thisbe had turned her back on all of them.

After Maiven gave Florence a quick tutorial on where they were, Florence called for everyone's attention. The ghost dragons hovered above her, for there was no place onshore large enough for them to land between the lake and the mountain that rose up sharply. Florence worriedly eyed the mind-controlled dragons overhead. And she still hadn't decided what to think about Fifer's most recent message telling them not to come to her. Was it a trick? Everything that was happening seemed suspect, and there was no telling what was the truth.

LISA McMANN

209 « Dragon Slayers

The warrior trainer knew she had a lot of great minds in front of her, though. She recapped the situation and reread Fifer's messages to them. "Now that we've had some time to mull this over, what do you make of it?" she asked. "Who thinks we should continue to Ashguard's palace?"

About half of them raised their hands.

"And the rest think we should follow Fifer's order to go to the cavelands? Anyone else have an alternate idea?"

Aaron, who hadn't raised his hand at either suggestion, asked to see the thread of messages. He read each one carefully, looking for hidden clues that would indicate that Fifer was being coerced, but nothing jumped out at him. "My gut says we do what Fifer says." Like Rohan, his voice was dull. The truth of what Ishibashi had said earlier was starting to sink in. And he still felt strange about it. Like maybe he wasn't the only evil one in the family. And that thought didn't give him any comfort. Had his past influenced Thisbe in some way?

"Mine says we go to the palace," said Carina.

"I also think we should follow Fifer's command," said Ishibashi. "Go to the cavelands."

Sky spoke up. "How about we go to the cavelands to set

up camp, and then send a small team in the morning to do a flyover of Ashguard's palace and check things out?"

Florence nodded. "That sounds like the best plan so far. Gorgrun, is it possible for the dragons to hurt you?"

"It is not," said Gorgrun. "We are more ghost than dragon."

"But you cannot harm them, either, correct?"

"Under the Revinir's spell, they act like enemies, but they are the future of our land. You are correct: We cannot harm them. But we can do our best to protect you from them should the need arise."

"That's what I figured," said Florence. "So you'll at least give us a safe ride overhead, won't you?"

"Absolutely," said Gorgrun. "Perhaps they will hold their fire and listen to us. Though, if I recall, we have not found that to be promising with other dragons under the Revinir's mind control. If they have been given commands, they will follow through."

"It's a start," Florence said, looking at Simber. "Do you agree?"

"I do," said Simber. He looked at Maiven and Rohan. "And you?"

LISA McMANN

Rohan's face was haggard. He seemed startled to be asked, even though he'd been a part of the conversations all along. "I . . . have no opinion," he said.

Maiven pocketed his bent arm inside her own. "We defer to you," she said to Simber and Florence. "You know the twins better than we do." She glanced at Rohan. "Or so it seems."

Florence and Maiven exchanged a pained look. Rohan was taking this news harder than anyone else—not that the others were glossing over its severity. The confusion of it all kept hope alive for most, but it only seemed to drag Rohan down even farther.

"Let's go with Sky's option, then," said Florence. "Everybody back on your dragons. We're heading for the cavelands."

As she spoke, a dark purple dragon swooped low overhead. Most of the people ducked, but Simber saw who it was. "It's Drrrock," he said.

"Is he under the Revinir's mind control?" Florence asked, peering up at the creature.

"He's too farrr away to tell," said Simber. "Let's see what happens when we lift off."

The ghost dragons landed in the shallow water, and

everyone boarded them. Then they and Simber took off, trying to steer clear of the other dragons, which continued to fill the skies all around Dragonsmarche.

"They're like vultures waiting for roadkill," said Sky.

"I think we're the roadkill," Aaron muttered.

Gorgrun and Quince dodged and weaved between the mind-controlled dragons as they headed for their homeland. Simber kept Drock in his sights, which wasn't too difficult, because the dragon seemed to be staying fairly close without looking like he was traveling with them.

Florence had something else on her mind. She turned to Rohan. "I see how glum this has made you," she said.

Rohan tried and failed to smile. "I can't deny that."

"It's very serious," said Florence. "But until we know the truth, there's no sense giving up on the world over it."

"If I'm being honest, it's very hard for me to think that way at this point."

"What helps me is to remember that Fifer and Thisbe are incredible mages," said Florence. "They are smart and bold and brave. Perhaps there will be some surprises coming our way."

LISA McMANN

Rohan looked up, horrified. "More surprises? I don't know if I can take any more."

Aaron, who'd been uncharacteristically quiet recently, was listening in. He caught Rohan's eye. "If it's any solace," he said, "people can come back from grave mistakes."

Florence nodded. "All is not lost," she said. "No matter what."

Rohan studied Aaron. He'd heard the whole story of Aaron's past by now. "Do you put any stock in the dragon-detected levels of good and evil?"

Aaron was thoughtful. "I don't have enough information to go on. I only know that the dragons believe Fifer is more good than evil, Thisbe more evil than good, and Dev is exactly half and half."

"I am more good than evil," Rohan said. "And what about you?"

"I don't have a clue," said Aaron.

Florence frowned, as if she detected where the conversation would land.

Rohan rolled a question around in his mind. He knew asking it would be terribly rude and possibly hurtful. But he was completely out of sorts and desperate for answers. So he plowed ahead, hoping he could make amends later if necessary. "Aaron," he said. "Thisbe is thirteen. How old were you when you started down your . . . evil path? When you killed Mr. Today?"

Florence's jaw slacked. "Rohan . . . ," she said softly. "That's not . . ."

But Aaron saw the desperation in the boy's eyes and held up his hand to stop Florence from chiding him. He understood more than anyone just how Rohan must be feeling. Aaron was not only desperate, but he'd started feeling responsible for Thisbe's actions too. What if she was just like him? How could Aaron bear the shame of that? Seeing his own horrific choices and mistakes recurring like a reflection in a lake of oil?

"I was thirteen," he said. "Nearly fourteen. But that doesn't mean anything. She's not me."

Rohan closed his eyes.

"I mean it, Rohan," Aaron said, his voice catching with emotion. "Our upbringings were vastly different. She has everything good going for her."

"Except for things she can't control," said Rohan, opening his eyes. "Things . . . that might run in families."

Aaron understood what Rohan was implying. He didn't blame the boy, who was only looking to make sense of something that was unfathomable. "I don't know what to tell you."

Rohan couldn't take any more. He thanked Aaron and apologized for the probing questions, then removed himself from the area, going to the back end of Gorgrun to be alone.

Aaron let out a defeated sigh. Ten times the amount of guilt he'd had before rushed over him now. He wasn't the only one wondering it. Thisbe seemed to be following in his way of life, and no one had seen it coming, not even him. It was a mistake that could cost Artimé more than they'd ever risked losing before. A mistake that could end the future of an entire land.

On Tenterhooks

L ate that night Fifer applied another layer of the magical salve to Dev's burns and gave him another capsule to swallow. Florence hadn't responded, which left Fifer stressed out and worried about what was happening. She didn't want them coming here—the red dragons would likely destroy them as they'd destroyed Fifer's birds.

And she wasn't sure what Florence was thinking. Was she buying Fifer's story? Had Fifer and Thisbe misjudged how everyone would react to this plan? Feeling stressed out and unable to sleep, Fifer picked up one of Dev's new weapons and a small chunk of the meteor they'd found in one of the tower

LISA McMANN

stairwells. She brought them to the east window and used the stone to sand down the wood while she pondered and watched.

Not to mention Fifer was suddenly weary of this place. How long would she be stuck here, especially if her Artiméan people couldn't approach or attempt to rescue her, and the dragons were being hostile? Had Thisbe made it to the castle safely? How were things going for her? Was there any way Thisbe could communicate with Fifer so she and Dev would know what was happening? Did the Revinir buy Thisbe's story?

And now there was Dev, with his not-very-well-thought-out plan to penetrate the mind control and speak to the dragons . . . in *their* language. Which Dev didn't know. What if Dev had said something really horrible or offensive in his roar? Sure, it got the red dragons to pay attention when they normally didn't react to anything that was spoken to them by anyone other than the Revinir. But that was not the reaction Dev had been hoping for, nor expecting.

They'd both seen Thisbe mount the dragon and speak to him . . . somehow. Did she have some dragon communication ability that no one knew about? More likely it had to do with the specific instructions the Revinir had given the red dragons.

After all, the dragons most certainly weren't given any pointers on what to do with Dev, since the Revinir thought he was dead. But it was easy to see the Revinir instructing them to take Thisbe to the castle if she asked them to.

Fifer wondered if she would be able to get through to the dragons if she wanted to have them take her somewhere. Did they have instructions to listen to her, too? Was there any safe way out using that method?

She shook her head. What was she thinking? She'd just witnessed Dev getting flambéed! She was not about to have the same thing happen to her—at least not until she knew what rules the dragons were following.

Sitting down at the desk, Fifer took out a piece of paper and began to write down what she knew about the red dragons.

1. Paid no attention when Dev and I spoke to them by river

2. Totally listened when Thisbe roared at them, and did what she wanted them to do

3. Torched my birds and hammock with no warning

4. Burned Dev to a crisp when he tried to do what Thisbe did with the roaring

LISA McMANN

As Fifer looked up to think about what else to write, she caught sight of something moving outside the window in the darkness. She got up and went to look. It was the remaining front dragon going toward the river, presumably to eat and drink. The dragons did this at some point each day, but Fifer had rarely caught them in the act because they usually did it during the night when she was asleep. But because the other front dragon was away, this move left that entire side of the property unguarded!

Granted, if Fifer were to ever make a run for it, it would take about six gallops for a dragon to catch her. And there was no place to run to that would be safe. But knowing there was a tiny vulnerability here gave Fifer some hope. She had no idea what she might do with that information, but it seemed note-worthy. Perhaps it would allow for people to come in rather than for Fifer and Dev to escape. Which was also something they desperately needed, especially if the people coming in brought components. And maybe some food that wasn't fish.

The thought reminded Fifer that Florence still hadn't replied to her latest send spell telling them not to come. Was Florence still thinking about how to answer that? Or had something happened to them? Fifer thought about how much time had passed since Florence had told them they were on their way. They must be taking the volcano network in order to get here by morning.

A panicky thought struck Fifer. What if Fifer's send spell had gone out when Florence was in the volcano system? Would the spell ever find her? That seemed like the one place Artimé's spells wouldn't be able to penetrate on their own. But wouldn't it find her once she exited? Or would it just be confused and give up?

All the unanswered questions that flew around Fifer's mind were making her weary. She checked on Dev again and found him resting as comfortably as possible. Fifer would give Florence until morning to reply, and if she didn't, she'd have to use her last send component. Because the last thing Fifer wanted was to be responsible for the death of another Artiméan. And if there was any chance that Florence hadn't received the instructions not to come here, and the whole team of them came barreling in to save their head mage and were attacked, Fifer would never be able to forgive herself.

LISA McMANN

She dozed for a few hours. When the sun streamed in and Dev stirred and sat up, Fifer startled awake. She applied one more dose of salve to Dev's burns and moved to put away the healing kit in her robe pocket. When she slid it inside, it caught on something in its way. Fifer frowned and pulled the kit out, then reached inside to find out what was there. Her fingers found a small box wrapped in paper. She'd never seen it before. "What's this?" she murmured.

A Trial Period

The Revinir had seemed cautiously pleased with Thisbe's response, and the two had parted ways for the night, agreeing tentatively to meet again in the morning for breakfast. Thisbe sent her servant to the sitting room to sleep and spent a wakeful night wrestling with how to play the next act. She knew the plan had been for Fifer to send for Florence on the morning after Thisbe left. So they probably weren't here yet. Should Thisbe buy time to make sure the people of Artimé could be in the area? Or jump right into the agreement, which would surely set off another round of problems that she would pretend not to expect? All she knew was that she'd been enjoying playing this part.

By morning, in the magical moment between asleep and awake, Thisbe had a good feeling about what to do. Her instincts had been on so far. And even with Rohan throwing a wrench into things, it had ended up working in her favor. The Revinir had seemed to believe Thisbe even more after seeing the message from Rohan.

Her eyes flew open, and her stomach pinched. Rohan. Thisbe's heart ached. He must be falling apart—he'd said as much. But she could picture the pain in his eyes. It was a desolate feeling, as if all of their deep connections, their soul-binding companionship, had gone down the drain. All for the singular reason of Thisbe trying to get close enough to the monster to do away with her. It had to happen soon.

She went to the ballroom for breakfast. The Revinir was there with her servants. Was the dragon-woman ever alone in this place? It didn't seem so. Which wasn't good for Thisbe, but she didn't let on. Instead she walked with confidence and surveyed the large amounts of food on the table. Apparently the Revinir still preferred to eat at a table like a human, despite the fact that she was almost all dragon by now. Her curled

LISA McMANN

talons clinked the china plates as she shoveled great amounts of food into her toothy maw.

"Hope you saved some for me," Thisbe said. "We have a big day ahead of us."

The Revinir growled like a wild animal and ate like one too, which was a bit unsettling. And while the dragon-woman was half the size of an average dragon and tiny compared to a ghost dragon, she could still be extremely ferocious, and Thisbe didn't want to ever find herself too close to her chompers. She sat down near the foot of the long table, within reach of a large tray of crispy bacon, and helped herself.

The Revinir took a cloth napkin and wiped her mouth. "We'll meet at noon to declare our partnership," she said. "Once that's in place, we can talk about your request."

Thisbe laughed. "Um, no. That's not how this is going to work. I want a trial period of a week to make sure you treat me right. And if you don't, I'm not declaring anything."

"A week!" said the Revinir, lifting her head and straightening her neck to its full height. "Not a chance."

Thisbe paused, holding a slice of bacon in midair. She turned sharply to her servant. "Will you pack my bag, please?

I'll be leaving right after I finish my meal." She glanced at the Revinir, who was seething, then added, "I may as well fill my stomach first. I'm a very hungry girl."

"I can stop you from leaving at *any time*," said the Revinir. Flames curled up around her jowls.

"I know you *can*," said Thisbe. "But we both know that would be a terrible idea. That would seal the deal for me to *never* work with you. I know you're used to getting your way, which is why this is all so aggravating for you. But think about what you really want, Emma. What have you wanted from me since we first met? You had a plan, and you went for it. You knew you couldn't ever be a true human ruler of the land of the dragons. Even if you'd somehow colored your eyes to black, you knew that you didn't have the right genealogy to take that position. So what did you do? You turned yourself into a dragon." Thisbe paused for effect. "A dragon! Who does that? It's totally bonkers."

The Revinir narrowed her eyes. "Where are you going with this? And stop calling me Emma."

Thisbe went on as if she hadn't heard. "All you needed was a true black-eyed person, descending from one of the two original ruling families, to throw their support behind you. And what do you know? You found one. Here I am. And after all of that effort—and to be honest, Emma, I think you're stuck as a dragon for the long haul once you committed—after all of that, you are willing to let me walk out of here because I want a week and your word not to harm people in a totally different world? Honestly, after the way you've acted toward me, it seems fair to want to make sure you're not going to treat me like dirt in our very crucial partnership. A week is barely enough. Maybe we should do two. Unless you're ready to grant my request? I'd be ready to go forward with everything if you simply agree to that."

The Revinir was still seething, but some of what Thisbe said was making sense. It did seem silly to let this whole thing fall apart for that. She wasn't about to make the promise about the seven islands, but she supposed she could give Thisbe a few days to settle in. After all, the Revinir really did need a partner. And . . . she realized she wanted one too. She'd been alone in leadership her whole life. Having someone smart like Thisbe around seemed so refreshing. "I'll give you two days," she said.

LISA McMANN

227 « Dragon Slayers

"A week," said Thisbe firmly.

"Fine. Let's take it a few days at a time and reevaluate."

Thisbe sighed dramatically. But that was all she really wanted. "All right. If you haven't driven me out of here in a few days, we'll reconnect about that condition and move forward with our plans."

Thisbe's servant returned to the ballroom carrying Thisbe's rucksack and canteen. "Oh! Thank you, good person," Thisbe said. "I won't be needing these quite yet after all. But I can take them from here. I'm going on a walk anyway. It's such a beautiful day. And I've never seen the grounds without being on the run from some dictator or other." She wiped her mouth and tossed her napkin on the table.

"Your servant will go with you," said the Revinir icily. "You don't trust me, and I don't trust you. That's final. There will be no arguing."

Thisbe wrinkled her nose. That wasn't the answer she wanted. But maybe she could work around it. And she knew how to give a little too. "Ask her what her name is," said Thisbe impatiently. "Then I'll happily give her some time off work to explore the waterfall and lounge on the hills with me."

LISA McMANN

And, Thisbe thought, figure out a way to give Fifer an update . . . and maybe even reply to Rohan. There was a good chance that finding the right words to say to him would break her heart.

Puzzling Developments

Fifer unfolded the paper around the small cube that she'd found in her robe pocket and soon recognized it as a long note written in Thisbe's hand. The box rolled onto the floor next to Fifer. As she read the note, her eyes widened. She stared at the paper. And then she reached for the box and, with trembling fingers, picked it up and examined it from all sides, seeing the small, innocent-looking pebble inside. Carefully she tucked the cube into her component vest's inner pocket for safekeeping as Thisbe had suggested in the note. Then Fifer read the paper again, scrutinizing it to make sure she understood everything, from

LISA McMANN

how to get the box open to how the spell worked.

Thisbe had done a good job explaining it. And Fifer had read about the obliterate component that Alex had used long ago and vowed never to re-create because it was so dangerous. Now here was Fifer, holding one close to her heart. It was a bit unnerving, and Fifer wasn't sure she'd ever feel okay using it. But Thisbe had been very unselfish and possibly even reckless in giving it to her. Fifer would honor the gift.

"What is that?" Dev asked, looking at the back of the paper.

"It's a note from Thiz. I just found it." She explained what it had been wrapped around.

"Yikes," said Dev. "That sounds dangerous."

"About as dangerous as messing with a dragon," Fifer said, giving him a side eye.

"Hey," Dev replied sheepishly. "Have you heard from Florence?"

"I was just about to use my last send spell to check in with her. I wish I didn't have to, but she didn't reply."

"No sign of them yet, I take it?"

"Thankfully no." She pulled her last send component out and wrote:

Florence,

I wanted to make sure you got my last instructions. If not, please do not come to Ashguard's palace. There are three dragons here with large fire-breathing ranges, and they will attack.

Please go to the cavelands until we figure out what to do. This is my last send component, so please reply if you can. I am alone.

Fifer

She looked at Dev and smiled. "I'm glad I'm not really alone. This is tolerable with you."

"I'm glad you're here too," said Dev. He moved carefully and strained his neck trying to see his back. "I can't believe how much better this is feeling. Your magic is powerful."

"All thanks to Henry." Fifer sent the component and was surprised when she didn't see it zoom out to the east. There was no sign of it from any of the three windows they could see out of. "It must have gone north," said Fifer, running from window to window to make sure she didn't miss it.

"That would be the direction of the cavelands," said Dev.

"So that's a good sign." He looked around the library. "Where's my shirt? Is it totally destroyed?" He was just glad his skirt hadn't caught fire. That could have been embarrassing—once the pain went away, that was.

"I had to cut it off you," Fifer said, returning and sitting down next to him on the sofa. "I'm glad you don't remember it. It was pretty horrible. You screamed a lot."

"I did?" Dev asked. "Yeah, that's all a blur. I think I was in shock. Thanks . . . for taking care of me."

Fifer smiled. "I washed your other shirt. It's probably dry by now. Hanging on the bannister." She slid down and rested her head on the pillow, staying curled up so she didn't accidentally bump Dev's burns. "I'm going to take a nap. I didn't sleep much last night. Wake me up if you need anything."

"Sure." As Fifer closed her eyes and drifted off, Dev got up slowly. He stood for a moment, then tested how it felt to move. His wounds had been extensive, and without Fifer's medicine he'd be in excruciating pain right now. Instead the pain was tolerable, and the wounds were scabbing over properly. He walked slowly over to the bannister to get his shirt, then eased it on, not sure he liked how it felt against his raw skin.

Leaving it unbuttoned, Dev went toward the east window but paused in front of a book that was lying on the floor. He pushed it with his toe into the light and saw it was a book about dragons written in the ancient language. The cover illustration depicted humans slaying a dragon. Unable to bend too far without opening his wounds, Dev flipped the cover open with his foot and used his toes to turn the pages. He studied the drawings, noting the different weapons that the people carried. With the right kind of wood and a bit of metal, Dev could carve most of them. He already had a good start on a few.

Inexplicably the image of the gray-haired man returned to his mind, and that made him think of the drawings he'd found, especially the one of the girl in the orchard. He went over to the desk and found the book that he'd slipped that picture into so many weeks ago, and he pulled it out.

The sight of it struck him hard in the chest, and he knew suddenly why the girl looked so familiar. She resembled one of the other black-eyed slaves, whose name Dev had never learned because they'd been under the Revinir's mind control almost the whole time he'd worked in the catacombs. But he'd seen her in the hallways when he'd first gotten sent down there. He was sure of it.

He looked back down at the drawing. When had this been done? The edges were battered, and the image was yellowed with age. It couldn't have been just a handful of years ago—it had to be much longer than that. So did that make this someone's mother? Maybe Fifer would see the resemblance too, and know the name of the girl from the catacombs.

Dev felt a surge of hope, like he'd found a way to reunite the girl with someone, even though it was only a portrait. It was better than nothing. But his heart crashed just as quickly when he realized that if the drawing was of the girl's mother, it couldn't be *his* mother. And maybe that meant that this palace belonged to the girl . . . and not to him.

News from a Friend

Florence had a lot on her mind. Getting two ghost dragons, a flying cheetah, and a group of humans here was a great deal to tackle, what with the volcano network and all the flying in a strange land she'd never been to before. Then there was Thisbe to worry about. She'd been trying to stay calm about everything, to be the voice of reason, but this was a huge problem that she didn't know how to solve. And with that problem came intense heartbreak all around—including her own. But she couldn't dwell on it because she was leading this crew. And then Drock had shown up, staying close as they traveled but trying not to appear so. Was he under the Revinir's mind control or not? That had given Florence one more thing to address. Luckily, Simber soon found Drock to be of his own mind.

When Fifer's send component showed up in the cavelands, Simber and Drock were on the ground talking and Florence was in the midst of assigning everyone caves to settle into until further notice. Ghost dragons roamed around asking repetitive questions and making everything just a little more difficult, and Florence was eager to get back on Gorgrun, fly over to Ashguard's palace, and figure this whole mess out.

Florence opened the message and read it, and realized she'd never responded to the head mage to let her know that they were indeed going to camp out at the cavelands as commanded . . . for the moment, at least. So she hastily wrote back:

> Fifer,
>
> We're in the cavelands as you suggested. I'm coming to you later today on a ghost dragon to do a flyover and drop supplies. We'll stay high in the air unless it looks safe to land. Don't worry—those dragons can't hurt us. Anxiously

awaiting further instructions on how to get you out of there so

we can find Thisbe.

Florence

She sent it off, then shouted out a couple of orders and went over to greet Drock. "It's good to see you," Florence said warmly to the dark purple dragon. "You've managed to keep yourself from succumbing to the Revinir's roar. That's quite a feat. Watching all of these dragons fly around aimlessly is quite a sad sight." She patted Drock's side. "How are you, old friend?"

Drock's expression was as desolate as the cavelands. "I'm losing hope, Florence. How are you?"

The dragon's words cut deep. And even though Florence was energized and eager to help the people of Grimere, she thought she understood how bleak things must look from Drock's perspective. He was the only dragon that had retained control of his own mind, and it had been this way for months. His mother, Pan, and his four siblings didn't acknowledge him or even seem to know him. There was no one to talk to except the ghost dragons, and Drock couldn't stay in the cavelands for long without being missed. "I'm sorry," Florence said. "You must feel terribly alone."

"It's true," said Drock. "I was pleased to notice your party shortly after your arrival. Though I'm sure the Revinir has received word by now that you're here."

"Unfortunately that couldn't be helped," said Florence. "There was no way to hide being spewed from a volcano. Even if the ghost dragons had used their cloudlike hiding features, they wouldn't have been able to hide Simber or me. And it was too late—we were noticed from the moment we entered the area."

"She's likely been expecting you for some time," said Drock. He looked around the cavelands as if searching for someone but didn't seem to locate them.

At the same time, Rohan and Maiven approached the small group. They greeted Drock, and Rohan blurted out, "Is it true about Thisbe?"

Drock bowed his head. "I saw one of the red dragons drop her at the castle. She went inside. That's all I know." He hesitated. "It doesn't look promising."

Florence and Simber exchanged a glance while Rohan stared numbly ahead. "Thank you," he said quietly.

"So Fiferrr's message was accurrrate," said Simber. "As I thought."

"Is there any way you can find out what's happening with her?" Florence asked Drock.

"I was on my way back to the castle to see if I could circle around and eavesdrop when I saw your party arrive. And since I'm here now, there's . . . someone I need to check on. But I'll go back to the castle soon and see what I can discover."

"I'm going with you," said Rohan.

"No, you'rrre not," said Simber sharply.

Rohan was taken aback. "Why? Thisbe will listen to me. I need to speak with her."

"Rohan," said Florence patiently. "I know you're not thinking clearly, but if you are seen, you'll be captured. Everyone at the castle knows you."

"Then I'll go at night on a ghost dragon," he said. "We'll use the fog feature. I'll stay hidden."

Florence studied him. "That's actually not a bad idea," she said thoughtfully. "I'll think about it. But before I let you go anywhere, I need to see you put your feelings in a separate compartment for a little while and focus on what's right for our combined army."

"I can do that," said Rohan, standing up straighter.

"And speaking of our combined army," Florence said, "I'd like to hand over the leadership position to Maiven now that we are back in her land. Maiven, your word is law from this point forward."

"Thank you," said Maiven with a little bow of her head.

Florence shared her plan to do a flyover with Maiven and Drock. "It's wise to use a ghost dragon," Drock said. "I'd take you myself, but I'm not sure what the red dragons have been ordered to do. They might attack me or any other regular dragon. At least if they do attack, a ghost dragon won't suffer from it."

They dispersed to take care of their individual tasks: Maiven to address the people and give them an update, Drock to search the cavelands for Dev before heading to the castle, and Florence to prep for her trip and find a ghost dragon to take her to Ashguard's palace. She wanted to get moving as quickly as possible to get an idea of what they were dealing with so they could start fixing things. Or, at least, that's what she intended to do. But things weren't going great for anyone lately.

LISA McMANN

On Equal Ground

Thisbe and her mind-controlled servant, named Zel, strolled the grounds outside the castle. Thisbe asked the woman a few random questions, but Zel only responded to direct orders that seemed appropriate for a personal servant. So Thisbe soon gave up trying to chat, and they went in silence. Two dragons circled overhead, staying suspiciously close, which told Thisbe that the Revinir didn't trust her. But they were making progress.

That wasn't on Thisbe's mind right now, though. She needed to ditch Zel so she could send a message to Fifer without the Revinir finding out. And soon—she knew that

Florence and the rest would be getting here anytime. They might even be here already. She didn't want to put Fifer in a compromising position of having to explain to anyone else what an incoming send spell was all about.

Thisbe had thought about sending it from her room when Zel left to run errands, but she had no idea what route the magical item would take as it traveled through rooms and down hallways. And her balcony had potential, but she worried about being seen by dragons or other servants. It was safer to send it out here if Thisbe could find a remote place out of sight, but only if Zel didn't witness the act, for if the Revinir asked her about seeing Thisbe do anything suspicious, Zel would be compelled to tell her.

She wandered to the immense waterfall with Zel on her tail. The water shimmered and pounded, making Thisbe's chest vibrate. It was one of the first things she'd seen when she and Fifer and Seth had crossed over the gorge for the first time on Hux the ice blue. It was wide and powerful, falling off the cliff into the vast nothingness below.

The image in her mind of her mother had given her a tiny glimpse of what this used to look like before the worlds

LISA McMANN

separated. The gorge had once not existed, and this area had been part of the sea that led to the seven islands. Somewhere along here was where Thisbe's mother had been abducted by pirates, who'd somehow gotten help from Rohan's mother.

Rohan. His name was on Thisbe's lips in an instant, but she made no sound. She closed her eyes as her heart stabbed beat after beat inside her rib cage. How could she answer his message when she had no words? All she could do was hope he'd forgive her someday. She was keeping this secret for the purest of intentions, no matter how awful it made her look. She was protecting him and all the others from having to tell the truth to the Revinir if, somehow in this process, the dragon-woman managed to capture anyone and force them back into compliance. Like Zel, here. In her right mind, the young woman might be totally against the Revinir, but she could do nothing about it except report everything as she saw it back to the dragon-woman. It would be so easy to foil this entire slippery plan that Fifer had conjured up. Thisbe had to stay strong no matter what.

But it was hard to do. It seemed like every minute there was a mental fight. A temptation to give in and give up. How bad could life be with the Revinir perpetually in charge? With mind-controlled dragons and humans ruling over everyone? Thisbe and Fifer and Dev and the rest of them could just retreat, and maybe start life over in Artimé. There was always room for more there. But no . . . the Revinir had promised to take over the seven islands next. There was no place safe from her—not even another world on the volcano network, because the dragon-woman knew how to use that system too. It was up to Thisbe to stop everything now, before it was too late. They'd already needed to concoct this dangerous plan just to get close enough to the dragon-woman to take her out. It was this . . . or surrender. And then what? Locked in the dungeon to ride out their lives until there were no more black-eyed people left? Or . . . worse?

The thought brought fire to the back of Thisbe's throat. Her scales rose, and smoke drifted out of her nostrils. If that happened, this beautiful land would never be the same. It would never again be ruled the way it was meant to be. The Revinir would be the sole leader. The dragons would never be free. And the ghost dragons would never be allowed to pass on to the next life. Everything would be so messed up and wrong.

And if the Revinir got control of the seven islands, too, there would be no one left to oppose her.

Thisbe walked close to the rushing waterfall and saw that there was a narrow ledge behind it. Her heart thumped, and her stomach churned. Her fear of heights was ever present, no matter how many times she was forced to deal with it. She grew dizzy just thinking about stepping onto the ledge and quickly retreated. "I need to sit down," she told Zel, and stumbled ridiculously close to the edge of the world. Dropping to her hands and knees, Thisbe crawled to safety and found a shady group of trees to sit under. Zel followed diligently, seemingly unaffected by any fears. Thisbe shifted around the base of the grouping of trees, trying to partially shield herself from Zel. Maybe she could at least write a note and find a time to send it later.

Zel stayed standing, staring off at nothing. One of the curving tree trunks partially obstructed her view of Thisbe. Thisbe quickly opened a send component and started writing:

Fife,
It's working. Declaring allegiance together in two days, then
expecting the questions/confusion and hoping for a moment to

do the deed. All my love to you and Dev, and please take care

of Rohan when you see him—he's falling apart.

Thiz

As Thisbe held the component and quickly scanned the words, her stomach was in knots. If anyone read this but Fifer, the jig would be up. And Thisbe's life would be in danger.

A shadow fell over the note, and Thisbe looked up. It was Zel, standing over her. "What are you doing?" asked Zel. She reached out for the component.

Thisbe froze. If she sent it immediately, Zel would tell. What else could she do? She should never have attempted this!

"Revinir will like to see this," said Zel more firmly, placing her fingers on the end of the note.

Thisbe panicked. Then the heat in her throat thickened, and she yanked the component away. She let out a blast of fire, incinerating the spell and sending the ashes to float on the air.

Overnight Journey

Drock didn't find Dev, but he found a ghost dragon named Astrid who looked familiar from the day Drock had brought Dev here. She seemed to have a faint recollection of a boy who'd stayed a night or two. After Drock described Dev, Astrid began to remember a little more, until she recalled a strange moment when she said Dev had tied a long braid of grass around her talon. She couldn't remember why, though.

"That's strange," said Drock. "Where did he get long grass around here?" The cavelands bordered a desert. The forest was beyond it, but not conveniently close to the area where the ghost dragons dwelled.

Astrid squeezed her eyes shut, thinking hard. And then they flew open. "It wasn't here!" she exclaimed. "It was by the palace! Yes! The Devastator—that's what I called him. He's at Ashguard's palace. And he told me to tell some dragon named Drock to find him there."

"That would be me," said Drock. "Many thanks, Astrid."

"The recent stuff is more difficult to remember," said Astrid.

"What do you mean?"

"I mean things that just happened are impossible to recall. But I can tell you what happened forty years ago."

Drock smiled kindly. "Perhaps you could do that sometime."

Astrid looked at him. "Do what?"

Drock's smile didn't fade, but he changed the subject. "I was wondering if you would like to take another trip to the palace to look for Dev. Our friend Florence needs a ride. She's standing right over there, the tall black warrior statue. We want to give Gorgrun and Quince a little break after all the flying they've done lately."

"I would be delighted," said Astrid. Together the two dragons walked over to where Florence was gathering up items to take with her. She had some ropes from their supply chest and a sturdy sack of components for Fifer, including plenty of send components so they could stay in touch without worry. Drock introduced Astrid and let Florence know that Dev had last been seen at the palace too.

"That's strange," said Florence. "He's not there now. Fifer said she was alone."

"Perhaps he's hiding in the surrounding area if there are dragons there," said Drock, looking worried. "I hope he's all right. I told him to stay out of Grimere at all costs. The Revinir thinks she threw him out the tower window to his death, but I managed to grab him just in time."

Florence gazed at the adolescent dragon. "You've turned into quite a hero, Drock," she said. "We are grateful for all you're doing to help us. And we're eager to get your mother and siblings out of the Revinir's grip."

Drock seemed uncomfortable yet pleased with the praise. "I

want that too. Thank you. I'll be going now—I can't stay away from Grimere for too long. Back to the castle. I'll let you know if I find out anything."

"Maiven will be here awaiting news. Simber, too. I'll be gone for a day or so, but don't be surprised if you see a ghost dragon in fog formation moving near the castle with a rider or two."

"I'll be on the lookout for an unusually low-flying cloud of fog," Drock promised. With a good-bye to Astrid, the dark purple dragon took off and sailed low toward the forest beyond the strip of desert.

Florence reintroduced herself to Astrid in case the ghost dragon had forgotten her and warned her that she was quite heavy. But Astrid didn't seem troubled by it. "Do you know where Ashguard's palace is?" Florence asked her, even though she knew Astrid had been there recently.

"The palace," said Astrid. "Oh yes. It's a beautiful place. Red and purple and gold. It's not far beyond that line of mountains. Would you like to go there?"

"Indeed I would," said Florence.

"Then climb aboard." Astrid dipped her wing and used her

tail to help Florence climb on. When Florence was settled, Astrid turned to look at her. "Where to, madam?"

Florence and Simber exchanged a smile and nodded their good-byes. "To Ashguard's palace, if you please," said Florence. "It's just over those mountains." To Simber she said, "I'll see you in a day or so." She glanced at Rohan, who seemed to have pulled himself together a bit after the pep talk and was chatting with Seth while they ate dinner. "If Maiven sends Rohan to the castle, suggest someone go with him."

Simber nodded. "I will. Be carrreful."

"Count on it."

By the time they headed out, it was dark. Florence sent Fifer another message to let her know she was on the way and to expect her in the morning. And then she settled back for a long ride.

In the palace library, Dev began whittling a new long spear while Fifer paged through the book about killing dragons, looking at the drawings. They discussed what to tell Florence about preparing for an attack, since they hadn't heard any news from Thisbe.

"Are you sure the dragons can't hurt your warrior trainer?" Dev asked.

"She's carved from stone. Fire won't hurt her. And she says the ghost dragons can't get hurt. I'm not going to argue. Plus, she's going to try to drop some components for me. When she gets closer, I'll tell her where to aim."

"She's going to have to throw them from quite a height," said Dev skeptically.

"She's got excellent aim. I'm not worried—wait'll you see her. You'll get what I mean. Besides, she can't be hurt, remember?"

"All right. If you say so." Dev didn't seem convinced, but he'd never met Florence before and had met only a few living statues in his life. "Why not have Simber come?"

"Simber is susceptible to very hot fires. I'm guessing that's why."

The most recent message from Florence came rushing up the stairwell. Fifer read it and looked up. "She'll be here in the morning. We should probably turn in. I could use some sleep. My nap ended too quickly."

"I guess that means I'm going to have to hide soon," said

Dev. "I'll sleep here tonight, but then I'll go to the alcove when Florence comes in case she gets a look inside the windows. I don't want to take any chances."

"Okay," said Fifer, feeling a bit melancholy at the thought. "And I'm glad you're feeling better . . . but please don't try talking to the dragons again."

Dev put down the long spear he was carving. He wasn't making any promises. As he made the rounds, checking the windows for unusual sights, he stopped at the east window. "Hmm," he said. "The fourth red dragon is back."

Bombs Away

Once Astrid the ghost dragon cleared the mountain range and the sky began to lighten, Florence strained to see the glorious palace Astrid had spoken about. She tried to imagine Fifer living alone in such a place. It seemed strange.

"It won't be long now," said Astrid. She sniffed the air. "I didn't know that Ashguard kept dragons."

"The dragons are under the command of the Revinir," Florence said for probably the eleventh time. "I'm pretty sure Ashguard isn't there anymore." Out of everyone, Florence knew the least about the history of this land, but she'd heard stories. "And from what Maiven Taveer told me, I don't think the palace has been kept up."

"Oh, that's right," said Astrid. "You mentioned that once before."

Florence blinked. "Right." A sliver of sun appeared to their left and Florence leaned forward, eager to see what they would be going up against. Astrid pointed out the forest and crater lake in the same direction as the sun and the deserted village with the palace straight ahead. It was surrounded by overgrowth and not easy to spot at first, but then Florence spied four red dots making a square on the ground. "Those red things are the dragons," Florence told Astrid. "Can you get a sense of how big they are? Or . . . how combative?"

Astrid was quiet for a long moment as she sampled the air. "They aren't large like ghost dragons," she said. "Maybe half the size—average for adults. A bit larger than that dark purple friend of yours, I'd say."

"Anything else you can detect?" asked Florence, feeling relieved that the dragons weren't as enormous as Gorgrun and Quince. Though they were still dragons. But Florence was betting on the fact that these were no different from the ones that flew aimlessly through the skies under the Revinir's mind control and would be somewhat oblivious to things. And even though they'd attacked Fifer's birds, perhaps they'd just seen them as food rather than intruders. Neither Astrid nor Florence looked like food.

"They seem docile," said Astrid. "But that could change."

Florence quickly sent a message to alert Fifer that they were approaching. Minutes later she received a response to drop the supplies through a hole in the roof if possible—that way the dragons wouldn't torch them.

There was still something fishy about the way Fifer was behaving. Perhaps it was just communicating through messages that was hard to get used to. Not being able to hear Fifer's voice or detect her tone made it difficult to tell how she was handling things. Her letters seemed quick and formal, and she didn't give Florence a lot of detail. She also seemed very matter-of-fact in this odd situation, which is partly what made Florence suspicious that perhaps Fifer was being forced to write like that. She couldn't tell what was up, and it was driving her crazy.

Where are you in the palace? Florence wrote back, and watched where the component went.

LISA McMANN

At the top of the center tower, inside the bulb, came the response. Her description of the building location matched what Florence could see. So at least that made sense.

Florence studied the broken-down palace as they drew close. It looked abandoned and unsafe. Sure enough, there were two holes in the roof, close together. Maybe there was a way to get a peek inside. "Okay, Astrid," said Florence. "Stay nice and high as we fly over the property. I don't think the dragons will do anything since you're a dragon too, but we want to be very careful."

Astrid agreed and stayed aloft. Florence could see the red dragons on the ground standing up and craning their necks to see what was flying into the airspace above the palace. They began moving but stayed primarily in their corners. Florence looked down at the roof. It was too far below them to guarantee an accurate drop of the components into one of the holes—they looked like dots from this height. Astrid sailed across the property toward the orchard. One of the red dragons took flight, then circled and settled again.

Astrid soared over the abandoned village and turned around. "Now what?" she asked.

"Let's return. A little lower."

Astrid flew back over the property, dropping slightly. Florence kept a close eye on the red dragons. They were definitely aware of the ghost dragon and her rider, but none of them seemed threatened enough to come for them. She took one of the ropes and tied the end around the sack of components. Perhaps lowering it would give it a better chance of hitting the right spot . . . and maybe Fifer could use the rope for something too.

Florence peered back at the south window of the onion-bulb tower as they crossed the property line. Sure enough, there was Fifer, pressed against the pane, seemingly alone. Florence waved, and Fifer waved back.

Once they made it without incident to the other side, Florence repeated the order, having Astrid drop a little farther and go a little slower. "I'm going to try to lower this sack of supplies through one of the holes in the roof," she explained. "If I miss, it'll get stuck on the rooftop and won't do anybody any good. So we need to get it right."

"I think we can make this happen," said Astrid. "I'm not sensing any serious animosity toward me coming from below. Just a little prickliness."

"Great. Let's get as close as you dare, then, and circle around the roof hole."

Astrid slowed her airspeed and dropped lower, doing her best to look casual about it to those below. Florence lay on her stomach across Astrid's back, arms outstretched and letting down the rope with the sack of supplies. Astrid circled and Florence kept the rope dangling as she waited for the perfect moment to let go.

Just as Florence was about to make the drop, movement at the back of the property caught her eye. One of the dragons had lifted off. It let out a roar and a blast of flames as it called to the other three.

Astrid jerked upward and abandoned circling. Florence cringed, forced to make a split decision, and let go of the rope. She watched as it barely missed its mark and stuck on the roof.

The other three dragons took flight and roared back to the first. They came straight for Astrid and Florence. "Hang on!" said Astrid.

The warrior trainer scrambled to sit upright. She reached for her bow and nocked a magical arrow as the four red dragons came at them from all directions. "Go, Astrid!" Florence cried, then let the arrow fly at the nearest dragon. It missed and soared over its head. She pulled another out as Astrid flew jerkily, trying to find her best path to safety without running into one of the attackers.

But the red dragons were faster. Florence aimed for the creature's open mouth and let loose another arrow. This time it hit, flying straight up the nostril instead and disappearing. The dragon shrieked and roared. Then its eyes rolled back into its head and it started falling, spiraling all the way down and crushing one of the corner towers. The palace shook.

Florence stared. She'd killed it with a direct hit up the nostril. Had it gone to its brain? Was that the secret? Was that the most vulnerable part of a dragon? "Move away from the palace!" Florence cried. She had to draw the dragons away from the structure so they didn't accidentally crush Fifer if they went down. Astrid did her best as the dragons roared at them from three sides, now. Florence took aim again but held off releasing the arrow until the dragons weren't directly above the palace. Astrid darted upward with one of the dragons on her tail. Florence, trying to keep her aim steady, took the shot and nailed the second dragon in the same place. It fell much like the first, narrowly missing the palace and landing with a hard thud on the property below.

The other two dragons were fully charged now, and they came after Astrid. One of them took the ghost dragon's neck in its mouth and yanked her around while the other barreled for Florence. Before the warrior trainer could get off another fatal shot, the dragon plowed into her, knocking her off balance. Her bow went flying out of her hands and fell to the ground. Florence grabbed on to the red dragon's face and pried its mouth open as its back end bucked. It roared, engulfing Florence in flames, but they only blinded her momentarily.

Then the red dragon reached out with its front claws and tried to grab the stone warrior, but its claws merely left long, shallow scratches in her. Florence hung on to it, frustrating the beast. It swung around violently, nearly throwing Florence into the air. Quickly she let go of it and grabbed for Astrid, but her fingers grasped only the ethereal cloudiness of the ghost dragon's body, and she started sliding. Astrid tried to help, but the second remaining dragon came roaring back and head-butted Florence off.

With an angry yell, the Magical Warrior trainer dropped like a bomb to the ground and smashed into a hundred pieces.

A Giant Puzzle

Fifer gasped when she saw Florence hit the ground. "Oh my God!"

Dev, who'd begun his careful but harried return from the alcove after witnessing the first red dragon hit the corner tower on its way down, came running into the library. "We need to take cover!" he cried.

"But look!" said Fifer, pointing out the east window to the ground. She couldn't bear to say Florence's name. The warrior's body had broken into chunks, and the impact had scattered the pieces over a wide swath of the yard like some horrifying art project gone wrong. None of the pieces moved. Nearby lay a writhing, dying red dragon.

"Holy—" Dev began, then stared. "What happened? Is that Florence? Is she . . . dead?"

Fifer gripped her head in shock. She'd never imagined anything more horrible than seeing the iconic Magical Warrior trainer and dear friend defeated and destroyed so violently. "I don't know," Fifer whispered.

"We need to take cover," Dev said again, more urgently. "The northwest tower is smashed to pieces." When Fifer didn't move, Dev grabbed her hand and pulled her to the stairwell. They went down a flight and crawled behind the stone and iron steps, hoping they were strong enough to protect them if anything else came slamming down from the sky.

Through the tower window, Dev and Fifer could occasionally see the remaining two dragons swoop by, and then they caught sight of the ghost dragon who was trying to fight them, knowing she wasn't allowed to kill them. "It's Astrid!" Dev said.

Fifer didn't know Astrid, and she didn't care about her either—not right now, anyway. Florence's body was destroyed and scattered across the front lawn. The shock was so great that Fifer was having a hard time believing what she'd seen. Could Florence really be dead? The warrior trainer had said the dragons couldn't hurt her. But she hadn't anticipated this.

"At least she got two of them," Dev said. "She helped us a lot."

Fifer cringed and buried her face, not wanting to talk about anything like that. "This is horrifying," she whispered. "Florence's death is the end of Artimé. We're nothing without her."

Dev was taken aback. How could Fifer feel so strongly about a statue? And how could Florence be so important to Artimé when she hadn't even been a part of all of the rescues the Artiméans had done in the land of the dragons? But he could see Fifer was shocked and stunned. After a while, glancing helplessly her way, he said, "This has to end soon. Let me know if I can do anything to help you."

Eventually Astrid lost interest in fighting, or forgot what she was doing, and flew away alone. The two remaining red dragons landed, one at the front and one at the back of the property, apparently settling back in to work. When all had been quiet for some time, Fifer and Dev went downstairs to the courtyard and tentatively poked their heads out. From there they could see pieces of Florence's body and one of the slain dragons. Fifer ventured outside a few more steps, not sure what to expect from the dragon guards at this point. She motioned for Dev to stay near the tower—she didn't want him to get attacked in case the dragons were still riled up over him roaring. And she went alone to the yard to assess . . . well, everything.

Fifer gripped her head, utterly blown away. Florence, broken into a hundred pieces, was even more tragic close up. She almost didn't want to see how strange it looked for Florence's head to be severed from her neck and split in two halves from her headpiece to her chin. She knelt. "Is there any way to fix this?" she murmured. Could she possibly bring the statue back to life again? If so, how?

There was a time when Simber had completely disintegrated into a pile of sand, but Aaron had been able to bring him back. Panther had split in two, and Alex had brought her back. Not to mention all of the other less debilitating things that had happened to statues over the years. Even Florence had lost her lower legs once, but Ms. Octavia had been able to repair them, and the warrior woman had been as good as new.

But this was a little different. Just looking at Florence's broken head made it obvious that Florence wasn't "alive" at the moment. Perhaps the trauma had been so great that it immediately put the statue in a resting state, as if the world had ended, until something could be done to fix her. Fifer had no clue how to do that. But maybe Aaron could tell her.

Unfortunately, the two send spells that Fifer and Florence had sent back and forth were unusable for Aaron—try as she might, the spell had Florence's name assigned to it, and that couldn't be changed. Fifer looked around the grounds, wondering if Florence had been carrying the bag of spells when she got knocked down. She didn't see it anywhere, though it was hard to find anything in the tall brush. If it wasn't inside the palace, she'd have to comb the entire property in case it had fallen somewhere during the fight. Hopefully, one of the dead dragons hadn't landed on it.

That was another problem. What were they supposed to do with these slain dragons? Maybe Dev had ideas. But that was the least of her worries. Fifer looked over her shoulder and saw Dev inching his way across the pavers toward her. The living dragons didn't seem to care a whit about him now. She motioned for him to come.

"Is it very bad?" Dev asked.

"Yes," said Fifer. "It's terrible. But there's a chance I can restore her. When it first happened, I thought she was dead for good. But now that I've had a chance to think, I remember other statues being brought back through a specific kind of spell. Unfortunately, I don't know how to do it. But I can find out, if we only had another send spell."

"Did Florence drop the sack of supplies?"

"I don't know."

"I can help look."

"I asked her to try to drop them through the roof holes. Do you want to start there?"

Dev seemed relieved to do something. "Yes. I'll let you know if I find them."

"When you're done, come back down. I'll need some help dragging pieces of Florence to put her back together. She's pretty heavy." Fifer hesitated, noticing for the first time that Dev had his shirt on and buttoned today. "How are your burns feeling?"

Dev nodded. "Much better. But I'll be careful." He hesitated. "I hope she'll be okay."

"Me too." Fifer pushed the two pieces of Florence's head together, being careful not to pinch any grass in between them. She found smaller pieces of her head ornament and laid them in the places they needed to go. Florence's arms and legs were all broken into multiple pieces. The quiver was miraculously in one piece, though the bow was hard to find, and the arrows were scattered about. The quiver was way too heavy for Fifer to lift alone. She peered inside and saw the spare robe tucked down inside, unharmed.

The two dragons didn't seem to have any problem with Florence now that she was broken into pieces and not moving. But what would they do if Fifer was able to bring her back to life? Would they attack her all over again? They'd have to cross that bridge when they came to it. But for now, there was no bringing her back to life if Fifer couldn't figure out how to make all the pieces come back together.

"Oh, Thisbe," Fifer moaned as she trudged through the overgrowth carrying a hunk of Florence's arm, "I really hope things are going better for you than they are for me."

LISA McMANN

Just then Dev emerged from the palace empty-handed. Fifer looked up expectantly, then deflated when she saw he hadn't found the supplies. "No luck?" Fifer asked him.

"I think I found the bag," Dev said, "but I can't reach it. There's a rope that wasn't there before hanging down through the hole. It's going to take a bit of work to get to it. But it's something."

At least there was that. "Good," said Fifer, glad that one thing was sort of going right. "Now, can you help me carry Florence's bum over to the right place?"

Making Big Plans

After Thisbe had torched the send spell she'd written, she scrambled for an excuse to give Zel. "Oh, I didn't actually write any words," she explained, trying to sound scientific and boring. "I was just testing my magical . . . flint . . . pencil. And it works great. Now I can quickly make a fire in the apartment fireplace tonight."

It was a terrible excuse—Thisbe could make a fire quickly enough without needing flint, but Zel didn't know that. In the end, it had been enough to calm Zel's alarm and throw off the mind-controlled servant's concerns. Unfortunately, knowing how closely Zel would be watching her now, Thisbe was

LISA McMANN

too paranoid to try to send anything again. She imagined what could have happened if someone had intercepted what she'd written. Thankfully, Zel hadn't had a chance to read it.

Later Thisbe returned to the ballroom to meet with the Revinir, ready to nail down some details of their new partnership and solidify in the Revinir's mind that she was truly on board with this plan. Getting the dragon-woman to trust her as much as possible was one of the most important goals Thisbe had. Perhaps she could lure her outside for a walk on the lawn without her entourage. Or somehow get her alone in a spot where no one else could be hurt if Thisbe used the obliterate spell on her.

The Revinir turned when Thisbe entered, then invited her to step out on the balcony with her to overlook the castle grounds. The ballroom balcony faced the back side of the property opposite the drawbridge and long driveway, so there was no hustle and bustle, only a few guards patrolling the hills. From this height Thisbe could see the city of Grimere off to the right, with a big open square not far from the forest. "What do you expect will change when we are co-rulers?" Thisbe asked, trying to sound casual.

"I thought you wanted to think it through," the Revinir said sarcastically.

"I'd like to know what to expect so that I can make my decision," said Thisbe. "You've had all sorts of time to envision it, but I haven't. What's in it for me?"

The Revinir shot Thisbe an approving glance. She continued to be surprised by the girl and appreciated her selfishness. To her, it was a sign of a good business partner. But she hadn't seen this side of Thisbe before, so it was a bit suspect. Perhaps this was the true Thisbe coming out—her evil side—which she hadn't allowed to show before. If so, this was going to be a great situation.

But the Revinir still had doubts, mainly because she couldn't read Thisbe the way she could read all the other black-eyed children. Which made Thisbe even more of a delightful challenge, despite the suspicions that came with it. Thisbe was complex, like the Revinir. And the dragon-woman was cautiously optimistic that things would work out for the betterment of herself and her land. After all, it wasn't called the land of the black-eyed rulers, now, was it? But that was a step that would come later. She needed Thisbe to think she'd be a

LISA McMANN

full partner in order to announce their agreement, take official leadership, release the dragons from their mind control, and send the ghost dragons to their next life. Once that happened, the Revinir could slowly push Thisbe out. Or maybe even lock her up in the dungeon and conveniently forget about her.

And while she needed at least a few of the black-eyed slaves as backup in case something happened to Thisbe, she didn't need them all. Especially Fifer. Now that Thisbe was here and things were looking promising, she didn't want Fifer showing up and wrecking it all.

The Revinir frowned. Fifer hadn't come after Thisbe. Was that bad? Or good? She hadn't sent any notes like Rohan had done. The Revinir turned sharply, ignoring Thisbe's question. "Why hasn't your sister tried to contact you with your little magical messages?"

"Because she doesn't have any," said Thisbe. "You emptied our pockets on the ride over, remember? That was right before you dumped us through a roof. That wasn't very nice, by the way."

"True," said the Revinir. "You seem all right, though."

"I was lucky."

"What about Fifer?" asked the Revinir, looking sharply into Thisbe's eyes.

Thisbe wasn't sure what the Revinir wanted to hear, but she went with her gut instinct, which seemed to be present whenever she was dealing with the dragon-woman. "She was hurt. But she'll live."

"Oh?" The Revinir turned away, hiding her expression. "How so?"

"She broke her wrist," said Thisbe truthfully, then embellished it. "And her ankle. She's not very mobile, but I made sure she could crawl to the river before I left her there alone."

"The dragons will feed her if she gets desperate," said the Revinir. "I instructed them to make sure you two didn't die."

"That was kind of you," said Thisbe, trying not to let her words drip with the sarcasm she felt. "It might have been nice to know."

"I couldn't let you think I had a soft heart," said the Revinir, and then she laughed. "Because I don't. I just needed you."

"I'm well aware of that," said Thisbe icily. "But as I said before, this partnership will be equal, or else I'm not participating. I fear that will be hard for you after the way you've treated

275 « Dragon Slayers

LISA McMANN

me. And that's why I wanted a few extra days to see how you handle it."

"I'm treating you fine!" the Revinir said, growing indignant. "What more do you want?"

"I want it to continue," said Thisbe, lifting her chin.

The Revinir averted her eyes. "It will."

Thisbe noticed. She crossed her arms. "You didn't answer my question. What do you expect will change if we join together?"

"You said 'when' before! Not 'if.'"

Thisbe hid a smirk. This was all going too well. Could it possibly continue? "When, then," said Thisbe amicably. "How do you envision it will all go down? I haven't heard the rules or history behind this type of rulership before."

"We just have to go together to publicly announce that we have agreed to co-lead the land of the dragons and restore the world to the way it was before the king and his people took over. One dragon and one black-eyed ruler. Then the ghost dragons will move on to their next lives, and the current dragons will be in power with me leading them."

"And the black-eyed rulers also leading," Thisbe said.

"Right. Obviously."

"Which means you'll stop enslaving them."

"Sure. I'll enslave other people instead."

"Um, no you won't."

"Whatever," said the Revinir impatiently. "I see no harm in putting the king's army to work. They never supported me."

"Us, you mean."

"Of course, us!" Fire shot from the Revinir's mouth, and Thisbe had to duck to avoid being singed.

"Watch it!" Thisbe warned, feeling her eyes spark and heat build in her throat.

"I'm sorry!" said the Revinir, not sounding sorry. She turned and went back into the ballroom, stomping as she went, which made the floor shake.

Thisbe touched the obliterate component box through her vest. It was so tempting. But if she used it now, she'd definitely die right along with the Revinir—either from the blast or from the balcony crumbling and a big chunk of the castle being obliterated with her.

"Let's take a walk outside," Thisbe suggested.

The Revinir frowned. "Why?"

Thisbe shrugged. "Because it's beautiful out there."

"Go take a walk with Zel. I don't like to be exposed. I prefer walls. To be honest, I miss being in the catacombs."

Thisbe's heart sank. This was going to be more difficult than she thought. "I think part of this process has to be showing the people of Grimere that we are unified. We should be seen together so they get used to the idea."

The Revinir turned to Thisbe. "You don't seem to understand that I don't care about them."

Thisbe held back an exasperated sigh. "Of course. I keep forgetting."

"But you asked what's in it for you. Power. You get to live here. And not be a slave."

"Generous," said Thisbe. "But you know that's not what I care about."

The Revinir moved slowly to the expanse of windows and looked out to the east at the gorge and the mist beyond it that hid the land of the seven islands from view. "And you can be assured that I won't make the promise you're looking for."

Thisbe was quiet for a moment, dissecting every word the Revinir had just said. Was that a flat no? It seemed . . .

intentionally vague. Which, in Thisbe's mind, left the door open for the promise she wanted. Because just in case Thisbe wasn't able to do away with the Revinir, she needed to be assured that her allies to the east wouldn't be put in jeopardy.

"All right," said Thisbe carefully. "I'll wait until you change your mind."

In the Cavelands

The shock of what Thisbe had done was starting to wear off, but the pain of betrayal was increasing for Rohan. Charged with nothing to do but wait for news upon Florence's return, he tried to keep busy. Sky was compassionate, and the two ended up fishing together most of the morning. Maiven and Simber kept an eye on him too. And while there had been talk of a castle flyby on a ghost dragon, they wouldn't do it until darkness fell. Simber wanted to put off those plans until Florence was back with information that could potentially give them insight, so the longer Florence was gone, the lower the chance of tonight being the night to make a move.

It was excruciating, really. Whenever Rohan allowed himself to think about it, he felt sharp stabs of pain like shards of glass raking through him. As the day progressed, he began to scan the sky to the south, looking for Astrid and Florence, until he could hardly do anything else.

Seth tried to help Rohan too, but to be honest, he was almost as out of sorts as Rohan. Thisbe had been one of his dearest friends since they were young, and he just couldn't see her doing anything like this. Out of everyone, Seth felt most like something else had to be going on that none of them could understand quite yet. Maybe he believed that because it gave him comfort or lessened the pain. Or maybe it was because he'd witnessed firsthand how the twins worked when their backs were up against the wall.

But inevitably, whispers about the levels of good and evil in a person began in earnest. Was there something to it? And was evilness genetic? Aaron kept to himself once he started hearing speculation from others about the very thing he'd been thinking about. He knew that what Thisbe had done wasn't his fault. Yet he caught the glances, like always. His past followed him everywhere. There was no escaping it, and he accepted

LISA McMANN

that he'd done something worthy of an infinite number of apologies. That was part of his punishment, in his eyes. There would never be a time when he'd be done apologizing . . . at least not as long as these people were alive. Maybe one day, when he was Ishibashi's age and all the people surrounding him were new, he would be able to escape judgment. Believing he might be immortal because of the seaweed that Ishibashi, Ito, and Sato had given him to save his life years ago, Aaron was forced to think about that, as well. What was worse than living a life full of apologies? Watching everyone you loved die and never getting to do so yourself.

A mood settled around him, bringing him way down. Not even Ishibashi could give him something good to ponder. Everyone was feeling it as they waited for Florence to return with something—anything—to soothe their worries. And Aaron had an increasingly bad feeling that what Florence was about to tell them wouldn't be good.

When a dot appeared in the sky, the anticipation increased. When they realized Astrid was riderless, they were struck with fear. Was Florence okay? She had to be, Simber assured them. They began to speculate: Had Florence been able to land

and see what was going on? Were the dragons as docile as they'd all hoped? Was she staying indefinitely?

But then doubts crept in. Why hadn't she sent a message telling them what was up? Would she really delay the conversation half a day by sending a message with a forgetful ghost dragon?

As the speculation turned dark, Aaron found Simber, and the two waited together, beginning to fear the worst. "This isn't good," Aaron said.

"Something isn't rrright," Simber said.

Finally Astrid landed. It took some coaxing to help her remember why she wasn't carrying a rider. But then she did.

"The red dragons attacked us," Astrid recalled. "Florence slayed two of them. But the other two fought and dragged her off my back, and she fell a long distance to the ground. She broke into a thousand pieces. Maybe a million. She's dead."

Simber gasped. Aaron, Maiven, Rohan, and the rest stared in disbelief. Florence dead? It couldn't be possible! But imagining the warrior trainer falling from a great height was stomach-churning. Everyone began talking at once.

"She's not dead," said Aaron firmly, above the noise. "I know how to fix her."

LISA McMANN

"You'rrre not going therrre," said Simber. "It isn't safe."

"Fifer can fix her, then. Why hasn't she contacted us? Didn't Florence drop the supplies?" He pulled out a send component and started writing.

"She dropped them as the dragons attacked," Astrid recalled. "I don't think they hit their target, though."

"I'm sending instructions now," said Aaron. "Good grief—I hope Fifer knows about the time we brought you back from a pile of sand, Sim."

"She knows," said Seth. "We've read all the books. She'll think of it." He was still horrified at the image of Florence breaking into a million pieces. How would Fifer put her back together? It would take forever! He hoped Astrid was exaggerating or remembering it wrong.

Meanwhile Rohan was getting anxious. Surely they weren't going to wait for Florence any longer in order to do a stealthy castle flyby. They needed to go now so they could travel both ways under the cover of darkness.

Once Aaron sent his message to Fifer and things settled down, Rohan spoke to Maiven. "I'd like to take a ghost dragon to the castle. Will you let me? Please, Grandmum . . . we have to do something."

Maiven nodded. "Oh yes, we do," she said. She didn't like waiting any more than anyone else. She called to Quince, who was camped nearby, and asked if he felt up to a nighttime mission. The ghost dragon was eager to help.

Rohan ran to grab his rucksack and canteen. But before he returned to the dragon, he stopped to rummage through a small suitcase that the black-eyed children kept their extra things in and pulled out a few supplies. Then he went to Quince and climbed aboard.

Maiven followed, grasping the dragon's bony wings and climbing up after him.

"What are you doing?" Rohan asked.

The queen looked up. "It's my castle," she said. "I'm going with you." She turned to Simber and Aaron. "We'll be back by daylight. Hopefully with answers."

Sticks and Stones

Try as they might, Fifer and Dev couldn't budge Florence's left leg. It was mostly intact and had broken off at mid-thigh, which was great. But now that they had assembled the rest of the body puzzle fairly well, they didn't want to have to move everything all again over to where the leg was.

Fifer, sweating and breathing hard from the exertion, stood up straight to ease the strain on her back and took a moment to survey the situation and think about what to do. "It's not going to happen. We'll have to leave it here. When I bring Florence back to life, I'll have her scoot down to the leg so we can reattach it then."

"Won't that hurt her?" said Dev. "Wow, she is huge." He wiped his temples with the sleeve of the new shirt he'd found—a cool white linen blouse with a pattern of pale lavender flowers. While the burns on his back had healed enough to wear something over them, the work they'd been doing had broken the delicate skin in a few places, and small red splotches of blood stained a couple of spots between the flowers. He looked around, and the dead dragon nearby caught his eye. He gazed thoughtfully at it.

"I don't think moving will hurt her," said Fifer. "She had her legs lopped off one time before when she was alive and it didn't faze her." She pulled out and reread the message Aaron had sent her about how to bring Florence back to life. It was a relief to know that Astrid had made it safely back to the Artiméans and had remembered enough to tell them what was going on.

Aaron's instructions on how he'd brought Simber back to life when he'd been a pile of sand didn't quite match the situation with Florence, who was in chunks. But Fifer was the head mage of Artimé, and she'd find a way to adapt the spell. She didn't want to send a reply to Aaron yet, though, because when she did, the instructions he'd written would go with it.

LISA McMANN

She needed to memorize them. But now that Florence's pieces were almost all reassembled on the lawn, she and Dev needed a break. "Let's catch some fish. I haven't eaten all day."

Dev nodded, but instead of going to the river, he went over to the slain dragon and peered up its nostril. He could see the end of Florence's arrow way up there. Though Dev didn't want to take any of Florence's unused magical arrows that remained in her quiver or had been scattered about, he didn't think she'd mind if he borrowed one that had already been shot. But that would mean he'd have to stick his arm far inside the dead dragon's nose. The thought made him queasy, but he steeled himself for the task. "If you want to get fish, I'll try to collect the sack of spells. I've got an idea."

"Deal." Fifer glanced worriedly at the bloody spots on Dev's shirt. But she'd asked him multiple times if he was okay, and each time he blew off her concerns. He was going to do what he wanted to do, and Fifer would treat his new injuries tonight. They really did need those components. "Wait. What are you doing?"

"I'm going to retrieve this arrow." He took off his shirt and tossed it on the ground.

LISA McMANN

"Oh, that is so disgusting. I'm out." Shaking her head, Fifer went to the river.

Dev reached into the dragon's sticky nostril up to his shoulder. He gagged once reflexively, then closed his eyes and felt around. His fingers landed on the nock end of the arrow. He pinched it between his thumb and forefinger and tried to get a better grip to pull it, but his arm was in as far as it could go. Wiggling the arrow loosened it, and soon Dev could feel the point give a little. He climbed up on top of the dragon's snout to get a better angle and shoved his arm in again, until the ridge of the nostril was touching his neck. He grasped the arrow in his hand and yanked it with all his might.

With a gurgling slurp, the point of the arrow let loose from the dragon's brain. Dev pulled the arrow out and scrambled away as gooey sludge rushed from the dragon's nose.

Trying not to think about what he'd just done, Dev grabbed his shirt with his clean hand and took the arrow to the river. "I got it," he said to Fifer.

Fifer choked at the stench and refused to look. "I can't believe you did that! You know, Florence shot one arrow and missed. We could have looked for that in the yard."

"I still plan to," said Dev, leaning so his whole arm submerged in the water. He scrubbed vigorously. "But I figured she could use that one again, and I didn't want to ruin it."

Fifer dared a glance at Dev. He was clever. And he was also being really thoughtful and considerate regarding all of this. How had he ever been such an annoying jerk? He'd really changed a lot since their first meeting. While he had his shirt off, Fifer peeked at his wounds. The bleeding ones seemed minor, and she rested a little more easily.

Once he and the arrow were clean, Dev put his shirt on and picked up the arrow. "If you hear any loud thumps or yelling, come rescue me," he said with a little laugh.

Fifer smiled and adjusted the net, seeing a plump fish heading her way. "You got it."

Dev headed for the storeroom off the courtyard, where he kept various things he'd found since he'd first arrived. On the way he practiced one of the magical spells Thisbe and Fifer had taught him in their time here—invisible hooks. Glad that he could still do it, he gathered boards and ropes and headed for the stairwell. Before going upstairs, he peered around the back of the steps. It was empty.

The foxes hadn't returned since the dragon fight. Dev hoped they weren't too scared to come back, but those dragons lying dead on the ground were a pretty frightening sight. He wasn't sure what to do about them.

Dev climbed to the fifth floor, which was the top floor if you didn't include the bulbs. It had the flat, rotted roof and ceiling that Fifer and Thisbe had fallen through when the Revinir had dropped them. Dev knew the floor was rotted too. Both girls had broken through that as well. So he had to be very careful to stay at the edges of the room, where the joists were the sturdiest.

He eyed the length of rope that hung temptingly from the hole in the center of the roof. Then he placed two magical invisible hooks on the wall at about knee height and rested one of the boards across them, securing it to make a step. He placed two more and secured another board higher up the wall, and then did it a third time. After adding more hooks above the top step and placing Florence's arrow across them to use as a handhold, he climbed up carrying the longest rope he had. Then he aimed for a spot at the wood ceiling about half-way between him and the hole, where the creeping rot didn't appear to have reached yet. He placed a couple of hooks in that area, then took the long rope and made a loop in one end. He hung on to the arrow with one hand and, with the other, began to throw the rope like a lasso at the ceiling in an attempt to catch one of the hooks.

After several tries, while Dev held on to the other end, the loop caught and hung there.

He let out a breath. Not being able to see the hooks was unnerving. The rope appeared to be hanging suspended from nothing. And if the hook didn't hold, Dev would go crashing down through multiple floors like Thisbe and Fifer had done.

Standing on the top step, Dev tied a loop in the other end of the rope. He'd thought about wearing it around his chest to keep his arms free but knew that the rope could rip up the burns on his back, and that sounded awful. So he stuck one arm through it.

After a few deep breaths to steady his nerves, Dev let go of Florence's arrow and grabbed the rope tightly with both hands. He jumped, emitting a frightened shriek as he dropped. Then he swung wide out over the gaping hole in the floor and sailed up toward the hole in the ceiling. As he neared it, he reached out precariously for the rope. His fingers brushed it, but he couldn't quite get it before the momentum switched. He began to spin slowly in the air as he swung back down and approached the makeshift wall steps. Trying to right himself, he kicked wildly and managed to push off the wall and build up speed. This time, when he neared Florence's rope, he was just barely able to snatch the end of it. He pulled the sack through the ceiling, and it swung behind him. "Yes," he whispered.

When Dev neared the wall a second time, he jumped and grabbed for Florence's arrow and the makeshift ladder. His fingers connected, but he fumbled and couldn't hang on. With a wild yell he landed unceremoniously in a pile on the floor as the sack of spells slipped down the center hole. "Ack! No!" Dev lunged for the sack's rope and got it just in time. The floor creaked and groaned beneath him.

He lay on his stomach, heaving, still gripping the end of Florence's rope. Then he slid backward across the floor as one might do when stuck on thin ice, trying to reach the shore. After a short distance Dev hit a soft patch. The floor began to groan and crack beneath him, and his body sank a few inches. Panicked, he quickly spread his arms and legs. He stayed as

LISA McMANN

293 « Dragon Slayers

still as possible, praying he wouldn't break through. After a long moment, he began moving again, sliding a little at a time. Eventually he reached his makeshift ladder. With a breath of relief, Dev held on to a hook and pulled himself to a sitting position. Slowly he reeled in the sack of supplies.

Triumphant, Dev tied the supply sack around his hips. He released the hooks on the ceiling and retrieved the rope that hung from them, then unhooked Florence's arrow and disassembled the ladder. As evening shadows fell over the palace, Dev carried his supplies carefully, staying along the edge of the floor, and made it to safety.

Fifer came flying up the steps holding a flopping fish. "Dev!" she cried. "Are you all right?"

Dev met her in the stairwell and gave her a quizzical look. "I'm fine," he said, setting the boards and arrow down and holding out the bag of supplies. "Why?"

Fifer's lips parted, and she nearly dropped the fish. "I . . . I heard you yell. I thought something terrible had happened . . . again. I'm glad you're okay." She went over to him and hesitated, then embraced him, the fish somehow getting caught up between them.

Surprised by the move, Dev stood stiffly for an instant, then slid the fish out from between them and hugged her gently in return. "Nothing terrible happened," he said softly. He closed his eyes and let his cheek rest against her hair, steeling himself for when she pulled away.

Ghostly Fog

Rohan and Maiven hid in the folds of Quince's foggy shape. The ghost dragon appeared the same as always to them because they had black eyes, but they knew he was activating his hiding feature, which made him look to others like a thick spray of fog drifting through the air. As long as Rohan and Maiven stayed flat on the cloudlike back of the dragon and Quince kept his hiding feature activated, only black-eyed people could detect that anyone was there at all.

They rounded the castle and discovered Drock sticking close to the back side of it, as if trying to get a look through the vast windows and balcony doors that lined the exterior of the guest-room wing. Quince floated over to Drock undetected. The dark purple dragon didn't notice anything unusual until Rohan lifted his head.

"Drock," Rohan whispered. "It's Rohan. Maiven and Quince are here with me. Do you have any information? What's happening?"

Drock seemed momentarily puzzled that he couldn't see Quince at all but remembered what Maiven had told him in the cavelands and accepted the explanation. "That balcony, just there, leads to the ballroom, where the Revinir spends most of her time. Sometimes Thisbe goes out on the balcony with the Revinir. And I've finally figured out that Thisbe stays in this room over here. She has a private balcony too, but I haven't seen her use it yet."

Maiven sat up. She knew the castle well. "That was my dressing room long ago. Have you overheard anything?"

Drock glanced around to make sure none of the mind-controlled dragons were noticing him. "I have," he said grimly. "They've been making plans."

Rohan cringed. "What do you mean? What kind of plans?"

LISA McMANN

"Plans to announce their partnership," said Drock. "I'm . . . I'm so sorry. For you and for all of us."

Maiven seemed skeptical. "But they can't officially take over just by announcing that," she said.

"I know," said Drock. "But I also overheard the Revinir say something about how the other black-eyed people will be coming soon. I think she must know she needs them to vote for a leader."

"Maybe Thisbe is planning to convince us to vote her into the position of leadership," said Maiven. She winced. She still had a hard time believing her beloved granddaughter had taken such a sharp turn like this. But the evidence was growing that Thisbe wasn't as innocent as everyone had thought her to be. Perhaps her time in the catacombs had taken a much deeper toll on her psyche than anyone had realized.

Rohan stared out toward the castle, wishing only to have a glance at Thisbe. He'd be able to tell from her eyes if she was truly with the Revinir. All signs pointed to it, but there was still a part of him that believed something else was factoring into this equation. He wondered if Seth had been onto something when he'd guessed that Fifer and Thisbe were plotting together. It still didn't make sense, though.

"I need to keep moving," Drock said as other dragons got a bit too close for comfort. "Sometimes the two of them come out on the balcony at this time of night." The queen and Rohan ducked back down as Drock continued on his aimless flight.

"Let's float closer," Rohan directed Quince.

"Closer to what?" asked the ghost dragon, who seemed to have forgotten his purpose for the moment.

"To the castle," Rohan said.

"And . . . where is that?" asked the ghost dragon.

"It's that building," said Rohan, trying to be patient. "Go toward that big balcony."

Quince spied the area and flew toward it.

"Nice and slow," Rohan said. "Remember, we're being stealthy."

"Oh," said Quince. "I'm glad you told me."

Rohan and Maiven exchanged a worried glance. As they drew close to the ballroom balcony, the doors swung open. The Revinir ducked her head and stepped out. Right behind her was Thisbe.

"Don't speak to them!" Rohan said in a harsh whisper to Quince. He was worried about everything now that they were

LISA McMANN

within earshot of the two. He looked at Maiven. "Stay low," he reminded her.

"You too," she whispered.

Rohan lifted his head an inch, trying to catch the slightest glimpse of Thisbe without being seen.

"My, the fog is thick tonight," said the Revinir. "You know the old saying? A change in the weather brings plans together."

Thisbe didn't smile. She'd seen Quince immediately. Her face went gray as she realized the Revinir couldn't see him, and she deduced that Quince was floating outside in stealth mode. Was he alone? She couldn't see anyone else just yet in the darkness. "I think you just made that up," she said.

Rohan's eyes widened to hear her speak like that.

The Revinir cackled uproariously, and Thisbe flashed an uneasy smile. Quince had to be here to eavesdrop, and Thisbe had to give him proof to take back with him. "Our plans will come together as soon as you agree to my stipulations," she said. "I'm ready to proceed. I want to be your partner! But you're standing in your own way."

"Your demands are unreasonable," the Revinir purred.

"Everything about you is unreasonable," Thisbe retorted.

LISA McMANN

"But that's why you like me," the Revinir shot back. "You do like me now, don't you? I can feel it—a bit of admiration, no?"

"Oh," said Thisbe, jamming her fists into her pants pockets, "oh, yes. Your intuition is strong—it always has been." Thisbe abruptly turned. "Let's go back inside. This . . . fog . . . is making my hair frizzy."

Rohan couldn't believe what he was hearing. Thisbe was complimenting the Revinir. The two had laughed like friends. Rohan knew that Thisbe was a good actor. But was she this good? And for what purpose? He was more confused than ever. And now she was leaving the balcony. Obviously she must have seen Quince since she had black eyes too. But was she trying to keep away from him? Rohan lifted his head another inch, and then another.

The Revinir didn't seem pleased about going in, and she stayed in place, blocking the doorway so Thisbe couldn't get in either. Thisbe looked annoyed and nervous. She glanced at Quince and narrowed her eyes.

The ghost dragon stared back, surprised, because this was the friend of the ghost dragons—they answered to her call.

LISA McMANN

Didn't she recognize him? Or couldn't she see him in stealth mode? In his confusion, Quince's body slowly materialized from the fog, revealing two human shapes on his back in the process. One of them slipped out of sight, but the other lifted his head. Light from the ballroom revealed Rohan's face.

Thisbe caught sight of him and gasped. The Revinir turned to look and gasped too. "That patch of fog—it was a ghost dragon in disguise? And *Rohan*! What is the meaning of this?"

Maiven, who had slid to the far side of Quince, stayed hidden under the base of his wing. But Rohan was caught. He ducked down and muttered under his breath. He hadn't realized Quince had returned to his normal form.

The Revinir snarled. "Rohan!" she said again. "What do you think you're doing?"

Thisbe didn't know what to do except stay in character. "Get him!" she cried. "The little sneak!"

The Revinir lunged over the railing and took flight. Before Quince could change course, she reached and grabbed Rohan by his shoulders and his rucksack.

"Augh!" Rohan cried. He squirmed and whispered, "Don't wait for me!" to Quince and Maiven over his shoulder. The

Revinir yanked the young man over the balcony railing and into the ballroom. She dropped him to his feet and shoved him to the floor, spitting bits of fire everywhere in her anger.

Thisbe's heart split into a thousand pieces. *Why did he have to do this?* But she kept her face from showing any emotion. She steeled herself, then followed the Revinir and Rohan into the ballroom. Then she stared down at the person who completed her soul in every way.

He saw her. "Thisbe," he pleaded, shielding himself from the sparks and trying to crawl over to her. "What are you doing?"

Thisbe didn't answer. She averted her gaze, looking instead at the Revinir, who seemed to be watching Thisbe very carefully to see what she would do. "Amateur," she said lightly to the dragon-woman, and laughed. "He's harmless enough, isn't he? More good than evil, you always said. What shall we do with him? Kick him out of here? I can't imagine he'll come back. Will you, Rohan?"

"I highly doubt it," Rohan muttered.

The Revinir's concern melted from her face, and she laughed too. "We should at least offer him some tea before we decide. And," she added in a darker voice, "find out what he knows about the locations and activities of the others. Keep an eye on him."

The Revinir called for hot water and went to the sideboard. She rummaged around in a cupboard, setting up tea for three.

Thisbe was hardly able to function. She stood frozen. She couldn't look at Rohan.

He could have made a run for it. But Rohan stayed on the floor. "Thisbe," he whispered.

Thisbe's bones melted. But somehow she remained strong.

"Thisbe," he whispered again. "You're breaking my heart, *pria*."

Thisbe felt a moan about to burst from her chest. But she stopped it with the fire in her throat. "Don't speak to me," she snapped, a bit harsher than she'd intended. But she had to show the Revinir that she was annoyed by his presence.

Rohan's mouth slacked. He could only stare.

The Revinir brought the tray of tea to the table and commanded Thisbe and Rohan to join her. The two did as they were told.

"Sugar for your tea?" the Revinir asked, poised, then dropped a cube in each cup without waiting for the answer and stirred them. She passed the cups out, then lifted hers to her lips and sipped. "Tell us where you've been, Rohan. What do you know?"

"I know that Thisbe betrayed our people," he said, tight-lipped.

Thisbe's brain was frozen. She shrugged, hardly able to feel the movement. She still couldn't meet his gaze. "I'm doing what's best for me," she said. "You'll benefit in the long run, when you don't have to fear being kept a slave anymore. I'm sorry if you can't see that, but it's obvious to me."

"Oh, Thisbe," Rohan said.

His voice dripped with disappointment so thick that Thisbe could hardly stand it. She lifted her cup and took a long sip, hardly able to taste anything but needing the distraction. What was she supposed to do now? What was the Revinir going to do to him?

The Revinir kept a close eye on both of them, realizing that this was a pivotal moment in her ability to trust Thisbe as a partner. So far she was passing every test, and the Revinir was admiring her quite a lot. But there was one more test she needed to pass.

LISA McMANN

"More sugar, Rohan?" the Revinir asked. "Too hot? Perhaps some cream?"

Rohan's eyes were crazy with emotion, and he could hardly think straight. "No," he said dully, then sipped his tea, trying to buy time and figure out what was going to happen next. Imprisonment?

The tea was soothing, and he drank the rest, worried that in the dungeon he might not get a meal for a while. A strange warm feeling came over him. When he set his cup down it bobbled in the saucer, and the table wavered in front of him. He sank back in the chair.

Thisbe looked up at the sound and saw the Revinir staring intently at Rohan with a small smile on her snout. Thisbe glanced at Rohan and gasped. Scales sprouted on his arms. And his eyes glazed over. Confused, Thisbe stood up and looked at the sideboard where the kettle of hot water still steamed. Beside it sat two empty vials.

Changing Plans

Thisbe turned to the Revinir, failing to mask how desolate she was feeling. "What have you done to him?"

The Revinir tilted her head. "Are you upset? I thought this would be a much easier way to find out the truth about . . . things."

Thisbe narrowed her eyes. "Things? What things?"

"And it's nice having him as a backup in case the agreement with you doesn't work out."

"In his right mind, he'd never agree to what I will do for you," Thisbe retorted. "And both the dragon and black-eyed ruler have to be of sound mind in order to make an agreement."

"Oh really?" The Revinir tapped her chin with a talon. "I thought you didn't know how this worked."

"You're the one who told me that," said Thisbe icily. But she was rattled. And lying. She needed to pull it together if she was going to keep the ruse going.

"Did I?" asked the Revinir lazily. "I don't recall that."

Thisbe shrugged like it wasn't a matter to quibble over. "What shall we ask him?"

"Why don't you start?"

"Will he listen to me? I thought people under your mind control only listen to you."

The Revinir preened with power. "The red dragon listened to you, didn't he? It's because I commanded him to. But only if you said you wanted to come here."

"Tricky," said Thisbe.

"Rohan," said the Revinir, turning to him, "I command you to listen to Thisbe and answer her questions as truthfully as you would me."

Rohan blinked. "Yes, Revinir," he said.

Thisbe felt like vomiting to hear him say that. To speak in that voice. Things had been going so well, but now, with the constant reminder of what she was doing sitting right next to her, she felt like quitting. She shifted in her seat and thought she saw a ghost dragon floating by the window, farther away now. Was Quince still out there? "Okay, um . . . ," she began. "What, uh, what made you come here, Rohan?"

"I had to talk to you," said Rohan in a monotone.

Thisbe's hands started sweating. Was Rohan sold on the plan that she and Fifer and Dev had concocted? Had he somehow gotten the truth out of Fifer or Dev in the past few days? Thisbe didn't know where he'd been or who he'd been with—anything could have happened between the time he'd sent that message to Thisbe and now. But the Revinir was most certainly testing her, waiting to see if Thisbe would ask real questions. Thisbe plowed forward. "Talk to me about what?"

"I wanted to tell you not to betray the black-eyed people by making a deal with the Revinir. You can still change your mind. It's not too late."

Thisbe sucked in a breath. *Okay.* She looked up at the Revinir. "Your turn?"

The Revinir seemed pleased with the answers so far.

"Rohan," she said, "does Thisbe want to rule the land of the dragons with me?"

Thisbe frowned. "What kind of question is that?" she said. "I thought you wanted information about where everyone is and what he and the others are doing."

"No, that was a bluff," said the Revinir. "I want to know if you're lying to me. If there's anyone besides Fifer that you've confided in, it would be Rohan. So I want the truth."

"So that's why you put dragon-bone broth in his tea? Because you want to know more from him about *me*? That's disgusting. I've told you the truth."

"I didn't get to this position by trusting people," the Revinir said lightly. "Rohan, answer the question. Does Thisbe truly want to rule this land with me?"

Thisbe's heart flew to her throat. Rohan was emotionless, which was somehow even worse than seeing his face filled with pain.

"I . . . don't know for sure," Rohan said. "I believe she does."

The Revinir lifted her chin. "Has she recently indicated that she wants to trick me?"

"No," said Rohan.

"Has she talked about me lately?"

"Yes."

Thisbe froze. What was coming next?

"Has she ever talked about overthrowing me?"

"Yes."

Thisbe didn't know if she should speak. If she jumped in to protest, would that only make her seem guilty? If she stayed silent, would that mean she wasn't shocked to be accused? She knew that Rohan would tell the truth as he knew it—that's all he could do under the Revinir's mind control. She stayed silent and kept her eyes on Rohan's face.

"When did she talk about that?"

"In the catacombs."

The Revinir eyed Thisbe and snorted. "Well, who down there didn't wish that? Am I right?"

Thisbe grinned uneasily. "Pretty much everybody cursed your name regularly."

"That's what makes a ruler become great," said the dragon-woman. She waved the conversation off as if it were beginning to get tiresome. "Look, Thisbe. I expected you to want to overthrow me at some point. You wouldn't be human if you hadn't expressed that. And that's the kind of fire I find so appealing in a partner. I saw it in you long ago."

"So you keep saying," Thisbe reminded her. She was sick to death of hearing it, but she didn't add that part.

"I saw the pain on Rohan's face when he spoke your name," the Revinir continued, softer now, sounding almost . . . compassionate. If that were possible.

Thisbe looked up, surprised at the change in tone, and found the Revinir gazing out through the balcony doors at the night sky.

The dragon-woman continued. "I even dare say I felt some sort of reminiscent pain when he looked at you. He was feeling so betrayed." She hesitated, then opened her jaws and threw back the contents of her teacup.

"Reminiscent pain?" Thisbe knew immediately what the Revinir was talking about, and she knew she had another chance to play a card right here. "You mean, back when you were Emma?"

The Revinir's expression flickered, and she turned to give Thisbe a warning look. "I told you to stop calling me that."

Thisbe conceded with a nod. "Back when Marcus and Justine betrayed you?"

The Revinir closed her eyes and sighed. "So you know about that. I suppose everyone has read my diaries by now—I didn't hide them. Is that how you found out?"

"Yes. But . . . I'm the only one who has read them. I've kept them private."

"You have? Why?" The Revinir opened her eyes and studied Thisbe.

"Because," Thisbe said, scrambling to read the dragon-woman's intentions so she would know how to answer. "Because as much as I despised you for what you did to me, I begrudgingly respected your game. So I went looking to find out more about you while I was away. And that . . . respect . . . helped change my mind." Thisbe held her breath and looked at the table. Had she said too much? And even more of a chilling question: Was it true?

But the Revinir had gone somewhere far away in her mind and didn't respond. After a long while, Thisbe nearly nodded off at the table. She pushed her chair back and got up from the table. "I'm going to turn in," she said quietly. "Good night." She glanced at Rohan, sitting quietly, staring at nothing. Thinking no thoughts. A shell of a person.

"Wait a moment," said the Revinir, rousing from her reverie. She put a hand on Rohan's shoulder, then looked at Thisbe, calculating her next move. "My kitchen staff has been asking for Zel to return. So . . ." She narrowed her eyes. "I'd like you to have Rohan as your servant. Send Zel back to the kitchen." A flicker crossed the evil dragon-woman's face, as if she regretted offering. But Thisbe knew that this was also a test. If asked, Rohan would tell the Revinir everything Thisbe did, just like Zel would. And maybe the Revinir thought Thisbe would try to communicate more with Rohan because he'd been her friend.

Could this get any more painful? The last thing Thisbe wanted was to have Rohan as a servant. It was hard enough having him show up here and seeing him in this state. Thisbe's worst nightmare had come true. But, thanks to Fifer's insistence, Rohan knew nothing about the true plan and hadn't foiled it for them. Thisbe had to hand it to Fifer for being firm about that. It could have been disastrous if Thisbe had told Rohan the truth.

But Thisbe was breaking through the Revinir's walls, and she needed to keep tying their emotional strings together so she could get what she wanted. So she could keep Artimé safe. And so she could get the Revinir alone in a place where she could destroy her.

"All right," Thisbe said coolly, giving the Revinir the side eye to convey that she was totally aware of the dragon-woman's antics. "Thank you." She turned to Rohan. "Come on."

A Strange Turn

Thisbe walked stiffly down the hallway to her room with Rohan following along behind. She hated this. Hated everything about it. She was steaming mad about the Revinir spiking Rohan's tea with the dragon-bone broth. That was one of the most underhanded, despicable things she'd ever done.

And why did Rohan have to come here in the first place? He could have messed up everything. Luckily his answers were good. He'd actually made the Revinir believe Thisbe even more, but it could have been very bad. Surely she'd discussed overthrowing the Revinir multiple times with him since they'd

LISA McMANN

been in the catacombs. In fact, they'd talked about it extensively on the way to Artimé—so why didn't he say that? But Thisbe had also noticed that the Revinir hadn't asked him the question quite right. And words mattered. She'd asked him when Thisbe had talked about overthrowing her. Not the most recent time, but "when." That would technically include times before the most recent ones, and he'd answered truthfully. So that little technicality had saved her. She turned the corner and blew out a breath, knowing she was out of sight of the Revinir.

As she neared her suite, she glanced behind her to make sure that Rohan was still obediently following her. It was pathetic seeing him like this. And now she had to treat him like a slave. Like the very thing he'd been so valiantly trying to fight against. The same efforts he now believed Thisbe had turned against.

She'd hurt him so deeply. Would those wounds ever heal? The only thing that gave her comfort is that he wouldn't remember this part of things later. But was there a way Thisbe could track down some ancestor broth to use as an antidote? Or would that only complicate things until Thisbe had secured her position and done away with the Revinir?

LISA McMANN

"Thisbe," she chided. How could she even think like that? If she had ancestor broth in her possession, she'd have no choice but to give it to Rohan immediately and face whatever consequences followed. But she had none, and she was pretty sure there wasn't any in the catacombs anymore . . . not that she could disappear for a day in search of some. She'd have to make a new batch. Somehow. There had to be a way. But of course the Revinir would find out.

Thisbe was so tired. When she found Zel sleeping on the floor outside her door, waiting for her to come back from her meeting, she shook her awake. "The Revinir wants you to go back to work in the kitchen," Thisbe said softly, her voice catching. "Maybe just go to your room for now and report there in the morning, okay?"

Zel didn't respond. She got up and left, and that was that. Thisbe entered her living quarters and left the door open. She wasn't quite sure what to do with Rohan, other than send him to sleep in the sitting room as she'd done with Zel. She didn't need him to do anything for her. Or . . . perhaps he could sleep on Thisbe's balcony—there was a comfy lounge chair out there. That way if Quince returned, he could see that

Rohan had been forced under the Revinir's mind control . . . and maybe even take him back to the others.

"That's it," Thisbe said under her breath. She could get Rohan out of here. And maybe the others could help him . . . somehow. . . . Ugh. Of course they couldn't. Not without ancestor broth.

Thisbe looked up when she heard the soft click of the door closing. Rohan turned and leaned back against it. He crossed one leg over the other and folded his arms over his chest. His eyes focused, and he glared at her. "I demand you tell me why you are doing this."

More Than Too Much

Thisbe stared. "What's happening?" she whispered. She stepped toward him and confirmed that his eyes were no longer glazed over. He wasn't under the Revinir's control. But he had brand-new scales on his arms where none had been before. "I saw your eyes glaze over! You have scales!"

Rohan didn't smile. He looked furious. But he remained quiet and collected. "You might recall I ingested a few extra doses of the ancestor broth back when we escaped the catacombs together. Remember?"

Thisbe was confused. But then it became clear. Rohan had

LISA McMANN

taken the ancestor broth multiple times, but he had never actually ingested any dragon-bone broth until today. The antidote was already present inside him. And while the build up of ancestor broth apparently couldn't stop the scales from appearing, it kept him from succumbing to the Revinir's mind control. Thisbe sank to the bed, rattled. "So you faked it? How did you know to do it?"

"It didn't take a detective to see she was up to something with that whole tea bit. I could tell she was pouring something in. And obviously when the scales popped out, I knew for sure. So yes. I faked it." His expression didn't soften. "Now you. What are you doing? And why? I can't . . . I just cannot believe what you've done. You've hurt me more than anyone ever has." His lips, pressed firmly together, trembled, and his eyes filled with angry tears. "Explain yourself," he said, his voice ragged. "Now."

Thisbe closed her eyes. A wave of nausea rolled through her. She'd imagined this moment multiple times—imagined having to hear his wrath, his pain. She had hoped it would come after everything was over so she could tell him the truth and beg for forgiveness. But she couldn't do that yet. She had

LISA McMANN

to keep this ruse going or it could cost them everything. And Rohan couldn't know the truth, especially when he was here in the castle with the sneaky Revinir pouring dragon-bone broth into tea. Sure, he'd taken in enough of the ancestor broth to fight the two vials of dragon-bone broth this time. But there was a one-to-one ratio of effectiveness with the broths. If he ingested a little more of the dragon-bone broth, he could fall under her mind control in an instant. What if she put it in *everything* he ate or drank while he was here, and he really did fall under her control? Then everything Thisbe would say now could be repeated later. She had to keep going, even if it killed her. She had to lie to his face. She had to stand here and get Rohan to believe that she really wanted to join the Revinir in ruling this world. She opened her eyes and slid off the bed to her feet, trying to compose her character once more.

"I've made my decision," Thisbe said, lifting her head and staring into Rohan's eyes. "I'm joining the Revinir, and together we're going to take over Grimere."

"Thisbe, you know that's not possible!" Rohan whispered. "You know how this works. It doesn't make sense!"

"It's my mostly evil side coming out, I guess," Thisbe said, choosing things to say that could be repeated to the Revinir, just in case.

Rohan was steaming mad. "But you aren't addressing the truth. It's not possible for the two of you to succeed!"

"Actually, it is," Thisbe lied. "We found a way." She dropped her gaze. "I'm sorry . . ." She paused, trying not to cry. Trying to sound cold. "I'm sorry I hurt you. I didn't want to do that, but there was no other way."

Rohan stared. He frowned and shook his head in disbelief. Then he looked around the room. "Are there people hiding in here? Are you being coerced? Compromised? Is she making you say this?"

Thisbe swallowed hard and shook her head. Rohan wasn't making this easy. "None of those things. This is all me. My choice. My decision. I want this because I'm selfish and horrible."

Rohan gripped his head in anger and frustration. "Did you just, like, wake up one day and decide this? Fifer said you had some sort of fall and you weren't making sense before you left. Are you injured? Have you taken any medicine for it?" He started pacing. "I just . . . I cannot fathom any of this. We had

LISA McMANN

plans, Thisbe. I thought I knew you. You were my soul mate one day, and just like that, a switch flipped in your mind? Is everything we've had together done? Is it over? Or have you been playing me from the start?"

Thisbe reeled. She turned and grabbed the back of a chair to steady herself. This was horrifying. So much worse than she could've imagined it. How could she go on after this was over? How could she keep pretending?

But she had to for his sake. This was so much bigger than Thisbe and Rohan. This was two worlds on the edge of disaster.

Thisbe stumbled to her balcony and opened the doors. She stood for a second as the cool night breeze caressed her face, and she looked for Quince but didn't see him. "You need to escape," she said softly. Then she sucked in a breath and turned, hoping her voice had been lost in the wind, because she couldn't have him repeat that to the Revinir. "Rohan," she said in a formal voice, "my good servant, I think you should sleep outside on the balcony and watch for the fog rolling in." She paused. "I'll come up with . . . I mean, I'll explain your disappearance to the Revinir."

"What? No way."

"Rohan," Thisbe said, her voice catching. She pointed to the balcony. "Go."

Rohan stopped pacing. The look of hurt and despair on his face said everything. He stood for a long moment, then picked up his rucksack and walked to the balcony. At the doorway he paused to look at Thisbe. His black eyes shone from tears and starlight. "So this is over?"

Everything in Thisbe's mind screamed "No!" She could hardly hold herself together. But the words that came out of her mouth were the last words she'd ever wanted to say in her entire life to the boy standing next to her. "It's over."

Rohan bowed his head. Then he went outside and dropped heavily into the lounge chair. His rucksack spilled open, and he didn't bother to pick the items up.

Thisbe's tears welled up. She gazed at him for one last moment, all the sorrow of the world building a permanent home inside her. Then she closed the doors.

Grasping Blindly

Thisbe took her hands from the doorknobs and stumbled backward, falling half onto the bed and sliding to the floor. The sobs rushed out in horrible waves. She didn't care if anyone could hear her. She didn't care about anything anymore. She'd just said good-bye to Rohan, sending him away, explaining nothing for fear of the truth getting to the Revinir's ears in a nefarious way. And even though she still had a tiny bit of hope that her relationship could be repaired someday, chances were growing every day that there was no coming back from this. Thisbe was causing too much damage.

LISA McMANN

If Rohan's reaction was this bad, how would Thisbe face everyone else? One by one they'd want to have this same conversation. They would be so disappointed in her. This had been the worst, but it was just a hint at how it was going to go. All the hurt looks, all the spite . . . the anger, the tears. It was way too much for Thisbe to handle. She realized that now. She had to act before anyone else could confront her. Including the Revinir, because how was Thisbe supposed to explain Rohan's disappearance without causing the dragon-woman's suspicion to flare up again? There was no way to do it—it had been a stupid mistake to force Rohan to leave. But she couldn't bear to have him around after what had just happened. Was there any method she could come up with that would allow her to tell him the truth but still keep him safe?

There was only one way. She had to take out the Revinir now. There would be no declaration, no more "growing closer" to put Thisbe in the best position to get the Revinir alone. It had to happen immediately, and it might even have to be messy. Thisbe needed to get her alone and do the deed.

Taking an obliterate spell out of her vest and the pebble from its box, Thisbe wiped her eyes and went out into the

LISA McMANN

hallway. If the Revinir was anywhere she could access, she was going down. Right this moment.

Thisbe stalked the hallways. Peered into rooms on her way to where she'd last seen the Revinir. But the ballroom was empty, the balcony vacant. The Revinir had gone to her living quarters for the night, surrounded by guards.

Thisbe entered the Revinir's hallway and saw the small army standing there. She stopped and watched them for a moment, contemplating, rolling the pebble between her fingers. Then she turned and, with a heavy heart, went back to her room.

Brokenhearted

Thisbe replaced the obliterate pebble and put it safely away in her vest pocket. She fell on the bed and tossed and turned almost feverishly until sleep came.

When she woke, a feeling of dread overcame her again. Tears spilled down into her hair, and another wave of sobs came. She'd never been so devastated in all her life. Her conviction wavered. Fifer had no idea how hard this was—wouldn't she understand if Thisbe's will caved? Because none of this was worth what she'd had to do to Rohan.

She cringed. Yes, okay, it was worth it for the sake of the worlds. For the greater good. For all of the other people. Just . . .

LISA McMANN

not for Thisbe. She couldn't imagine offering up a greater sacrifice than this. Having no one realize it for what it was made it all the more difficult. That's why this had to end soon. She would take whatever reasonable risks she had to take. But she was glad she hadn't made an impulsive move last night. With so many servants around, it could have backfired terribly.

But how could she do it? Thisbe thought about the Revinir as Emma, the little girl who felt betrayed by her older siblings. She thought about how the Revinir had shared a little piece of herself with Thisbe earlier. It had been so strange to realize that the Revinir had feelings.

At first Thisbe had thought of her as one-dimensionally evil, but she'd learned that the dragon-woman went deeper than that. Still, it wouldn't be hard for Thisbe to put an end to her. She'd done some of the most heinous things Thisbe had ever heard of.

Perhaps there really was a way to slay the dragon-woman while she was in the ballroom—on the balcony. The impact could rip apart that area of the castle, so it would be risky. And a couple of servants could go down with her, because there was always someone standing nearby to address the Revinir's whims. That would be a shame, but this really couldn't go on any longer.

Thisbe wiped her eyes and got out of bed. She cleaned up and got ready. And then, with a start, she realized that she was currently without a servant's watchful eye over her, and she had a near-perfect opportunity to send a message to Fifer. She pulled out the component and wrote:

Fife,
Things will have to happen soon. Alert the troops.
Thiz

She wanted to write more. She wanted to pour her heart out to one of the two people who actually knew what she was doing. But she couldn't risk it. A wave of emotion passed over her again, but she didn't have any tears left. Would Fifer even understand her pain? She was probably living large in the palace with Dev, having a grand time.

As she turned to go to the balcony, a shadow passed in front of the glass doors, followed by a quiet knock.

Thisbe's heart sank. Was Rohan still out there? Didn't he

get that they had ended everything? A lump rose to her throat at the same time the truth came crashing around her. He was still here. Quince hadn't come for him. She had to stay strong. She went to the doors, took a deep breath, and opened them.

Backlit by a pink morning sky, Rohan stood there, ragged, with tears streaming down his face. In one hand he held his rucksack.

"Rohan," Thisbe whispered. "What are you still doing here?" His tears made her weak.

He caught her gaze and held it. "I figured it out."

Thisbe swallowed hard. "You . . . What?"

"I figured out what you're doing," he said. "Seth thought that maybe . . . and then me drinking the broth . . ." He shook his head—it was too much to explain right now. "Never mind that." His haggard face held a hint of warmth. "I have an idea."

Coming Together

Thisbe dropped the send component she'd been holding. Rohan picked it up and handed it to her. She hesitated, then stepped aside to let him in. "Explain," she said quietly, trying to sound cool and collected but failing miserably. She pocketed the component. "There's nothing to figure out. I don't . . . I don't know what you mean."

"Yes, you do." Rohan came inside and closed the balcony door. Then he turned back to Thisbe and clasped his hands in front of him. "I get it now. I just can't believe it."

"Rohan, we've been over this."

"No, no, no. Not *this*. Not you making a crazy decision

out of nowhere to join ranks with a monster. Because I cannot believe you have that in you, no matter how much you insist otherwise. You can't convince me that I don't know you, because I do." He ripped his hand through his hair, impassioned. "Look. I sat on this balcony freezing all night, and I finally figured out what you're doing."

"Well, what am I doing, then?" Thisbe demanded. He couldn't possibly have guessed.

"You can't tell anyone the truth," Rohan said, watching her face closely, "because of exactly what just happened to me with the dragon-bone broth."

Thisbe felt the blood drain from her face. She said nothing.

Rohan, encouraged by her silence, continued his theory. "You can't tell me what you're doing because I'm vulnerable. Just like any of us. If we are forced to drink that dragon-bone broth, we could give away the secret. And Fifer is in on it. Seth was right. Why doesn't anyone listen to him?"

Thisbe held up her hands. "What secret?" she said weakly, feeling like she ought to keep the plan going if possible. Maybe Rohan was all wrong.

Rohan spoke in a soft voice. "You're faking it. You're pretending to join with the Revinir."

"That's ridiculous," Thisbe said wearily. "Why would I do that?"

"So you can kill her."

Thisbe took in a sharp breath. The earnest, eager look in Rohan's eye seemed an odd contrast to the tears still drying on his cheeks. Thisbe wasn't sure how he'd figured it out, but it was true he knew her best of anyone. And he kept going on about Seth, who was right up there. It wasn't too surprising that between them, they'd figured this out.

She dropped her gaze and turned away to hide her confusion. She needed to think this through. How would his knowledge of this affect him if he ended up being truly compromised later? Would her refusal to confirm it help save him if something awful happened? If Rohan thought he knew what she was doing, and he actually got it right, was there still a way to protect him from the Revinir in case she fed him more broth? This was getting way too confusing.

"Thisbe," Rohan said, his voice pleading. "Please say

LISA McMANN

something. I'm delirious with exhaustion and sorrow. But I know I'm right. I have to be. Or else I have to question every truth I've ever known."

"No," Thisbe lied, because she didn't know what else to do. "I'm sorry, but you're wrong. I really do just want to be like the Revinir." But she couldn't get herself to make him leave again. She'd lost her stamina. She dropped onto the foot of her bed and sat there feeling thickheaded with all the questions swimming around. She didn't know the answer to anything.

Rohan narrowed his eyes. "You're lying again. But I get it. You can only say things that are safe for me to repeat in case I get mind controlled." He stepped toward her, then dropped to one knee. "Listen to me, Thisbe. Please. I have a solution that should satisfy you and make you feel better about telling me the truth."

Thisbe glanced at him. "What is it?"

Rohan opened his rucksack. He reached inside and pulled out a handful of vials. "Prindi took these, remember? When we all escaped the catacombs together. It's ancestor broth."

Thisbe sat up straighter. Sure enough, it was the deep, rich, golden-colored liquid with bits of herbs floating inside.

LISA McMANN

She remembered now, shoving that sack of them at Prindi. Thisbe's mind began to whir. "I forgot we had them."

"Well, I didn't. And I brought them along purposely because I know how sneaky the Revinir is."

"And?" Thisbe began to figure out his plan, but she was still so hesitant. She didn't want to say anything that could cause problems later.

"And I can drink as many of these as you want me to."

Thisbe closed her eyes as pain and hope swirled together inside her. "Why, though?" she whispered, even though she knew the answer.

Rohan could tell she was struggling mightily and explained the obvious. "To cover against any accidental or forced inges-tion of the dragon-bone broth. And this way I can stay here and keep playing your servant, and I can help you if you need it." Rohan hesitated, looking terribly aggrieved. "But please, will you acknowledge that this is what you're doing? Because if it's not, I'm going to lose my mind. Please, Thisbe. I . . . Just please say it!"

Thisbe opened her eyes and looked at Rohan, her chin trem-bling. It was the thing she wanted more than anything—to

LISA McMANN

337 « Dragon Slayers

have Rohan know and understand what she was doing. To have him accept her and forgive her for the anguish she'd caused. But everything was so confusing, and she couldn't think it all through. Was there anything that could happen to him now if she admitted to everything? He already had his guesses. And he had the ancestor broth. It seemed useless to carry on with the lies now that he knew that's what they were.

Before she could answer, there was a thumping noise growing louder in the hallway, followed by a hard knock at the door. Thisbe panicked. She shoved the vials of broth into Rohan's bag and chucked it under the bed. "Act like a servant," she hissed. Then she went to the door and opened it a crack.

The Revinir pushed the door open wide and seemed surprised to see Rohan standing there, methodically folding Thisbe's sweater.

"What's going on?" Thisbe asked, trying to breathe normally.

The Revinir lifted her snout. "I heard a rumor from some dragons that Rohan had escaped from your balcony. I thought that sounded awfully suspect, since humans under my mind control would never think to do such a thing."

Thisbe frowned. "Escaped? Obviously not. But I did make him sleep on the balcony." She tapped her lips. "Hmm. Perhaps that was part of the confusion? They saw him out there, and then he was gone, so they made the wrong assumption?"

Rohan finished with the sweater, then stood still and gazed at the wall next to where the Revinir stood.

The Revinir eyed him suspiciously. "He doesn't look very well rested."

"I suppose it was a bit chilly," Thisbe said agreeably. "Maybe tonight I'll give him a blanket."

The Revinir laughed. "He's survived worse."

"Isn't that the truth," Thisbe said, laughing too, though she wanted to punch the dragon-woman in the snout.

"All right," the Revinir said. "Well, breakfast is being served in the ballroom, Thisbe, so come along with me. Rohan, you can get your gruel in the kitchen. It's one floor down from here."

"Great," said Thisbe, forcing herself not to look at Rohan even though everything between them was up in the air.

The dragon-woman turned around in the hallway, thumping against the walls and knocking artwork off them. Before

Thisbe followed her, she flashed Rohan a stressed-out look. She wanted to warn him not to eat or drink anything until he'd taken some of the ancestor broth to act against any sabotage the Revinir had planned. But Thisbe had no way to do so without setting off alarm bells in the Revinir's head. So they parted ways, not sure what to expect for the day.

Thisbe had never been more determined to use her obliterate component at the first opportunity. But she also needed her Artiméan army to come as backup just in case a war broke out because of it. With a sinking heart, Thisbe realized the message to Fifer was still in her pocket, unsent.

Confusion in the Cavelands

Maiven Taveer and Quince returned to the cavelands to a million questions, mainly about Rohan's whereabouts. Maiven stayed on Quince's back and raised her hand in the air for silence. Then she explained.

"Rohan and I were able to listen in on a conversation between the Revinir and Thisbe," Maiven said. "It seems our worst fears are confirmed. Thisbe is all in with the Revinir, and they are planning some sort of takeover." She lifted her chin. "Rohan was discovered and seized by the Revinir. He's inside the castle. As he was being captured, he told Quince and me

LISA McMANN

not to wait for him. If he isn't immediately imprisoned, I believe he will do his best to try to reach Thisbe on a different level, to talk to her and find out what is prompting this treasonous action." She paused for breath. "If there is anyone who can get through to her after so much has happened, after Fifer herself has failed, I believe Rohan is the one. And so Quince and I left to report back to you as we assured you we would do."

She turned to Simber. "And now I'd like to meet with Simber and Aaron in my cave. And Ishibashi, too, if you please." The queen had taken a liking to Ishibashi's intelligence and calm manner, and she appreciated his insight.

Maiven descended the ghost dragon in a style that was uniquely hers, by sliding down the dragon's tail, holding her military swagger stick in one hand and a sword in the other for balance. She went to the river first to clean up from her journey. Then she found Simber, Ishibashi, and Aaron waiting at her cave.

"Things seem dire," Maiven said in greeting.

"Indeed," said Ishibashi. "This is very serious."

Aaron shook his head in disbelief. He'd been hoping for good news. But it sounded like Thisbe had truly gone to the evil side. Is this how people had felt when he'd done the same thing? Because it was excruciating. He had a sudden wave of regret when he thought about Alex, who'd never given up on him, even in the darkest times. How he missed his brother! The thought of never seeing him again was too much to take. If only he could have a moment with him now.

Aaron glanced at Ishibashi. The man had stuck by him as well when he needed a parental figure in his life. It seemed Aaron needed to step into that role now, with Thisbe. It didn't matter anymore what people thought of him. He needed to be the person who believed in Thisbe when everyone else wrote her off. To be there for her when no one else trusted her.

"What are you thinking?" Ishibashi asked Aaron. "I can see the determination in your eyes."

"I think we can turn this around," said Aaron. "I know this isn't Thisbe's path to the future. It can't be! She still has a chance to redeem herself, if we can only get her to stop this nonsense before something terrible happens."

"I believe in you to be there for Thisbe," Ishibashi said quietly, giving Aaron a meaningful look. He turned to Maiven. "And you, Queen Maiven. What are your thoughts?"

"I have many," said the woman, stabbing her swagger stick into the soft ground.

"Things arrre trrricky, though," Simber said before she could begin to list them. "We've lost Rrrohan and Florrrence, two key playerrrs. And we'rrre camped out herrre in this desolate place, of no help to anyone."

The others looked at him. "What are you suggesting?" Maiven asked him. "That we send ghost dragons to Artimé to pick up the rest of our warriors while we head to the palace to slay the two remaining dragons and rescue Fifer? And then we all take on the castle to free our loved ones and try to talk sense into them?"

Simber was rendered momentarily speechless, for that was exactly what he was thinking.

Ishibashi lowered his eyes and tried to hide the merriment on his face.

Simber gazed at the queen as if he'd underestimated her all this time, because, truth be told, he probably had. "Yes, Queen," he said. When Maiven let a smile play at the corner of her lips, Simber bowed his head and continued. "I'll . . . get rrright on that."

Making Their Own Plans

Now that Dev had retrieved the sack of components, Fifer possessed all the send spells she needed. The first thing she did was call on Maiven Taveer to speak to the ghost dragons about how to respectfully remove the dead dragons from the front and back yards. Hopefully, they would know how to properly care for and dispose of the bodies, and had the strength to do it.

There was still no word from Thisbe, and Fifer and Dev were on hold and feeling skittish. They were both worried about her, but they didn't talk about it much. And neither of them knew quite what to do next other than continue to wait

LISA McMANN

for Thisbe's instructions, as they'd agreed upon. Fifer would then call on Maiven and the others to bring in the whole army, saying she couldn't allow it to go on any longer. Then they'd all go to the castle, and hopefully, one way or another, they'd be able to remove the Revinir from power.

It would be nice if Fifer could go along with them, but the way things were looking, she and Dev were going to be stuck here indefinitely unless they could figure out how to get rid of the remaining two red dragons. She hadn't ever been taught how to use a bow and arrow, and Florence's bow was almost too heavy for Fifer to lift, much less use properly. Dev offered to carve a bow and some arrows for her, but Fifer was pretty sure it was the magic in the arrows that had caused the fatal blows, not just the vulnerability of the nostril area.

Of course she'd also thought about bringing Florence back to life so that she could shoot down the remaining two. But it was too risky to bring her back now, especially since she would be without one of her legs and unable to position herself to shoot like she was accustomed to. And if Fifer stuck around to help attach Florence's leg, she would be putting herself at great risk. No one could predict what the dragons would do if they saw the warrior trainer move even a little bit. Sure, they might not be able to hurt her if she stayed on the ground . . . but if they attacked her and grew frenzied, there was no longer any doubt that they would come after Dev and Fifer. There were a lot of factors, and Fifer wasn't about to risk anybody's life if she could help it. Besides, they were safe here for the moment.

And Dev was making things happen. He'd whittled two long spears so far and was working on a third. "If a well-placed magical arrow can kill a dragon," he told Fifer, "maybe a long spear can come in handy. That's what they used in that book you found. And if you somehow put some magic into it, it could be almost as powerful as Florence's arrows."

Fifer had ideas as well. She knew that the front dragon would go to the river in the middle of the night to eat and drink, and that would put her near the back dragon for a short time. She couldn't tell how close the two got to each other without going outside and following them, which could trigger an attack— she wanted to be very careful not to assume anything after the catastrophes with Dev and Florence and the birds. But if she could get them close enough to each other, would she be able to get both dragons with one obliterate component?

LISA McMANN

The last thing Fifer wanted was to lose out on a chance to help Thisbe. So she and Dev needed to make a move on the red dragons to give themselves every opportunity to help when the time came. Maybe tonight would bring their dragon-slaying moment.

When Dev finished the long swords, he brought them to Fifer. Fifer stared at the sharp points, concentrating, trying her best to figure out how to instill magic in them. It wasn't the last time that the young head mage would be trying out magic she'd never done before.

Making a Deal

The thing the Revinir wanted most was to have the people and dragons of Grimere obey her without being under any sort of mind control. And if she became the true dragon ruler, in harmony with the black-eyed humans, all of that would fall into place. She just wanted to be an adored leader. Like Marcus had been. Even Justine, early in her reign. Marcus hadn't had to force his people to love him. They still loved him long after he was gone. And he'd done some pretty rotten things before he turned it all around.

Back when she'd been Queen Eagala of Warbler, the Revinir

had few adoring fans, if any. She'd forced everyone there to obey her by keeping them silent with the golden thorn necklaces. And she'd put her orange-eye brand on them so they'd be easily identifiable in case any of them escaped, because they definitely wanted to. The dragon-woman realized that nothing much had changed since then except the methods the Revinir was using to keep her people, and now her dragons, in line. It was all force and had been since day one. It was enough to make a dragon-woman weary.

So much of the joy of being the ruler had slipped away from her over the years. And ruling over these zombies was getting tiresome. It almost felt like . . . cheating. Not that the Revinir was against cheating. She admired a good cheat, which was why she had almost liked Dev before she threw him out the window to his death. She felt a twinge of regret over that, truth be told.

But ruling over people she'd forced into obedience just wasn't bringing much joy anymore. She'd come to that stark realization in a striking way last evening. Having Thisbe here for the past few days, not under any kind of spell, had been . . . lovely. It had been the nicest time the Revinir had ever experienced since she'd been a child.

She remembered her previous best day when she was young. She'd been regularly spying on Marcus and Justine and Eva Fathom and Gondoleery Rattrapp, all of them trying to do magic in their own ways. One summer day they'd relented and let her join them. The sun was shining on the rocks and stream where they often met up. Gondoleery had managed to make a tiny pool of water freeze, despite the heat. There had been a minnow trapped in that cupped area of the stone, and when Gondoleery had frozen the water without a thought for the minnow's well-being, it had given young Emma a chill of horror and wonder. It had opened up her eyes to all the possibilities in the world that went beyond her usual way of thinking. She'd realized that people had more opportunities to do so many things—good or evil—than they actually took. That she had choices she'd never considered because they were outside the realm of what her normal day-to-day activities had consisted of. It was a breathtaking realization, and Emma would recall that revelation again, many times.

Remembering it now made the Revinir think hard about what she was doing. The two best memories of her life were spent with people who weren't being coerced or controlled.

Thisbe had wanted to be there with her last evening, and they'd laughed multiple times together. She'd enjoyed it so much that she'd taken a risk and had given Rohan to Thisbe, sort of as a gift—a thank-you, in a way—for liking her for who she was.

The Revinir had regretted it almost immediately, but she'd realized there was nothing Thisbe could do now that Rohan was under the mind-control spell. She'd had all the remaining ancestor broth destroyed after Dev had spilled that important information in the tower. And she had plenty of dragon-bone broth stashed around the castle to feed him just in case.

But the truth was that the Revinir didn't think she'd need the dragon-bone broth for much longer, because she was just about ready to agree to Thisbe's demands. She'd thought about it—leaving the seven islands alone. And she'd realized that all she really had to do to get what she wanted was to tell Thisbe she wasn't going to touch her precious islands— even though Warbler was already technically hers. And they could do the agreement thing and become the true leaders and release all the mind-controlled dragons and people and let the pesky ghost dragons die, and then the Revinir would be adored by all because she'd restored the land after forty

LISA McMANN

years under the control of that dumb king and his usurpers.

And after that, she could go take over the seven islands anyway.

As she and Thisbe sat down to breakfast, the Revinir peered at the young woman. "How did you sleep?" she asked, because she supposed that was something friends might ask each other.

"Great," said Thisbe. "You?"

"Fine." The Revinir thought Thisbe seemed slightly preoccupied. Was she having second thoughts about their partnership? "I wanted to see you this morning because I wished to talk more about our agreement," the dragon-woman said.

"Oh," said Thisbe, perking up. "Good. I'd like that as well. I've been thinking a lot about it, actually. And like I've told you, I'm ready to join you in going forward with it."

"On your condition, of course," the Revinir said dryly.

"Well," said Thisbe, "yes, obviously. But I wonder if you've really taken in how very large the land of the dragons is. There's so much to explore and expand here. There's that other village down the mountain. The forest, which is huge. The cavelands, which will be empty once the ghost dragons are gone. And the whole palace and village where Ashguard's property is that could be restored and repopulated. Plus the crater lake and the entire city of Grimere, of course. That's a lot of land to rule over. And . . ." She hesitated, looking into the Revinir's eyes. "It seems like it might be just the right size for a dragon and a black-eyed ruler to enjoy together without having to always keep an eye on things that are so far away. The traveling is so tedious, isn't it?"

The Revinir almost smiled. Thisbe was growing very sneaky, and she liked that about her. This girl was someone who could keep up with her. And this partnership was actually going to work—the Revinir could feel in her dragon scales that things were moving in the right direction. It didn't take much for her to see that all she had to do was agree to the terms and renegotiate them later, once things here were running smoothly. She made it appear like she was thinking very hard about this and wrestling with it.

"All right," the Revinir said finally. "You've worn me down on this, and I can see you aren't wavering. I want to enter into this agreement with you, and I'll give you what you want. I'll leave the seven islands alone." *For now.*

Surprisingly, Thisbe's expression didn't change. But that was one more thing the Revinir liked about her—that she didn't show her emotions easily. She was a shrewd negotiator.

"Very well," said Thisbe. "Shall we designate a time and place to make our announcement to the people of Grimere? Perhaps outside the castle on the drawbridge? I've always pictured us standing together with the castle behind us and having the people gather all around." She made it sound dreamy.

"Dragonsmarche seems more appropriate, doesn't it?" said the Revinir with a gleam in her eye. "It's where we first met."

This time a flicker crossed Thisbe's expression. The Revinir knew it was horrible, but she had to have something to retain the upper hand after giving up all the seven islands.

"You forgot our meeting when I was two years old—I killed your pirate-captain friend," she said coolly. "But Dragonsmarche is also the spot where I set all of the black-eyed children free from the catacombs. Sounds perfect. Tomorrow? Next week?"

The Revinir gave a delighted snort. "Well played. It shall be so. But let's not wait. Let's go today." She didn't wait for Thisbe to object. "Guards! Sound the trumpets and call everyone to

LISA McMANN

the Dragonsmarche Square. We have a major announcement to make to all the people and dragons."

With the servants scrambling to make things happen, the Revinir turned to Thisbe. "When this is through, I'm afraid I might have to ask you to make some more ancestor broth to wake everyone up. I hope you don't mind."

This time Thisbe snorted, and not just because she knew this probably wouldn't work—she was banking on that happening once the Revinir was dead. But she played along. "Bring the proper bones to the kitchen, and I'll teach the staff what to do with them."

The Revinir smiled. "I will indeed." This was the most spirited, fun conversation she might have ever had. She was more excited for the future than she'd ever been before. And for the first time, it was only partially because of the power that went with it.

Scrambling

Thisbe's appetite for breakfast left her. *Now?* This was all happening *now*? Obviously she wanted to get moving on this, but where was Rohan? And had he eaten or drunk anything? Was he okay? They'd been in the midst of a crucial talk when the Revinir had shown up, and Thisbe had tossed all the ancestor broth under the bed. Now, with his orders to go to the kitchen, Rohan couldn't get to it. And if he'd eaten or drunk anything that the Revinir had spiked, he wouldn't know he'd be in need of it. If everyone was suddenly heading to Dragonsmarche, neither of them would be able to retrieve the broth anytime soon.

LISA McMANN

It would probably be okay, Thisbe reasoned. The Revinir wasn't nearly as focused on him today as she'd been last night. And now she had a lot of other things to keep her busy, like organizing this big announcement, which would lead to . . . absolutely nothing.

Ugh. That was another problem. How would the Revinir react when she found out that the agreement didn't magically just make everything become perfect, the way she expected it would? Thisbe would have to act like she was just as surprised. Unless there was a way to take out the dragon-woman before the announcement even happened.

"Why so troubled?" the Revinir said. "Having second thoughts?"

Thisbe looked up and mellowed her expression. "I was just thinking about how fun it was to have Rohan as my mind-controlled servant. I'll miss that when we bring everyone back to their right minds." She shrugged. "But I can't have everything."

"I think you'll find the mind control becomes boring over time," the Revinir confided.

"Really? Interesting," said Thisbe. "Well, I imagine he'll be annoyed once we bring him out of it, but he'll get used to it over time. Like the others." She turned sharply. "By the way, did you really kill Dev? Or did you just say that for effect?"

The Revinir twitched. "I really killed him," she admitted. "I wish I hadn't acted quite so rashly. I was beginning to appreciate him."

"Oh well," said Thisbe, dabbing her mouth with a napkin. "It's regrettable. But there's nothing you can do now, I suppose." She set the napkin down and got up from the table. "I'll run to my living quarters to see if I can find something more royal-looking to wear for the occasion. I noticed several things hanging in the closet—whoever stayed in my room before must have left in a hurry. Shall we meet in the grand entryway in an hour?"

The Revinir nodded. "I will find you there."

Impulsively Thisbe reached out and touched the Revinir's claws. "I'm glad we're doing this."

"As am I," said the dragon-woman. And she actually meant it.

In the privacy of her room, Thisbe took a moment to sort her thoughts. There was one thing she absolutely had to take a chance on before she did anything else. She went out to the balcony and climbed up on top of the lounge chair. Then she reached for the overhanging roof, pulled herself up onto that, and scrambled to her feet. From there she could see clear skies to the west, which was the direction her send spell to Fifer would need to go. If the direct path it took was over the castle rather than through its hallways or around its outsides, there was a better chance it wouldn't be noticed, especially with all of the excitement that was happening in preparation for a procession to Dragonsmarche.

Thisbe took the component out of her pocket and reread it. Then she added *We're heading to Dragonsmarche today to announce our partnership. Don't reply.* And then, with a moment of concentration, she sent it off and watched it soar between two towers and fly through the air, just as she'd hoped. In two seconds it was out of sight. "Whew," she muttered.

Thisbe inched down the roof. She eased over the edge, dangled there for a moment, trying to ignore her fear of heights, then dropped onto her balcony. The drop made her old ankle injury flare up, and she couldn't walk for a second. When she could put weight on it, she went back inside her room and gave a little shriek. Rohan was standing there.

His eyes were glazed over.

"Ugh, Rohan!" Thisbe exclaimed. "Are you kidding me? We don't have time for this. Be smarter, please. Sheesh." She limped over to the bed, reached under it, and pulled Rohan's rucksack out. She took out several vials of ancestor broth and opened the first one. "Here you go, Rohan," said Thisbe. "Drink this."

Rohan didn't turn. "The Revinir instructed me not to drink anything you give me," he said in a mechanical voice.

Thisbe paled. "What?" She hadn't anticipated that. "Well, I'm telling you to drink this anyway. You—you work for me."

"I cannot." Rohan didn't move to take it. Then his face relaxed. "Aw, I'm just messing with you. Be smarter? Really?"

Thisbe's face exploded. "This is not a good time for jokes!" she hissed.

Rohan shrugged and shot her a half grin. "Sorry." He took the broth and gulped it down. Then he steadied himself as the wave of images tore through his mind. "Blech." He held out his hand for another.

"Take all of these." Thisbe gave him three more, still shaking her head at his shenanigans. "I need to find a dress or something," she said. "Did you hear what's happening?"

"I heard the announcement. What are you going to do when you declare your partnership and nothing happens?" He chugged the next vial.

Thisbe hesitated to answer. She'd been so programmed not to tell anyone anything that she was still wary about putting Rohan in danger. But he was in the know whether she wanted him to be or not. And he was downing ancestor broth like a happy little cannibal. So he was protected. Finally she said, "I'm going to be exactly as surprised as she is. And then I'm going to demand we find out what went wrong."

"So you're admitting my theory is correct?" Rohan said, stopping his vial sipping for a moment to look at her. "I still haven't heard your answer."

Thisbe paused in the closet. She turned her head, conceding everything in one look. "Yes, Rohan. And . . . I'm so sorry. I'll explain more later if you like." What she didn't tell him was that there was still a conflicted part of her that was enjoying this time she was spending with the Revinir.

Rohan took in a breath and closed his weary eyes for a moment. "Thank the gods," he murmured. Then he went back to finishing his next vial.

Thisbe felt a great weight lift off her heart, but she still felt the urgency of getting ready for the announcement. She ripped through a bunch of dusty clothes in the closet, most of them looking like they might actually fit, which was curious. She searched for something suitable for a leader that wasn't too ugly or frilly. Then she happened on a charcoal-gray uniform that had only a few small moth-eaten holes in it. She took it out and looked at it. It was like Maiven's. Could these clothes belong to her grandmother? Being consumed by moths up here while Maiven was wasting away in the dungeon? There wasn't time to speculate further.

"This," she said, and hoped it would fit. She ran with it into her washroom and slammed the door behind her, then tried it on over her component vest. When she looked in the mirror, she took in a breath. She looked so much like Maiven. She hadn't noticed the resemblance before. But now, with the same suit on and a similar cap perched on her head, it was more than clear that the two were related. Tears sprang to Thisbe's eyes. She felt like she was betraying everything that Maiven stood for by doing such a terrible deed while wearing the uniform of a black-eyed warrior. "Please forgive me," Thisbe whispered.

LISA McMANN

"Is it a good fit?" came Rohan's voice through the door.

Thisbe blew out a breath and adjusted the jacket, then smoothed her hand over the moth-nibbled area on the lapel. "It's perfect," she said. She opened the door.

Rohan, holding four empty vials, nearly dropped them. "My, you do resemble her, don't you?"

"I was thinking that."

"You look very smart," he said quietly. "I believe . . . if Maiven knew what you were doing to save us, she would feel very good about this."

"Do you really think so?" Thisbe asked. She turned to him.

They held each other's gaze for a long moment, all of the angst between them being shoved aside. Rohan swallowed hard, his eyes brimming. Then he slipped his fingers along Thisbe's cheek, slid them into her hair, and pulled her close. Thisbe's eyes closed, and their lips met and moved together. When the two broke apart, Thisbe wrapped her arms around Rohan's neck and held him. "I'm so sorry for hurting you," she whispered in his ear. "And I'm so glad you figured it out, or I might have died."

"Thisbe," said Rohan, overcome. He wrapped his arms

around her waist and held her. "That was the most horrible time of my life," he confessed. "But I'm grateful you were willing to sacrifice everything for the land of the dragons. For us. For our future."

"Next time, we do this together," said Thisbe.

Rohan nodded, though he said, "I hope there aren't any more next times."

Reluctantly they broke apart. Thisbe straightened her suit and tidied her hair once more. "You're coming with me now, right? You'll be there with me?"

"I'll be right by your side."

"But," warned Thisbe, "if you see me reach inside my jacket and pull out a tiny box, I want you to run away from the Revinir like you've never run before."

On the Move

A team of ghost dragons, with Carina aboard to remind them where they were going, began their journey to Artimé to collect the rest of the army of fighters. Maiven, Aaron, and the remaining team members from Artimé prepared to head for Ashguard's palace to bust up some dragons. Aaron sent Fifer a note letting her know they were on the way to attempt to free her so they could be ready to fight the Revinir and stop everything that was happening.

That wasn't the only note Fifer received. As she and Dev finished lunch in the library, another send spell arrived. Fifer read it, then looked at Dev. "Finally! It's from Thisbe. She's okay. And she says we need to get ready to go and call the others in. Good thing they're already coming. But I'm worried about the dragons attacking them."

Fifer studied Thisbe's note again, then looked up at Dev. His black eyes bored into her, not angrily but soft around the edges, making her catch her breath. A strange feeling swept through her, something she'd never felt before. She wasn't sure if it was uneasiness or just a bad fish for dinner, but whatever it was made her feel weird.

Dev realized he was staring and dropped his gaze. "We have a big job to do, I guess," he said. Then, softer: "I'm sorry I was staring at you."

Fifer wasn't sure what to make of the strange feelings she was having lately. "It's fine," she said. She smiled in a friendly way to let him know she wasn't bothered by him staring. And then she started to think they were making way too big a deal out of all of this when they had dragons to slay.

Dev got up quickly and cleaned up the remains of dinner. Then the two sat together in front of the fireplace to go over their plans. Dev checked over his three finished long spears,

LISA McMANN

adding a bit of melted tin to make the spear points sharper and sturdier, and hoped the magic Fifer instilled in them would help things out.

Fifer reread the instructions for the obliterate spell to make sure she absolutely knew how to use it. Now they just needed the dragons to take their places in the middle of the night. By the time Maiven and Aaron and the rest of them arrived, hopefully the dragons would be taken care of and Florence would be up and moving around like old times.

As Fifer was folding the instructions and Dev was getting up to put his spears by the staircase for later, Dev glanced outside the south window. There was something moving in the orchard, bigger than the foxes.

He went to the window. "Fifer!" he said, and beckoned her to join him. "Come look." There was a herd of deer picking its way among the apple trees. A sight hardly ever seen outside of the forest. "They must have heard about all the fruit on the ground out here," Dev said jokingly, then pointed them out to Fifer. The animals were moving slowly past the boundary to the bright green grass, near where the pieces of Florence lay.

"They're beautiful," said Fifer, who'd never seen a deer

before, much less several of them together. "Look at how they step so carefully. And that little one, tilting its head!"

Dev was looking at Fifer and the joy on her face. But then his gaze moved beyond her through the window, and he saw a spot of red. A really, really big spot of red. Heading from the front of the property straight for the deer. Dev turned and glanced at the back of the property and saw the dragon at the back coming too. "Oh no," he said softly. "You might not want to watch this."

But Fifer caught sight of them as well. "Yikes," she said, looking away and turning toward Dev. Their faces were inches apart. And for some reason, the thought of kissing someone Fifer had become such close friends with didn't seem quite as weird as it had felt before. But this was not the right time for thoughts like that. Because the two red dragons were standing really close together, paying attention to something that wasn't them. "Grab your spears, Dev," said Fifer. "It's time to go."

Danger, Danger

The two friends ran for the stairs. Dev grabbed his long spears, and on the way down, Fifer pulled the obliterate spell from her vest. She held it tightly until she had a moment to pause at the bottom of the steps to open the little box. While she did so, the dragons rushed in to devour the herd of deer. Fifer cringed, trying not to listen to the sounds the deer made. She removed the innocuous-looking pebble from its safety box and pinched it between her fingers. "Stay behind me," she told Dev.

Dev nodded. "Be careful."

"I will." They moved toward the action.

The dragons were enjoying their rare feast. Fifer rolled the pebble between her thumb and forefinger, trying to get a sense of its weight and power. Trying to decide where to place it. Should she aim between the dragons? Or closer to one to ensure eliminating at least one of them? She decided on that. "Be ready to run for the library if I mess this up," Fifer said. "Don't worry about me."

"You don't worry about me," Dev said, more defiantly than he'd intended. But he didn't exactly like Fifer telling him to run and hide if he didn't feel like doing that. Or if he felt like sticking by her . . . just in case. He kept moving and hid his eyes from the deer carnage.

Fifer crept forward, concentrating. She kept her eye on the nearest dragon, who was fully invested in its meal. Then, signaling Dev, she stood up straight, took aim, and threw the pebble straight and true at the near dragon's head. "Obliterate!" she cried.

The pebble found its mark. It detonated, throwing Fifer and Dev backward as if they were rag dolls. The palace and the grounds shook. Fifer rolled to a stop and twisted to get back to a standing position. Dev scrambled up too, and both of them peered at the scene, half-deaf from the explosion and unable

LISA McMANN

371 « Dragon Slayers

to see anything because of the smoke. When the air cleared enough for them to see, one red dragon lay motionless and headless on the ground. The other was roaring and squirming on its back, trying to get to its feet.

"Oh crud," whispered Fifer. "Cover me! Don't attack unless you have to," she shouted to Dev, and ran over to Florence.

Dev grabbed his spears and stood in front of Fifer, waiting for the second dragon. They weren't about to stop fighting now, but he only had three spears, and he had to be smart.

Fifer laid her hands on the statue's leg that was in line with the rest of the body. She spoke the words Aaron had told her to say. "Be alive. Live." Over and over again she said it at each of the breaks, going as quickly as she possibly could. The pieces of Florence's body melded together.

The remaining red dragon slowly recovered, and he got to his feet. Dev recognized it as the one that had burned his back so terribly. He stayed near Fifer, one spear in hand and the other two on the ground at his feet.

The dragon started toward them.

Fifer moved at a feverish pace, putting Florence's pieces back together.

Dev focused on the dragon like Fifer had told him to do. When it got within spear-throwing range, he hoisted the spear and gripped it loosely in his hand, and concentrated on his task, which hopefully would ignite the magic part of the spear. Then he ran at the beast, getting as close as he dared, and let the spear fly.

It found its mark, burying itself inside the left nostril of the dragon. Dev's mouth dropped open. He'd nailed the beast right where he'd intended to. Dev's strength couldn't land it deep enough to prove fatal, but it did make the dragon furious. The ferocious enemy roared and spewed fire in a long arc in front of him, singeing Fifer and nearly hitting Dev, but the young man was too quick this time. With fire percolating in his throat— inadequate against these monsters as it was—Dev raced back for his second spear. "Hurry!" he cried to Fifer. "The dragon is advancing! I can't throw hard enough to lodge it deeply!"

"You're doing great!" Fifer shouted to him. "Don't get hurt!" She turned back to Florence and continued her process. "Be alive!" she said desperately. "Live!" She moved on to the next section. And the next. In a race against time, she felt like she was losing. She looked up and saw the red dragon with

LISA McMANN

two spears sticking out of its nostril and Dev diving for cover as the dragon advanced with fire spraying everywhere, igniting part of the orchard and the spiderweb-covered garden. "Be alive! Live!" Fifer went on, as sobs started to break through. "Be alive! Live!"

Fifer looked up and saw the dragon pressing forward. "Dev, run! Hide in the library!" Then she went back to Florence with the last few pieces of her neck and her head. Each time she said the words, the cracks would fuse together. And when the warrior trainer's split head was finally fused, her body came to life. Florence's eyes opened.

"Florence," Fifer said intensely, leaning over the startled statue, "I need you to nock an arrow and shoot that dragon up its nostril right now."

Florence, having no idea what had happened, sat up. "Where's my leg?" she said.

"Do it, Florence! Just roll over and do it from sitting if you can. Hurry!" She looked at Dev. "Look out, Dev!"

Florence reached for the bow that Fifer had placed near her and grabbed an arrow. She wore a pained look on her face. She nocked the arrow, twisted her hips, and took the shot. It hit the dragon's neck, lodging between the scales, but it didn't go deep enough to stop the attack.

"One more, please!" Fifer commanded. The dragon lunged for them. Dev scrambled for his third long spear.

Florence pulled another arrow out and aimed as the dragon's face was looming large. The arrow found its mark and sank deep into the nostril. The dragon roared. His tail whipped around like a rope. It caught Fifer's legs, and he threw her high into the air. With a strangled shout, Fifer went sailing and landed with a thud fifty feet away.

"Nooo!" shouted Dev. He ran at the beast as it began to stumble and threw the third spear, but overshot in his haste. When its face neared the earth, Dev leaped over flames and grabbed one of the spears sticking out of its nostril. He heaved and shoved it as hard as he could into the dragon's brain. He did the same with the other spear.

Finally the beast's eyes rolled back. He slumped, and his giant head flopped down on top of Dev, trapping him. Dev screamed, then went silent.

Florence had no context for what was happening, but that wasn't going to stop her. She dragged herself over to the dying dragon and shot one more arrow up its nostril, quickly ending its life. Then, biceps bulging, she shoved its head to one side and pulled Dev out. She dragged herself and the strange boy to the courtyard and laid him under the protection of the center tower stairs. Then she went to get Fifer.

Fifer wasn't moving. She looked . . . flattened. Some of her skin was blistered with burns. Florence picked her up gently and cradled her in her arms. "Fifer," she said gently. "Fifer, you did it. Please wake up."

But Fifer didn't wake up. Florence scooted along the ground to the palace, avoiding the small fires that smoldered everywhere, or putting them out with her stony backside. She kept her eye on the dragons, but both now appeared deader than dead, just like the first two she'd killed with her arrows. How much time had gone by since that disaster?

Florence didn't have a clue. She only knew that she'd fallen a long way and had hit the ground. And now she was missing a leg. Was that fall an hour ago? A week ago? A year? She had no idea. She only knew that Dev had been crushed and Fifer was unresponsive in her arms. But as long as Florence was alive and moving, that meant Fifer was alive too. And that knowledge was all the strength she needed to sort things out on her own at this dilapidated palace.

The Partnership

Thisbe took a seat in a small carriage, pulled by a horse. The Revinir walked next to her on the left. Rohan, who still hadn't slept, trotted along on the right side of the carriage, available to Thisbe for whatever she might need. And the rest of the Revinir's company surrounded them, front, back, and on all sides. There was no possible chance to obliterate the Revinir without taking many casualties with her.

Thisbe was going to end the Revinir's reign today. But she wanted to get the Revinir alone.

Okay, part of her wanted that. But, to be honest, another

part of Thisbe wanted to never have to use this obliterate component against the Revinir at all. It was . . . complicated.

It's not because the dragon-woman deserved anything. She had done terrible things to the black-eyed children. To all of Grimere. She'd put hundreds of innocent soldiers under her mind control, as well as dragons from all the lands far and wide. She'd caused tremendous injury to Thisbe and Rohan and Dev, and all of their fellow future rulers. If she'd known Maiven Taveer still lived? She'd have buried her. There was no question in Thisbe's mind.

But.

The Revinir had just started to reveal herself in some convoluted way. And she wasn't 100 percent evil. Just like Thisbe. Or Dev. Or Rohan. Or Aaron. Or any of them. She had a mix of evil and good in her. And while the good bit was probably tiny, it still made her extremely complex. After Thisbe had taken a turn as a perceived supervillain and had witnessed a little of the wrath that came with that, she'd developed a slightly more forgiving attitude.

The Revinir was unlike Frieda Stubbs, who had seemed like the most one-dimensional, fear-mongering villain to ever cross

LISA McMANN

the path of any Unwanted. But the dragon-woman had layers and layers of history that somehow worked to give her a mysterious, intriguing life. She just hadn't revealed any of it until now.

Thisbe wished she hadn't revealed it at all, because it was only making this job harder. She slipped her hand inside her jacket to her vest to make sure she could access the small component box easily when needed.

As they traveled, trumpets sounded every quarter hour, calling the people of the land of the dragons to come to the square. The Revinir let out an unexpected, earsplitting roar once they drew close, making Thisbe and Rohan wince. Both felt the tug of the Revinir's call even though they were already with her. Both saw their usual images flash before their eyes— Rohan for the first time when a roar occurred. Soon a cyclone of dragons whirled around above them.

Thisbe eyed Rohan. Things weren't looking good for getting the Revinir alone and away from everyone else. With a sinking heart, she couldn't see how she would possibly be able to take the dragon-woman down during this event.

But if she could, it would be so convenient. Everyone was

already gathered in Dragonsmarche. After the deed was done, Thisbe could address everyone and explain what was going on before rumors spread wildly. Still . . . that would be a traumatic experience to witness. Not something Thisbe wanted others to have to suffer through. No, it was best to wait. Find the Revinir alone. Do it safely. Don't endanger anyone.

She sighed and realized she felt a twinge of relief, which was alarming. Why was she feeling relieved not to have a chance to take the Revinir down, when this was the thing she'd been so set on doing for such a long time?

They arrived in the square. The stage was set—the same stage Thisbe and Fifer had been tied to and auctioned from more than a year ago. Thisbe shuddered at the sight of it. She averted her gaze, but her carriage kept going toward it. Thisbe remembered that day clearly. She and Fifer, chained to posts. People gaping at them, ready to bid. The twins had set up magical glass barriers around themselves to keep the strangers from getting too close. And then Simber, unknowingly, swooped in and crashed through the glass trying to save them. Fifer had been seriously injured—she still had scars from all the glass cuts. Thisbe had been snatched away by the Revinir

LISA McMANN

and taken down into the catacombs through the elevator.

When the carriage came to a stop, Rohan held a hand out to Thisbe to help her down. She took it without looking at him, and he gave it an extra squeeze of support, knowing what must be going through her mind. But he had his part to play, and the Revinir was watching everyone. Thisbe walked up the steps to the stage, and the Revinir climbed onto it directly next to her.

People began gathering around them. Some of them were speckled with scales and wore the glazed look of mind-controlled citizens who'd been subjected to the dragon-bone broth. Others had clear eyes. Suspicious eyes. They didn't know Thisbe or what she was doing there. But they knew the Revinir and her oppressive ways. They knew what she'd done so sneakily to so many people in their community. They saw the dragons flying aimlessly. Soon those in the front rows noticed Thisbe's black eyes, and murmurs began.

The Revinir, who was a small dragon, still made the center of the stage bow under her weight. Thisbe stood next to her and tried to appear calm and confident. But there were a lot of things freaking her out right now. Being on this stage was giving her the stress of horrible flashbacks. Pretending to do this partnership thing was making her anxious about what everyone would think. And trying to plan the ultimate takedown without hurting anyone else was giving her hives, especially when she was having these twinges of doubts. This was definitely not the right time or place for them. Yet she couldn't get these things out of her mind.

As more and more townspeople gathered and filled in every available inch of the square, Thisbe's eyes strayed to the forest, which began just on the other side of the road they'd traveled to get here. She remembered taking the path to Alex's grave. Finding that mound of dirt with unopened seek spells hovering above it. Having such weird feelings about it. Those feelings continued today. And while she'd made some progress, she still hadn't fully come to terms with the guilt she carried. She and Alex had been in a fight the last time she'd seen him. And now she was doing something awful. How would he feel about it? Could he possibly somehow sense what she was doing, even in death?

A pang of dread ripped through her as Fifer came to mind. Thisbe didn't know why her thoughts were torn away from everything else in that instant and forced on Fifer, but it was

LISA McMANN

strange enough to raise her fears. Then Thisbe realized she was a lot closer to the palace now than she'd been in the castle. Was she back in telepathic range? Immediately she tried to communicate mentally with her twin. She focused on two short sentences. "I'm in Dragonsmarche. Ready to declare partnership." She thought them over and over, but there was no sense that the words got through like she'd felt before when she and Fifer had practiced this. She must still be too far away. But the thought of Fifer stayed with her, a sharp-edged worry. Perhaps it was because of their location on this stage and the memory of what had happened.

The Revinir's big face loomed and came into Thisbe's space. "I'll do most of the talking," the dragon-woman said.

"That's fine," said Thisbe, trying to smile.

"But I want you to say something too, so the people know that we are in agreement."

"Of course."

The Revinir studied Thisbe. "All right. I'm ready to get started."

Thisbe nodded, trying to look encouraging. Trying to appear like she wanted to be here.

"People and dragons!" shouted the Revinir. "People and dragons!"

The crowd quieted.

"People and dragons," the Revinir said a third time, "I am here today with exciting news. As a dragon, and your current leader, I am happy to announce that I have come to an understanding with one of the few remaining black-eyed rulers. We have agreed to officially take back this land from the usurpers who have reigned these past forty years. We will restore our world to the way it was meant to be!"

She paused as murmurs rose up all around them. A few shouts rang out, but they were drowned by a smattering of applause.

The Revinir held up both front legs and rested on her haunches. Her tail swished around from side to side, occasionally curling around Thisbe's feet as if to warn her there was no way out. She waited for silence. Eventually it came.

"I declare here and now that I, as ruling dragon, have entered into a partnership with Thisbe Stowe, the ruling black-eyed human. We agree to come together for the good of our land. Thisbe is a competent leader and . . . she is my friend. We will work very well as a team."

LISA McMANN

Thisbe was surprised by the Revinir's soft, complimentary words. She glanced over and noticed the dragon-woman almost had a sheen in her eyes. She'd really meant it. And while that was touching, it was also a little strange, seeing as how Thisbe had been playing her hard all this time. She almost felt guilty. But then a new thought struck her: Maybe the Revinir was playing Thisbe just as hard. That helped chill Thisbe's heart a little.

The Revinir was staring at her, and Thisbe suddenly realized she was supposed to speak now. "Yes," she said loudly, and glanced around, looking for Rohan. He was on the ground nearby, staring vacantly into the crowd. "I am excited to represent all people in this fine land," she said. "Our partnership restores a symbiotic system that has almost been forgotten. A ruling body that is unique to this land. And I'm honored to step in as co-leader with . . . my friend, the Revinir." Thisbe's eloquent words drew light applause. She turned to the Revinir but continued as if to the crowd, "And so I declare that our partnership should commence immediately."

"Commence the partnership!" said the Revinir, with great flair.

The crowd waited. It seemed like something should happen, but the Revinir didn't know quite what.

Thisbe frowned. "Did it work?" she whispered.

"I'm not sure," muttered the Revinir. "I expected the dragons to return to normal, if not the humans—like I told you, we might need some of that ancestor broth for that."

"Are there any ghost dragons in the skies that you can see?" Thisbe asked. "If they're gone, that would be a sure sign it worked."

The Revinir frowned. "I don't see any, but they don't usually come around here. Except when you humans are up to your tricks." She eyed Rohan thoughtfully. "He's the only one of the black-eyed people present here who has lived in Grimere his whole life. I wonder if he knows the history of how the rulership works."

"Rohan," Thisbe said.

Rohan turned toward her like an automaton.

"Do you know what has to happen in order for two new rulers to take over this land? Is there any sort of ritual . . . or something . . . that we have to go through?" *Maybe in a deserted place where we must travel alone?* she wanted to add. "Perhaps it

LISA McMANN

has something to do with the ghost dragons," she speculated aloud, wanting to give Rohan a minute to think, "since they're the ones who want to be able to leave this life and pass along their duties to the next generation."

Rohan didn't waver. "You are correct. The two partners must go to the cavelands to announce their partnership before the ghost dragons and assure them that the next generation is ready to serve," he said. "It's in the history books."

Thisbe gave a mysterious shrug at the Revinir. "I guess we didn't read our history books, did we?" she said snidely.

The Revinir chuckled. "Why didn't we ask him in the first place? We're going to have to fly if we're to get there by dark."

"Do you want to dismiss everyone first?" Thisbe asked her. "We can just tell them it's done, right? They won't know the difference."

"I like that plan." The Revinir shouted out to everyone in the area that all was said and done. And she announced, "Everyone who has taken dragon-bone broth, please report to the castle in two days for a remedy." She turned to Thisbe and explained, "I have the bones being delivered from the catacombs tonight." And then the Revinir let out a little snarl. "I

LISA McMANN

suppose we should mingle as people are leaving so they think we're decent."

Thisbe nodded. "Good idea." But she was preoccupied. At least the Revinir wasn't too mad about nothing happening, but what would she do when nothing happened in the cavelands and the ghost dragons had no idea what was going on? Thisbe would have to take her chance there. Once this was all over, hopefully the red dragons around the palace would snap out of their mind control and leave, and Fifer and Dev could get out of there and rescue Thisbe and Rohan, who'd be stuck in the cavelands once all of the ghost dragons disappeared forever. Success was on Thisbe's mind now, squelching out the doubt.

In Rough Shape

In the palace courtyard, Fifer and Dev were limp and unresponsive. Florence, keeping up her no-nonsense warrior facade, did what she could to make them comfortable. Then she rifled through Fifer's robe and component vest pockets, looking for the healing kit. She found it but also found the empty cube that had stored an obliterate component and the paper on which Thisbe had written instructions.

After applying whatever first aid she could to the young warriors, Florence glanced over at where the dragons lay. The one she'd just helped slay was stuck with several sharp objects, like its face was a pincushion. But the other's head was blown clean

LISA McMANN

away, and the ground near it was marked by a huge hole. Fifer must have used the obliterate spell there. But what had possessed Thisbe to give it to her? Florence was glad Fifer had had it, but she'd told Thisbe under no uncertain terms that the magic was for Thisbe's use only—no one else had been trained on such a dangerous spell. It could have been a disastrous situation.

Not that it wasn't, under the current circumstances. As Florence continued to treat Fifer and Dev, she worried over the letter from Thisbe explaining the obliterate spell. If Thisbe had gone to join the Revinir's cause, why would she leave one of these monstrously dangerous components with Fifer? It was like giving the enemy ammunition to come after her. And it looked like Thisbe hadn't given the component to Fifer directly because of the detailed note. It seemed more likely that she'd left it for her right before she'd decided to sneak off. That didn't seem like something a person would do if they were turning their back on their people—giving them such a powerful spell that could be used against her. It didn't make sense. Maybe Seth had been right—that the twins had been in on something much bigger than anybody had figured out yet.

"Come on, Fifer," Florence muttered under her breath as

she gave her another dose of a magical healing concoction she'd found. She was trying hard not to break down. The warrior trainer wiped a tear from her eyes and kept up her commanding exterior because it made it easier to cope. But here they were again. Another leader was down. Near death. How often would this happen? It was horrifying. And if there was anything Florence could do to save Fifer, she'd do it. "Wake up, Fifer. Listen . . . you did everything right. Please don't leave us. We need you desperately to stay alive. Please . . . Simber needs you. I need you. All of Artimé needs you." She sat back and stared at the spot where her leg should be.

Florence turned to Dev for a follow-up dose of medicine. Fifer had said his name earlier, or the warrior trainer might not have realized who he was. She hadn't known there was anyone else here—Fifer hadn't mentioned Dev in her send communications. In fact, she'd plainly said once that she was alone. Had he just arrived? Why was his back covered with healing burns? They weren't from today's battle. Everything was a puzzle for now.

She kept them both alive. When the two seemed stable and there was nothing else Florence could do for them, the warrior scooted along the ground in search of her leg. She'd never repaired her own body before because it was always better to have someone else's trained eye to place a body part just right. But now she didn't really have a choice—she wanted her leg attached in case something else threatened them.

She found it in the yard not far from where Fifer had brought her back to life. After magically repairing the cracks, Florence maneuvered herself into the proper position to attach the leg to the rest of her body. When she was finished, she got up and tested it. There were a few blades of grass that had gotten trapped during the sealing process and they stuck out of her leg now. And it was a tiny bit crooked—which was why it would have been nice to have Octavia there to catch that mistake. But she walked around on it. Other than a minor limp, she was in good shape.

Now that Florence was back in one piece, she took stock of her location. The four dead dragons were a big eyesore, and so was the broken-down palace. She stomped out the few smoldering fires that luckily hadn't spread through the orchard. Florence could just barely see the village beyond the trees. She spotted the river in the back of the property and remembered how important it was for humans to drink, so she filled the two teenagers' canteens for them. Then she rummaged through

Fifer's vest pockets again and pulled out a send spell so she could contact Maiven. But it was one that had already been used. And it was from Thisbe.

Florence read it.

> *Fife,*
> *Things will have to happen soon. Alert the troops.*
> *Thiz*
> *PS We're heading to Dragonsmarche today to announce our partnership. Don't reply.*

This message added to Florence's confusion about what was really happening. Her suspicions about the twins grew. But there was something more urgent about this. "If this is recent, and the Revinir and Thisbe are heading to Dragonsmarche," Florence reasoned, "we want some eyes on them."

She found an unused send spell and wrote:

> *Maiven,*
> *I'm not sure how much time has passed since I went down, but I'm back up again. All four red dragons are dead. Fifer*

and Dev are both seriously injured and unconscious. If they
don't wake up soon . . . that could spell trouble. Where are
you? Can you send Aaron with more medical supplies? And
send someone to Dragonsmarche and the castle to keep an
eye on things there. Sounds like Thisbe and the Revinir are
making their pact in the public square.

Florence

She sent it off, noting it went to the north as she expected, which meant Maiven was still in the direction of the cavelands. Then she picked up Thisbe's note and send spell again and studied them, looking for clues to what was truly going on here. Fifer was somehow in on this, that much was clear— she was aiding Thisbe in this horrible takeover. But was it possible that they'd both turned away from Artimé? Or had Seth's hunch actually been accurate, that they were somehow plotting together against the Revinir? Either way, it was reckless, and it undermined the safety and future of Artimé. And Florence was beginning to get very worried.

LISA McMANN

Pulling It Together

Partway to their palace destination, Maiven read the send message from Florence. She commanded Gorgrun, Quince, and Astrid to land so she could address Aaron, Ishibashi, Simber, Seth, and Sky and their dragons. "I have mixed news for you," she announced once everyone was in hearing distance. "The good news: Florence is back up and working. They defeated the remaining two red dragons. But the bad news is that Fifer is hurt quite badly."

Aaron's face paled. "Any details?"

"No." The queen waited a moment while that news sank in. "Florence doesn't seem to know we're already coming. But

LISA McMANN

she also mentions that Thisbe and the Revinir are announcing their partnership in Dragonsmarche and suggests we send a spy out that way." She twisted her swagger stick, thinking. "Since we no longer have the red dragons to fight, I agree with her. But I don't like the idea of someone going alone. Let's send two."

"I will go," said Ishibashi, stepping forward.

"Thank you, Ishibashi-san," said Maiven. "I like having you there with your long-range weapons. Now someone else with strong magical skills." Her eyes wavered between Seth and Aaron.

Seth looked torn. Fifer was hurt, and he cared about her. But Thisbe was being awful, and he wanted to look her in the eye and see what looked back.

Before he could decide, Aaron stepped up. "I'm sick about Fifer, but I doubt there's anything I can do for her," he said. "I'd like to go with Ishibashi."

Seth nodded. "I'll do what I can to help Fifer," he said. "But tell Thisbe I'm really mad."

"Thanks. I will." Aaron glanced at Simber. "I assume you will stay with Maiven and go to Fifer?"

"Corrrect," said Simber.

Aaron gathered his possessions and turned to Ishibashi. "Shall we take Quince and head out? No time to waste."

Ishibashi nodded and collected his weapons.

"Don't engage unless you see an opportunity to catch Thisbe alone," said Maiven. "We don't need any more casualties. Quince, you must do better at staying in your fog mode. Riders, don't hesitate to remind Quince of that regularly."

Quince seemed slightly offended, for he'd forgotten his mistake by now, but he let it go.

Aaron and Ishibashi agreed and headed out on the ghost dragon while Maiven and the rest reboarded Gorgrun and Astrid and continued to Ashguard's palace.

The two men hadn't spent much time together lately except in battle. "I'll be glad when this is over and we can go back home," Aaron said to the scientist as they glided along. "I miss our quiet island. I miss Daniel and Kaylee. And Ito and Sato."

"There will be time for catching up," said Ishibashi, trying to smile but feeling weary. They both knew it was true—it seemed they had all the time imaginable. Ishibashi and Aaron hadn't talked much lately about the seaweed and how it potentially made them immortal. It was old news. And besides, Kaylee didn't know the truth, so there weren't a lot of opportunities to chat about it. Aaron was racked with guilt about not telling her, but how could he? That his life would extend forever while hers would end was heartbreaking.

"Are you holding up all right?" Aaron asked. The old scientist was slight, but he wasn't frail. Still, this had become quite a lengthy ordeal.

"I have never been better," Ishibashi said. "This has been a long journey, but I believe it will be a satisfying one. I'm glad I came along to see this beautiful world. I was thrilled to experience the volcano system—what a ride! And so happy to spend time with you, my son. I must tell you, Aaron, that I wasn't sure about you for a long time. But I am so pleased with the man you have become."

Tears sprang to Aaron's eyes. He hadn't been expecting praise, and the normally quiet scientist had caught him off guard. It was especially meaningful at a time when he was feeling guilty for Thisbe's actions and wondering if there was some family flaw that would plague the Stowes forever. If Aaron and

Thisbe had it, would Daniel someday turn to his evil side too? Aaron had so many questions, and Ishibashi usually had answers. But Aaron could only whisper, "Thank you."

It was as if Ishibashi could read Aaron's mind. The old man put his cool, wrinkled hand on top of Aaron's. After a moment he said, "Every day is a new day, Aaron-san. A chance to try again. We can't control other people's choices. But with our gift, we can continue to gain wisdom and be there for our loved ones forever to try to steer the way."

Aaron choked up. He hadn't thought of immortality as a gift like that before. He'd mostly thought of how it would affect him, not how he could use it to affect others. The old scientist had taught him something else new in that moment. He took the man's hand and gave it a gentle squeeze. "Thank you for steering my way and for sticking by me when I didn't deserve it. I will try to do the same for Thisbe. And . . . for all the rest to come."

"That is all you can do," Ishibashi said. "We will do it together."

"That's what keeps me going," said Aaron. "That I'm not alone in this." They rode in silence for a while, side by side and hands linked, until Quince sniffed.

"Is everything okay, Quince?" Aaron asked him.

"Oh," said Quince, turning his head to look at them. "That was such a beautiful sentiment. I . . . Thank you for having that conversation in my presence."

The two men smiled at each other, and Ishibashi spoke up. "I believe you have a similar story to tell to the next generation of dragons."

Quince didn't answer, but he seemed thoughtful. A while later he said, "I can't remember where we are going, but does it happen to have something to do with the Revinir?" It seemed like everything lately had something to do with her, so it was his best guess.

"It does," said Aaron. "We're looking for her and Thisbe."

"Well, they're right up ahead, flying toward the cavelands."

Surprised, Aaron sat up and peered in front of them. He could see a tiny dot far ahead, moving sideways across their path. "I wonder why they're going there," Aaron mused. It seemed strange, and he could think of no reason that would bring the two out to such a desolate place. But maybe this was the opportunity Aaron was looking for. If the Revinir was traveling without a fleet of dragons surrounding her, there could be a chance to speak to Thisbe. To pour his heart out, or even simply give her a signal. A look. Something to express that he wanted her to come back to them. That he would welcome her, no matter what she did.

He watched the dot for a few moments, wanting to be sure of the Revinir's flight path, then said, "Quince, let's turn and meet them wherever they're headed. It's time to go into stealth mode."

Delirious

Fifer lay perfectly still, seemingly unconscious as Florence tended to her. But in her mind, wrapped up in the tremendous pain that rocked her body, the same old things they'd all been discussing for months about the Revinir swirled around like a song she couldn't get out of her head. Emma. Queen Eagala. The monstrous dragon-woman. She didn't care who lived or died. She wanted to rule all of the worlds. She was selfish and greedy for power. What was her weakness?

Bits of Emma's journal pages wavered in Fifer's mind. The girl had been jealous. Left behind. Lonely. Thisbe had landed

LISA McMANN

on these notes and was out there trying to exploit them. And Fifer knew she needed to rouse herself and help. But try as she might, the injuries she'd sustained and the whirling thoughts pressed her back firmly into the pavers and left her body weighing a thousand tons, unable to move. Emma. Queen Eagala. The Revinir. What was the consistency that connected them? What were her fears that stayed with her?

Emma. Standing next to a stream with the others, watching them do magic, happy to be included for once. But also glad to be excluded in a similar situation. Queen Eagala, building dozens of ships that had no purpose. Ships that would go nowhere because she commanded everyone to stay in Warbler. Why?

Sky and Crow's story came to mind—they'd escaped from Eagala on a raft and told stories about how they weren't allowed to learn to swim because their queen didn't want anyone to be able to leave.

Eagala's huge loss to Artimé and what everyone believed to be her death, being sucked down the volcano. But she'd survived, and her power after that had multiplied.

Then came Dev's story about hiding in the river and the strange way the Revinir had communicated with the red dragon to collect fish for her—when a dragon's natural hunting tendency seemed to imply fishing for oneself would be an experience to savor.

There was also Thisbe and Fifer's most recent traumatic abduction—the Revinir from above the trees, but having an elaborate setup of six dragons hiding under water.

The memory of a sound of fear rang in Fifer's ears as she lay battling for her life. A strained little *whoop*. It had been a strange, frightful sound that the Revinir had emitted when Thisbe had escaped the Revinir's grasp and fallen into the sea. The Revinir, with Fifer in one claw, had scooped Thisbe up and had made that sound. Like she was terrified for a moment.

The images swirled into one story: The rocks next to the stream. The ships with no purpose. Allowing no one to swim. The volcano sucking her ship down. The fish at the river. The inadvertent fearful whoop when her talons had plucked Thisbe from the sea. Around and around these thoughts churned as the magical medicine began to do its work.

Fifer needed to talk to Thisbe. She tried to, in her mind. Tried to send a message. A single word over and over again. Was it going through?

LISA McMANN

The weight of Fifer's body was stifling. Suffocating. The weight of her thoughts even more so. She struggled against it, feeling trapped. Needing to escape. The pain was secondary to everything as she wriggled and pushed and slid out from the heavy unconsciousness. Her eyes fluttered and opened, and she gasped. "Water."

In an instant, Florence was there. She lifted Fifer gently around the shoulders and held the canteen to her lips.

Fifer was too weak to push it away. "Water," she whispered again, and closed her eyes as the suffocating weight returned.

At Last, a Moment

Thisbe and Rohan could see Quince plain as day, but they knew the Revinir could only see rolling fog. And though she'd figured out that the ghost dragons could hide like fog, they hoped she was too distracted by their plans to notice this patch.

From the dragon-woman's back, Thisbe strained to see if anyone was riding him. She detected two bodies nestled into the pillowy softness, but there was no telling who they were. In the distance, many other ghost dragons saw the Revinir and her riders coming and started toward them.

The Revinir landed in the strip of desert between the forest

LISA McMANN

and the cavelands. Thisbe and Rohan got down and stood with her as the ghost dragons approached.

"Obviously we were right, that nothing changed," the Revinir muttered to Thisbe. "The ghost dragons are all still here. Let's see what they have to say."

Thisbe walked with her. "I hope they have more knowledge than Rohan does, and can fill us in so we can get this partnership rolling."

The Revinir glanced at the girl. "I'll do all the talking," she said, reminding Thisbe of how greedy she was.

"That's fine," said Thisbe icily.

The Revinir noticed the rolling fog had stopped moving and was just sort of stuck in one place nearby. She narrowed her eyes at it. "Is that one of the ghost dragons doing that same weird thing it did when Rohan was on board outside the castle?"

"I don't know," said Thisbe.

"Let's see which of your friends is hiding this time."

"I'm curious to know as well," said Thisbe. "We know you're a ghost dragon," she called out. "Reveal yourself, please."

Seeing no reason to keep up the pretense, Aaron told

Quince to materialize. Aaron and Ishibashi raised their heads and sat up.

At the sight of her brother and one of the grandfathers, Thisbe's heart trembled and her stomach churned. Why did it have to be them? But Thisbe had to pull it together and handle this right in order to keep the Revinir believing her farce. "What are you doing?" Thisbe demanded. "I told you not to come after me."

"Thisbe," said Aaron. His voice shook, making Thisbe shake too. But he continued. "Ishibashi and I have come to talk, not fight. May we have a word?"

Thisbe narrowed her eyes and glanced at the Revinir. "I don't know," she murmured.

"It's just me and a one-hundred-and-ten-year-old man here," Aaron said lightly. "We're not interested in attacking anyone. I just . . . I just want to try to understand." He went quiet, then added, "Please, Thisbe. Just a few minutes."

Thisbe continued her glare. She knew the Revinir was watching her closely. After a moment she turned to the dragon-woman. "Do you mind if I just take care of this a moment?" Under her breath she added, "If you get my meaning."

The Revinir's eyes widened slightly. "Bold move," she said.

"Only if the moment presents itself, understand," Thisbe said carefully.

The other ghost dragons were still flying in and gathering around the Revinir. They seemed curious, and some of them bowed their heads slightly, which made the Revinir quite pleased. "Go ahead," she said loud enough for Aaron to hear. "Bring Rohan to listen in so I can find out later what was said if I need to. And tell them I'll kill them in an instant if they try anything."

"Of course," said Thisbe, then added snidely, "Since you obviously still don't trust me, Rohan is welcome to tag along."

The Revinir's face flickered. "I told you. I trust no one."

Thisbe started walking toward Quince. Rohan followed a few paces behind, a glazed look markedly present in his eyes. "Climb down from there," Thisbe called to her brother. "Both of you, please."

Aaron and Ishibashi made their way to the ground and met Thisbe and Rohan. Thisbe's pulse wouldn't stop pounding in her ears like a ticking bomb. She had to stay in character. She had to trick her brother . . . and dear Ishibashi, her acting grandfather. It would be nearly impossible.

The four stood together in a square, and Thisbe saw the sadness in their eyes that she'd caused. Aaron gazed at his sister for a moment, clearly emotional. He almost couldn't speak. And when he did, he said something that threw Thisbe off her game.

"This is all my fault," Aaron whispered. "You're taking after me. Please, please don't make the same mistakes I made. I'm here today to tell you that you will regret this for the rest of your life . . . like I regret my mistakes." He took a breath. "Every day I relive my past like a recurring nightmare. Every day I face people who still hold scorn for what I've done. And I deserve it. But, Thisbe, my dear sister . . . I want you to know it's not too late to come home. You have a chance that I didn't have. And I'm begging you to take it. Come with us."

Thisbe had no idea Aaron would take some sort of blame for her wrongdoings. She glanced at Ishibashi, whose eyes were glistening.

"This is your pivotal moment," Ishibashi said quietly. "What you do next will define you. I believe you will make the right choice."

Thisbe swallowed hard, over and over again, trying to clear

the lump that insisted on rising. And she held her eyes wide open, trying to get the wind to dry her tears. She spoke to herself silently, reminding herself why she was doing what she was doing. They were not done with this. The Revinir was thirty yards away and could kill any of them at any moment with a blast of fire.

"There's something else," Aaron said. "It's Fifer. She's hurt. I . . . I don't know how badly."

Thisbe took in a sharp breath. Her mind swam. What had happened to Fifer? Had the red dragons done something? She felt sick. But she was so close to getting this right. If she left with Aaron, the Revinir would never trust her again, and all their work would be ruined. She'd go to Fifer immediately after she took care of the Revinir. Gathering strength, Thisbe stared Aaron right in the eye. "This meeting is a waste of time," she said, trying to sound disgusted.

But then a whisper came from her left. From Rohan, whose lips barely moved. "Thisbe, quickly. She's standing alone. The ghost dragons can't be hurt."

Thisbe's eyes widened as tears slipped down Aaron's cheek. Keeping her back to the Revinir, she slid her hand inside her jacket and secured the obliterate box. With a whisper of magic she opened it and removed the stone.

Fingers trembling, she knew she had a fraction of a second before Aaron and Ishibashi would show surprise or fear on their faces—a fraction of a second to turn and aim and throw and kill the Revinir. The dragon-woman who had imprisoned her, who had nearly killed her and her friends multiple times. But who had also just revealed a little of herself for the first time. Thisbe's heartstrings twanged against her will. She fought against her hesitation, but her body began to shake uncontrollably. The Revinir had to be taken out. There was no other option. This was the moment. Her moment.

With the pebble pinched between her fingers, Thisbe withdrew her hand from her jacket. She turned and took aim. Then she threw the pebble with her shaking hand at the Revinir, crying "Obligerate!"

Her eyes widened as she bungled the word, and she hastened to fix it. "Obliterate!"

Rohan gasped. Aaron cried out, "What are you doing?"

The pebble soared toward the Revinir, whose jaw opened

LISA McMANN

in shock. Whose eyes showed her feeling of betrayal. The Revinir let out a cry as the pebble skimmed over her head, missing its target and hitting the ground just beyond her. It exploded on impact, sending sand and rocks flying and knocking the Revinir off her feet.

Thisbe had missed. The Revinir was not dead. Thisbe watched in absolute horror as everything she'd built up over the past weeks fell apart in an instant. She caught Aaron's eye in a pure moment as they both realized what was happening. But when the Revinir rolled and got up, Thisbe grabbed Rohan's wrist and yelled, "Everybody run!"

As Thisbe and Rohan ran for the edge of the forest, and Aaron fumbled for components, Ishibashi sent two throwing stars flying at the Revinir's face, striking her. He timed a third to soar straight into her open mouth, coinciding with her angry roar. It embedded into the back of her throat.

The dragon-woman let out a scream and a thick spray of fire that swept over the ground like a giant fireball, building in size as it went. There was nowhere safe for the two men to go. Ishibashi shoved Aaron behind Quince for cover, then tried to dive out of the fireball's way. But the old scientist wasn't fast enough, and the ball of flames engulfed him. His knees buckled and he fell to the ground.

Aaron stumbled, then regained his footing as a thin wall of flames passed over him. Scorched, he turned and saw his mentor on the ground. He threw his body on top of Ishibashi's to douse the flames and rolled him over. "Quince! Help us!" Aaron screamed.

The ghost dragon scooped up Aaron and Ishibashi before the Revinir could send another wave of fire. He took off at a velocity rarely seen in ghost dragons, heading south toward Ashguard's palace. As Thisbe and Rohan disappeared into the thick of the forest, the Revinir sent another ball of fire at the rising ghost dragon, but could do no harm to Quince's underside.

The rest of the ghost dragons surrounded the Revinir, raising their wings around her to trap her and delay her from going after either party. When Quince had moved out of the Revinir's fiery range, he used his tail to put the two men gently on his back, one at a time, as he continued flying.

Aaron, scorched and blistering, rolled to his side as the throbbing pain began and grew. "I'm coming, Ishibashi!" he

LISA McMANN

cried, his voice ragged. He pushed himself to his feet and stumbled across the dragon's back to the scientist. In the distance the Revinir let out a frustrated, bloodcurdling roar.

Aaron stared at Ishibashi's limp body, then quickly knelt by the old man's side. He checked the scientist's vital signs, cursing himself all the while for not bringing medicine with him.

But Ishibashi had no pulse. No heartbeat. Aaron bent his face near the scientist's but could detect no breath left inside him. The young man tried his best to revive Ishibashi, ignoring his own agonizing pain. But in time, Ishibashi's neck and chest grew cold beneath Aaron's hands. After too long, Aaron finally gave up. Heaving and exhausted, he looked at the man's face. Ishibashi . . . was dead.

Aaron's eyes widened as unshed tears burned them. But then a desperate, wretched sob escaped. He took in a sharp breath, and more sobs came. Sick, angry, broken sobs. Sobs that had never come when his own parents had died. But Ishibashi had been more than a parent. "No!" Aaron screamed. "No!"

An overwhelming feeling and an intense realization enveloped Aaron, pressing down like a weight on his chest. The man who'd rescued him. The man who'd taken him in. Who'd shown him love and had taught him discipline. Who'd promised just moments ago to spend the rest of forever with him . . . Ishibashi was *dead*. How could it be? He'd *died*.

As Aaron sat numb on the back of a ghost dragon with the scientist's body in his arms, his mind spun between sorrow and wonder. He felt the weight on his chest lifting and lightening. The soul of the beautiful old man seemed to leave its burned shell and rise to the air, moving far away to the east, taking bits of Aaron's sorrows and one of his biggest fears with it.

As Fifer and Dev struggled to survive at Ashguard's palace, and as Thisbe and Rohan ran for their lives toward the forest, something incredibly sad and horrible yet tremendously important had just occurred. And it changed everything for Aaron. For his future. For his life . . . and for his death.

Ishibashi Junpei, grandfather, scientist immortal, had died. But in the midst of deepest, darkest sorrow, grief, and loss, Aaron could squint and barely see a tiny ray of light. Leading Ishibashi home.

The Revinir broke free from her ghost-dragon prison. The two traitors were out of sight in the forest, but she could smell them easily enough. It would only be a matter of time before she had them back in her grasp. The question now was what she would do to them. As the Revinir rose up above the trees to track them, her eyes narrowed in anger and her heart grew colder than ever before. She'd let Thisbe in, and the girl had cruelly turned on her. How dare she? The dragon-woman wouldn't make that mistake again.

As Thisbe and Rohan stumbled through the forest, fleeing for their lives, a faint, desperate whisper of a single word fought to bridge the distance and found its way to Thisbe's ear. But then a furious roar from the Revinir revealed that she was closing in, and the word was gone on the wind.

Water.

Acknowledgments

I want to thank Brian Luster, the copy editor of so many Unwanteds books. If anyone knows my books better than me, it's you. You save me from embarrassment by suggesting I should change gristly to grisly (good call). You fix my comma issues time after time after time. (Or is that time, after time, after time?) We have a strange relationship—we've never met, and we don't communicate directly. But I've come to rely on you. And I'm really grateful that you've stuck with this series all these years. Just one more book to go! I don't know if you'll miss these characters, but they'll definitely miss you. An extra-large thank you to all the others who make my manuscripts shine. In the publishing world, authors don't often meet the people who make our books better, and we hardly know just how many hands touch these words to help tell the best story we can. I'm so grateful for all of you.

Thanks to Liesa Abrams at Aladdin, who guides the ever-growing big picture of these books. This penultimate book felt especially daring to me, and your support gave me the confidence to go for it. And thanks to the entire team at Aladdin, from editorial and education to sales, art and design to publicity and marketing. Special thanks to my publicist, Lauren Carr, for making everything easier, especially around tour time.

I'm unendingly grateful to Owen Richardson, who has stunned me with his cover illustrations a grand total of fourteen times over the past decade. Your iconic art has brought warm feelings to readers for years, and will continue to do so for years to come. When readers think back to the world of Artimé and the joy it brought them, they will picture your covers in their minds.

To Kilian McMann, who has provided various forms of art for The Unwanteds and Unwanteds Quests—posters, illustrations, pins, postcards, and art for my presentations—I'm so glad to have worked with you from the moment the idea for The Unwanteds began to form. Your dedication to your craft since then has made this journey in Artimé feel so much more special, and it has made my belief in the value of the arts that much stronger. I'm also extremely proud of you.

As always, I'm enormously thankful for my agent, Michael Bourret. Twenty-five books and counting, thanks to you. You're simply the best.

And huge thanks to my readers. Some of you are just finding this series, others shuffled through the gate into Artimé with the debut of The Unwanteds, and still others picked it up somewhere in between. I hope you see yourself in these books, and I can't wait for everyone to discover how it all ends in book seven.

Fifer's and Thisbe's stories continue in

THE UNWANTEDS QUESTS

BOOK SEVEN
Dragon Fury

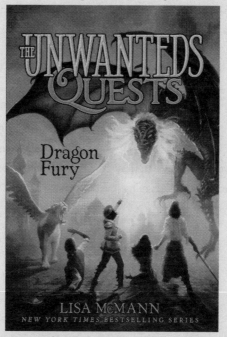

Turn the page for a peek. . . .

The Chase

Thisbe Stowe had failed to obliterate the Revinir.

Her spell had struck the ground and exploded behind the dragon-woman, knocking her down, but only for a moment. In seconds the Revinir was back up—and furious. While Aaron and Ishibashi exchanged fire with the Revinir, Thisbe and Rohan escaped into the forest of Grimere. But the evil ruler was soon on their tail again, roaring and spraying fire in all directions.

The two dodged the flames from the Revinir's blasts and kept running. They knew she couldn't see them, and she couldn't squeeze her body between the trees to go after them, but her random bursts of fire could still reach the fugitives—and all the timber surrounding them.

"You betrayed me!" the Revinir shouted down. Her voice hitched. To Thisbe, she sounded . . . devastated. And . . . possibly in pain?

Between roars and flames, the dragon-woman reached her claws into her mouth and scraped around, trying to dislodge the throwing star that Ishibashi had implanted there moments ago. The first two weapons that had hit her in the forehead had barely nicked her thick skin and bounced off, one of them leaving a trickle of blood. But the metal star in the back of her throat was stuck fast, and the tissue surrounding it was swelling up.

Below, Thisbe's expression flickered as thoughts about all that had just happened pounded her. What a terrible mess she'd made! She was devastated by her failure to use the obliterate spell properly. Now everything was in chaos. She'd put Aaron and Ishibashi in danger and left them to fend for themselves. And she and Rohan were about to get burned to a crisp.

The two didn't respond to the Revinir's shouts. They ran as quietly as they could for a while, then spied a large fallen tree and slid under its branches for cover. Too late, they realized the remaining dead leaves of the tree were brittle—the leaves would catch fast if the Revinir figured out where to aim her blasts. But their smartest option was to stay still and quiet.

"How do we get out of here?" Rohan whispered.

Thisbe looked back the way they'd come. "The desert is back there," she said, "so that means the road and the crater lake are this way." She pointed to the south, then frowned. "I think." Neither of them knew their way through this end of the forest. They were far from the castle and the city of Grimere. The thick expanse of trees spread through the entire center of the land of the dragons: One end was near the castle; the other was close to the cavelands where the ghost dragons dwelled. Dragonsmarche and the crater lake were somewhere between those two points on the other side of the road.

No matter where they were at the moment, Thisbe knew that they had to stay hidden in the thicker parts of the forest in order to keep the Revinir from diving down and snatching them up in her claws or blasting them with her furnace breath. They could hear her circling above the treetops.

"Rohan," the Revinir called, slurring her words a bit

because of the metal star in her throat, "I command you to stop Thisbe! Bring her to the dragon path where I can see her!" Then she muttered, "I should never have ordered him to obey that traitor."

Thisbe and Rohan's eyes widened. The Revinir still believed Rohan was under her mind control. She hadn't yet figured out that they'd been tricking her all this time.

"What should I do?" Thisbe whispered, her chin in the dirt. "The version of Thisbe I've been pretending to be would try to take control of the situation. Not apologize for almost killing her, but accuse her of hurting Fifer and telling her she deserved to be attacked. That would startle her, I think, in the right way. Should I tell her that's what I was reacting to, and declare that I'm sorry I didn't manage to kill her?" She paused and cringed. What would that lead to? "Or should I try to explain some other way?"

Rohan looked at her, concerned. "I . . . think it's over, *pria*."

"What? What do you mean?"

"This whole act you've been doing." He shifted in the detritus under the tree as ants crawled on them. "It's done. There's no coming back from what happened."

Thisbe stayed silent, the blood draining from her face as she tried to comprehend what he was saying. Rohan continued gently. "Do you really think you can go back to her and try to salvage this fake relationship? I just can't see it ever being repaired. It took you so long to get her to trust you, and after what took place back there—after what you just did to her— the farce is over. You tried to kill her, Thiz. And she's well aware it wasn't a mistake."

Thisbe's thoughts continued whirring as she attempted to come up with a way to reconcile with the Revinir and keep this going. She'd worked so hard to get here. Poured her heart and soul into this! But the damage had been done. Thisbe dropped her head into her hands. There was no explaining away her attempt to kill the dragon-woman—it had changed their strengthening relationship in an instant, and the Revinir would never forgive her, no matter what story she concocted to try to explain it. Thisbe had messed it up. The fragile trust had been broken. The Revinir was way too hardened, and this betrayal would only harden her more. There was no way to fix it. "It *is* over, isn't it," Thisbe said, resigned. She lifted her head to look at Rohan as the weight of it all came down on her. "Everything I've worked toward and all we sacrificed for this . . . I just messed it up in a single move."

"You still have one obliterate component," Rohan reminded her. "Do you want to try again?"

Thisbe peered up around the fallen tree, trying to locate the Revinir above the treetops. "Too many branches. I can't even see her. I'll miss again." She sighed and gathered her thoughts. "We need to focus on getting out of here, I think."

Rohan nodded. "Yes. Find the others and see about Fifer's injuries. I hope she's all right."

"The Revinir is going to round up her people and dragons," Thisbe said, thinking about what would happen next. "We need to be ready when she comes after us. Oh," she moaned, "what have I done? I've put everyone in so much danger!" She thought of the interaction with Aaron and Ishibashi. They hadn't fled with her and Rohan, which meant they probably believed Thisbe had turned on them for real. "They're going to hate me. And all of this damage . . . for nothing."

Rohan reached for Thisbe's hand and laced his fingers with hers. "We're going to figure this out," he said, but he didn't sound sure.

"And Fifer," Thisbe whispered, her voice catching. "I won-der what happened to her. We're going to need her help. And Dev's."

Almost as if on cue, an echo of a whisper filled Thisbe's ear. *Water.*

Thisbe turned to Rohan. "Did you hear something?"

He shook his head and put a finger to his lips. The random fire strikes were getting closer, and they could smell smoke.

Thisbe was certain she'd heard the word. It had to be from Fifer. Could their telepathic communication system reach this far? And why *water*? Perhaps, in her injured state, she was in need of a drink. *Somebody please give Fifer some water!*

In that quiet moment, the crackles of the forest around them grew louder and more consistent. Rohan shifted to look behind them, and he gasped. "The trees are burning," he said. "Lots of them."

Thisbe forgot the whisper in her ear and turned sharply to look at the areas of flames growing around them. The Revinir had set the forest of Grimere on fire. And Thisbe and Rohan were trapped in the midst of it.

Taking Care

Aaron, holding Ishibashi's dead body in his arms, could barely get out his instructions to Quince. "Fly as quickly as possible to Ashguard's palace." He choked, then added, "Please hurry." The rest of the team members would be there already. He looked down at the silent, small body of the man who'd taught him what goodness was. The man who'd loved him when he'd felt unlovable. Ishibashi had given him a second chance to make something good with his life. He'd died pushing Aaron out of the way of the Revinir's flames, even though he was immortal. Or so Aaron had thought.

He closed his eyes. "I'm so sorry," he whispered. "I hope you didn't suffer." After a long moment, Aaron lifted his head. He reached into his vest and found a send component. He opened it, took out the tiny pencil attached, and wrote:

Dear Kaylee,

Gather Ito and Sato. Brace yourselves for shocking, terrible news, and hold each other close, for I must tell you that our beloved Ishibashi has died. He was killed by the Revinir as he saved my life. It was a swift, unexpected attack, and I have minor burns but am otherwise all right. Shock is still muddling my thoughts, but I wanted to let you know right away.

Love,

Aaron

Aaron let out a ragged sob, then took a breath and blew it out slowly. He concentrated on his wife and released the send spell. It left a trail of smoke to the east and disappeared. Then he pulled out another component to tell a similar story.

Dear Florence,

Brace yourself for shocking, terrible news. Ishibashi and I ran into the Revinir, Thisbe, and Rohan. Thisbe confirmed our worst fears, but then she changed suddenly and tried to kill the Revinir with an obliterate spell. She missed, which is so unlikely, and the Revinir retaliated and killed Ishibashi. Thisbe and Rohan ran off into the forest. I'm unsure about where my sister stands, but I fear she's gone rogue against us all, and we've lost her forever. I'm on my way to Ashguard's palace with Ishibashi and Quince. If you have time . . . prepare a burial spot.

Your friend,

Aaron

He sat back, his skin on fire, burns weeping, body aching, and he closed his eyes again. Ishibashi had died, and that was not only shocking and sad, but confusing as well. To what extent had ingesting the glowing seaweed affected them? Aaron and the scientists had all thought it made them immortal. Ito and Sato were both over 115 years old by now and still functioning quite well. Ishibashi had only taken one dose in his lifetime, when he was already a middle-aged man. Aaron had been a teenager when they'd administered the dose to him to save his life. But it was apparent now that the seaweed didn't save them from everything. Perhaps the small amount had been ingested so long ago that it had made Ishibashi vulnerable. In that case, what did it mean for Aaron? And for the other two scientists?

It was something he'd have to discuss with Ito and Sato when he returned. *If* he returned. It was still too soon to know what was going to shape their lives in the coming days, but one thing was now painfully clear—there was no promise that Aaron would survive it.

Added to that, while he was worried about Fifer, he was extremely confused by what had happened with Thisbe. Her actions were inexplicable. She'd said horrible things to him, then suddenly turned and attempted to kill the Revinir, but . . . missed? Was she going for an even bigger power grab than anyone had imagined, taking on the Revinir *and* all of Artimé?

Or . . . had she missed the Revinir on purpose? It wasn't like Thisbe to mess up a spell. He didn't know if she'd ever done it before. As one of Artimé's best mages, Thisbe didn't make mistakes when it came to launching a spell she'd handled before. So what had happened there? And why had Rohan gone along with all of it? Did she have some sort of power over him? Had she figured out how to control people in the same way the Revinir had done?

Something felt terribly off. Thisbe had become someone they all might need to be afraid of. Did the people of Artimé have two enemies now, including the identical twin of their head mage? Was history repeating itself before Aaron's very eyes, but he'd been too stubborn to see it for what it was until this moment?

With Ishibashi gone in an instant, Aaron was deeply worried about the Revinir's vast firepower. She could've taken Aaron out just as swiftly. Would any of his other friends fail to survive whatever lay before them? Aaron had never felt so much darkness in all of his life. Things had gone too far—and the Revinir and Thisbe seemed unstoppable. What if there was no way out of the disaster that seemed to be steamrolling toward them?

On the Run

Thick smoke billowed through the forest and hung over Thisbe and Rohan. Sprays of fire scorched and ignited the trees around them. When flames crept to the fallen tree they were hiding under, setting the dead leaves around them ablaze, the two knew they had to run for it.

"This way," Thisbe whispered, trying to stay calm as smoke burned her throat. They held hands and kept low. Thisbe felt sick. This reminded her of when they were in the castle dungeon searching through the maze of passageways for Maiven Taveer while the drawbridge and building burned. If only the results of this venture turned out as well or better, maybe things would be okay. But that was a big if. Just thinking about her flub forced a groan from deep inside her. She'd been so close to ending the Revinir's reign, freeing the people and dragons of Grimere, setting the ghost dragons free to go to their next lives, and restoring the rulership to Maiven and the dragons. And she'd completely biffed it. It made her want to give up.

The two caught sight of the river but didn't take the time to get near enough for a drink. Instead they continued moving forward through the thick mass of trees and hoped the forest canopy would give them the best protection from the Revinir's keen senses. With any luck the smoke would shield their scent from the dragon-woman. They skirted around spot fires and ducked when another blast came through the foliage. When Rohan's shirttail caught fire, Thisbe shoved him to the ground to put it out.

She helped him to his feet, and they continued painstakingly, trying not to let the leaves and twigs crunch under their shoes. Hoping whatever sounds they did make were masked by the crackle of fire. Praying they were going the right way. How far would they have to travel before they spotted the road? Before the Revinir realized she was destroying her own land? Before the smoke completely disoriented them and they were lost for good?

As the forest became thick with smoke and the fiery sections more plentiful, Thisbe started to panic. Would they ever make it out? Were they even going in the right direction? Soon they could barely see ten feet in front of them because of the haze, and they struggled not to cough and give away their location. They came upon an entire section of the forest ablaze and had to detour around it.

When the trees began to thin and smoky sunlight filtered in between them, Thisbe realized the edge of the forest couldn't be too far off. She looked up, catching a glimpse of the Revinir's wings overhead. The dragon-woman snarled something about the forest fire, and then she belted out a mighty roar.

Thisbe and Rohan cringed and ran as the roar triggered images to flash in their minds. "This is bad," whispered Rohan as the new, real scales on his arms and legs stood on end. "She's calling in more dragons. We'll never get out of here without being seen."

Many of the dragons were already close by since the Revinir had roared in anger at Thisbe for trying to kill her. As the first ones circled around her, the Revinir shouted an order. "Get water from the river and the crater lake! And put this fire out before my entire land is destroyed." She was quiet a moment as the air swarmed with more arriving dragons. Then she added, in a menacing growl that was more to herself than to the dragons, "If you see Thisbe Stowe, don't bother bringing her to me. Just kill her."